DATING IN THE DEEP END

She's swimming with the only man who can sink her...

LYNDSEY GALLAGHER

Copyright © Lyndsey Gallagher 2024

All Rights Reserved

All rights reserved. No part of this publication may be reproduced, stored in a retrieval system or transmitted in any forms or by any means, without the prior permission in writing of the publisher, nor to be otherwise circulated in any form of binding or cover other than that in which it is published.

All the characters in this book are fictitious. Any resemblance to any actual persons, living or dead, is purely coincidental.

ASIN: B0CLDD24ZW

Chapter One
SAVANNAH

Masculinity rolls from Ronan Rivers in undulating waves. Watching his taut, tanned torso ripple and glide through the Olympic-sized swimming pool is like watching porn.

Ahem—poetry, I mean.

When he reaches the edge of the pool and stands, tiny beads of water glisten and drip across his exposed flesh. Broad muscular shoulders taper down over a marble-sculpted chest to a narrow waist. A fine smattering of fair hair dusts the smooth skin beneath his belly button before disappearing into fire engine red swim shorts.

What's he storing down there? Eight, maybe ten inches? It's hard to tell today, but from the footage I saw from his Olympic days, there was a sizeable package in those budgie smugglers.

It's just a crying shame the man is a complete wanker.

Well, maybe not technically. I'd be surprised if he had anything left in his balls that he'd need to empty alone. Ronan has been photographed with a ridiculous number of women - but never the same one twice.

But personality wise, he's an unequivocal wanker.

From the second we laid eyes on each other, he's done nothing but torment me. I suppose I did accidentally write off his Aston Martin with my Range Rover.

His arrogance knows no bounds. I suppose he does have two Olympic gold medals tucked beneath his belt. Or budgie smugglers.

I shift in the plastic poolside seating and press my thighs together, will my eyes to focus on my twin daughters splashing in the deep end, and not their insanely attractive but infuriating swimming instructor.

I've created a multi-million euro blogging empire from my situation as a single mother. I haven't dated since... since my last boyfriend knocked me up, then knocked me down with three soul-shattering words, 'I'm actually married.'

But I'm still a red-blooded woman.

'See something you like?' Ronan calls from the edge of the pool, raking a hand through his damp, dirty blond hair and shooting me a wink.

If goading me was an Olympic sport, he'd have won a million gold medals.

I peel my eyes from his perfect pecs as a hot flush strikes my cheeks. 'No. I was merely disapproving of the scratch marks on your chest,' I lie. Really, I'm wondering about the woman who put them there. Specifically, what he was doing to her to make her claw so crazily.

'Do you scratch, Sassy Sav?' He wiggles a pair of thick, fair eyebrows.

Irritation flares my nostrils. He knows well my blog handle is Single Sav, but he's always called me Sassy Sav.

His thumb roams over his chin thoughtfully. 'I bet you do. In fact, I bet you claw, and scratch and scream.'

As much as I hate him, what I hate more is that his filthy mouth incites baser feelings in my groin. I cross my denim-clad legs and toss my hair from my shoulder. 'You'll never find out.'

'Never say never, sweetheart.' His navy eyes twinkle. 'I'm biding my time until you finally overcome your man-hating ways.'

I'm not a man-hater.

I've just been burned.

Badly.

Adopting an air of boredom, I pretend to examine my pink painted nails, even though his filthy mouth sets my heart racing like a wild stallion thundering across an open prairie. 'Oh, I can safely say I'd rather jump into the middle of the Irish Sea without a life raft than jump into bed with you.' And I can't swim.

'Is that right?' His plump lips lift into an infuriating smirk. 'Maybe that will cool your flaming face down.'

'Is that an appropriate way to speak to the mother of the children you're being paid to teach to swim?' I bite out, furious with him for inciting a reaction in me like this, and even more furious with myself for letting him.

'I'd say it's about as appropriate as said mother salivating over the man she's paying to teach said children to swim.' He folds his powerful arms across the sharp curves of his chest and cocks his head.

I sigh in disgust. 'In your dreams, dickhead.'

'I won't even deny it.' Ronan's voice is suddenly serious.

My daughter Eden saves me from having to wonder why. She chooses this precise second to shout from the deep end of the pool. 'Watch this, Mammy.'

My head flicks up as she dives gracefully beneath the clear blue water. My twin daughters might be identical in appearance, but in personality they are worlds apart. Where Eden strives to please, Isla strives to make mischief. Second child syndrome is real, even though there's only a couple of minutes between them.

'That was rubbish!' Isla exclaims. 'Watch this, Mammy.' She dive-bombs into the pool, ass first. Water sprays four feet in every direction before she emerges with a raucous cackle.

God help me when the hormones hit.

'Bravo, girls.' Ronan claps his palms together and nods approvingly. Both girls beam at his praise. Isla whoops and holds her hand up, offering him a gleeful thumbs up. Eden simply gives him a shy smile.

I might think Ronan's a dickhead, but my daughters adore him. And as much as it pains me to admit it, he's ridiculously good with them. He indulges them when they climb on his back (Isla, obviously), praises them when they venture into the deep end, and wipes the water from their eyes when their goggles aren't sitting right.

Ronan teaches swimming at St Jude's Girls' School during the week as part of the school curriculum, but the girls prefer these private one-to-one lessons every Saturday morning because they get to shamelessly monopolise him for forty-five minutes. I'd pay for them to come every day if Ronan had the space, but these classes are like gold dust. The fact Ronan somehow always squeezes my girls in somewhere every Saturday is a wonder.

'That's it for today,' Ronan calls, glancing up at the huge clock mounted on the wall behind the diving board.

'Ohhhhh,' the girls groan simultaneously and reluctantly drag themselves out of the pool.

The perving session, I mean swimming/sparring lesson, is over, for another week at least.

Ronan's baby blues settle on mine again. 'I'll text you a time for next Saturday.'

'Morning works best for me.' I uncross my legs and rise from the uncomfortable chair.

His biceps flex as he hauls himself out of the water. I will my eyes to look anywhere but at those damn pecs, scratches or no scratches. 'Yeah, I thought you'd be a morning type of person.' His lascivious tone conveys a clear innuendo.

Does he see me as a challenge?

Is it because I don't date?

No, Ronan flirts aggressively with every woman he meets. Hence the never-ending supply of paparazzi shots the papers are always publishing.

I roll my eyes at him and take a step back to put some distance between us. 'Think about me a lot, do you, manwhore?'

'Usually when I'm in the shower.' He grins and shakes the water off himself like a dog before stepping closer to me.

My tongue clicks against the roof of my mouth, primarily because now that specific image is imprinted into my brain for evermore. 'Have you no shame?' I nod towards my approaching shivering daughters.

'Absolutely none.' He winks again. 'See you next week.'

Chapter Two

SAVANNAH

In the changing room, I help the girls shower and then dress in matching denim jumpsuits. Eden blow-dries her own hair. Isla screams in protest as I run a brush through her long, dark locks.

My daughters have my heart-shaped face, high cheekbones, and button noses, but they have their father's dark hair and hazel eyes.

Not that they know that.

They've never met their father.

He-Who-Has-Never-Been-Named wanted nothing to do with them.

A memory of the last time I saw him plays through my mind like a low-quality blurry video recording.

'I'm pregnant.'

A frown furrows on his brow as he backs towards the door like an animal looking for its escape. 'You're what?' Panic tinges his words.

'I'm pregnant.'

'You can't be. How?' This isn't the reaction I'd been expecting. Shock - absolutely. This level of horror - no way.

Nervous laughter bubbles in my throat. 'You know how babies are made.'

'You're supposed to be on the pill.' His nostrils flare as his gaze narrows.

'I am. It's not one hundred per cent effective though, and you've certainly been testing its abilities lately.'

'How could you let this happen?' The man who stares back at me is unrecognisable. Bitterness twists his face. 'Don't go through with it, Savannah. If you do, you're on your own. I can't help you.' He clears his throat. 'I'm actually married.'

The shock, along with the first trimester nausea, is enough to send me hurtling towards the bathroom.

By the time I'd finished throwing my guts up, he was long gone. So, I fled home to Dublin, broken and ashamed, and started a blog documenting my life as a single mother, sharing tips and journaling the highs and lows of the journey.

Within a few weeks, I had a hundred thousand subscribers. Within months, I was offered an advertising contract from Bella Baby, Ireland's biggest supplier of baby care essentials.

Now, six years later, I have more than a million followers on Instagram.

Almost half a million paying subscribers to my blog.

I've written a best-selling book, *Single Sav's Guide To Winging Parenthood Alone*.

I've designed my own infant clothing range, stocked by Brown Thomas and plenty more luxury boutiques around the country. I'm hoping to open a flagship shop on Grafton Street next year.

It's ironic how one of the worst things that's happened to me became the best thing that's ever happened to me. I have my gorgeous daughters, my two best friends, Ashley and Holly, and my business. I don't need *him*.

But that doesn't stop red-hot rage sizzling through my

veins every time I see his smarmy face popping up on TV. He wasn't famous then, but he is now. He's never once reached out to even ask about the girls, or to offer them a single cent. Sometimes, in my worst nightmares, I dream he turns up here in Dublin. But why would he? He didn't want the girls then, and he doesn't want them now.

'Can we get something out of the vending machine?' Isla runs towards the well-stocked machine in the reception area like it's a foregone conclusion. Eden hangs beside me, tugging on the straps of her rucksack to tighten it.

'Sure.' I fumble in my jeans pocket for some change.

My phone rings from the Bottega Veneta handbag that's draped across my shoulders. I need more hands. I slip the girls a few coins each and rummage past chewing gum, old receipts and six different lipsticks before I locate it.

It's an unknown number. Probably work. Despite having a virtual PA and an agent called Cassandra, I still can't seem to escape weekend work calls.

'Hello?'

'Savannah?' a female voice coos into my ear. 'Savannah Kingsley?'

'Speaking.' I watch as Isla selects the biggest bar of Dairy Milk from the top row of colourful confectionary.

'My name is Susie Silver. I work for a company called Coral. You may have heard of them?'

Of course I've heard of them. Coral is an Irish brand, manufacturing high quality, elegant swimwear which is stocked world-wide. Their range is exquisite and ultra-exclusive. A bikini retails for three hundred euros. The pieces are iconic. They go out of stock faster than the manufacturers can produce them.

Lucas Beechwood, the CEO, is the son of one of the world's most famous models, and he has the bone structure to prove it. That guy's been plastered all over the media since he was a kid, and he has used his face, and his connections, shamelessly to build his brand.

'I'm familiar with the brand.' It's an effort to keep my tone neutral. I send up a silent prayer that she's calling to offer me some merchandise to promote on my social media platforms. I'll even do it for free; I just *need* one of those ass-sculpting bikinis.

'Then you'll be aware that we have a women's range called Coral Chic.'

'I am.' Isla tears open the chocolate and drops the wrapper on the floor. I motion for her to pick it up, praying the bar will keep her quiet until I get to the crux of this conversation.

'We're looking for a real woman to model our swimwear. Someone who's had children. Who is athletically healthy, but not model skinny. Someone with a large female following of their own.'

My jaw drops.

Is she seriously asking me?

'We'd like to offer you the position of brand ambassador. The contract is worth a million euros.' She pauses. 'I'm sure you'll have to think about it.'

'I'll do it!' I exclaim. A million euros and the ass-sculpting bikinis have nothing on the exposure that a contract like this will offer the Single Sav brand.

A chuckle resounds through the phone. 'Fabulous. I'll email you the details straightaway. We'll be shooting the promotional images in a couple of months.'

'Fabulous. Thank you so much for thinking of me.' I glance between my daughters. 'Where is the shoot?'

An image of white sandy beaches and clear turquoise sea lapping the shore springs to mind. Me sipping pina coladas on a day bed by a shimmering pool.

To some people, this might be heaven.

To me it's hell.

One, I already mentioned I can't swim. Two, I won't leave my daughters to go any further than the UK.

A niggle of worry worms its way through my stomach. What if something happened to either of them and I wasn't here? What if I couldn't get back quickly enough?

My dads are brilliant. Yes, you heard me right, dads. Plural. I'm adopted. Steve and Stuart Kingsley took me in when I was only three-weeks-old. I consider myself exceptionally lucky. They're fantastic parents and amazing grandparents. But I won't fly across the world and leave my daughters with them for weeks on end.

'It's here, in Ireland.' Susie's confident tone is pleasantly reassuring.

Relief seeps into my soul. 'In a studio?'

'No, in the sea.'

'The sea?' I parrot.

'Yes. As you know, at Coral we pride ourselves on being Irish. We'll be shooting all the promotional images in this country. Don't worry, the water will have warmed up by June.' Her chuckle sends chills down my spine.

'You want me to get into the Irish Sea?'

Careful what you wish for, right? Not twenty minutes earlier, that's almost exactly what I said to Ronan.

'Yes. You can swim, right?' Concern etches into Susie's voice.

'Absolutely.' Lies. Lies. Lies. But I have a couple of months to learn, and to get over my fear of water. I'll have to because there's no way I can pass up an opportunity like this.

No way in the world.

'Wonderful.' Susie's tone brightens again. 'I'll email you the contract. Sign it and send it back at your earliest convenience. Include your measurements for sizing.'

'I will,' I promise.

'You're everything Lucas is looking for. Wholesome. Hard working and a brilliant role model for women,' Susie says. 'We're excited to have you on board.'

My cheeks flush. 'Thanks, I'm excited too.'

Excited and terrified.

Do I need the money? Honestly, no. Besides my clothing range, book royalties, and paid blog subscribers, I have five luxury properties I rent out. Money isn't an issue these days. But the exposure will be phenomenal.

What I need is swimming lessons.

And I'm going to need the best instructor in the country.

On the plus side, I know the perfect guy.

It's just a shame he's such a cocky manwhore.

Chapter Three

RONAN

An image of my younger self fills the sixty-inch TV screen in the living room of my penthouse apartment. Watching reruns of my last race isn't healthy, but I can't help it. One minute, I'm the most successful Olympic swimmer this country has ever seen, the next I'm a glorified swimming instructor passing the time with expensive whiskey and faceless women.

Okay, I get paid a ridiculous amount of money to teach at the most exclusive girls' school in Dublin, the only school in Ireland that has a full-sized Olympic pool, and I actually enjoy the craic with the kids. Even so, it's a huge lifestyle change.

One that I couldn't have transitioned into without the help of my friend, Jake Nolan.

Jake and I trained together every day of our lives for years. For each of my gold medals, he secured the silver. There was always a fierce rivalry between us, but it was always good natured.

Unlike me, Jake adjusted to his retirement seamlessly. Probably because it coincided with his wedding to his childhood sweetheart, Jessica James. They bought an old house in the west of Ireland and divide their time between renovating it and swimming in the sea. Jake might not have secured the gold, but he's certainly winning at life.

When I was in training, my routine was watertight - pun intended. Now all I have is time and I have no idea how to fill it, apart from partying with my brother and serial shagging, but both pastimes are wearing thin.

I have my medals.

The memories of glory.

The sense of achievement.

But when it comes to something more meaningful, it all boils back to the same thing, the Olympic-sized hole in my life.

There's only so many first dates a man can endure.

Only so many dull, repetitive questions a man can answer.

Only so many faceless fucks a man can sustain.

I have a ferocious appetite for sex. Nothing compares to the sensation of a woman's body bucking and writhing beneath mine, legs wrapped around my waist while I drive us both to a decadent finale. But lately, nothing, or perhaps I should say no one, has been able to quench my appetite.

I'm looking for something more meaningful.

The problem is, the only woman I really want, I can't have.

I have been obsessed with the same woman for two years, one month, and fifteen days.

A woman who never dates.

A woman who has carved out an entire career on being single.

A woman with long blonde hair, a body to die for, and two adorable daughters who I could hang out with all day.

Yep - you heard me right. I am obsessed with Savannah fucking Kingsley, "Single Sav," the man-hater herself.

Why?

I have no idea.

There's just something about her. Something deep inside of her calls to something deep inside of me. I've wanted her from the very first day I laid eyes on her, even if she did unapologetically write off my Aston Martin in the school car park. She crashed into my car, crashed into my life, and somehow hijacked my head and my heart.

But I can't have her.

Savannah has cultivated her entire brand based on being single.

That said, the woman oozes sexuality, from those sultry come-to-bed-eyes that dart away every time I catch her staring at me, right down to her long, toned legs.

It's just a shame they remain permanently crossed.

She acts like she hates the ground I walk on, but she was staring at my pecs like she wanted to devour them earlier. The scratches on my chest stemmed from helping my brother move some sharp-edged furniture in his apartment, but the heat flooding her cheeks as she imagined an entirely different scenario was almost adorable.

Does a woman like her really abstain from sex completely?

Her full, round breasts are too fucking perfect not to be touched.

The womanly contours of her ass were made to be grabbed and groped.

And those lips, rosy pink, are so fucking plump, it's criminal not to make use of them.

It's great that she's a champion for women, and for single mothers, but not all men are bastards.

Not all of us need to be put back in our box.

Not that I'll ever convince her of that.

Which is why I'm stuck in the first date/ faceless fuck

cycle, hoping that one day, one of them will affect me the same way Savannah does.

She calls me a manwhore. Maybe I am. But it's only because I can't have what I really want – her.

Winding her up, watching her cringe, watching her cheeks flush crimson, is the highlight of my Saturday. She assumes my sexual innuendos are a joke, but there's nothing funny about the way I silently will her to take me up on one of them.

My phone buzzes on the glass coffee table. I hate that coffee table. I've banged my shin on it more times than I can count, but it was a housewarming gift from my sister, Rachel, and I can't bring myself to get rid of it. If she called in and it was gone, she'd be hurt, so I keep it and regularly hurt myself on it instead.

I rock up from the couch, praying it's not the weather girl I fucked a few weeks ago. I told her it was a one-time thing, but she got my number from somewhere and has been stalking me ever since.

No, given it's Saturday night. It's probably my brother, Richard, wondering if I'm going out. He's more than happy to act as my wingman, especially when it provides access to the VIP section of every exclusive nightclub in Dublin.

Unlike me, he's showing no sign of tiring of the serial dates and faceless fucks.

My brow tugs upwards at the sight of Savannah Kingsley's name flashing across my screen.

Hope sparks in my chest for a split second before spectacularly crashing and burning.

She's probably calling to bollock me for flirting with her in front of the twins. They were out of earshot. I'm not that careless.

I reach for the remote and flick off the TV before swiping to answer her call.

'If you're calling to help me out in the shower, you're half an hour too late.' I force my tone into a lazy drawl to hide the giddiness at the unexpected chance to hear her velvety voice, even if she is calling to berate me.

'You're disgusting,' she exclaims.

'No, I'm a man with needs. Taking care of them is the most natural thing in the world. Tell me Savannah, do you take care of your needs? Or is the reason you're so aggressive because you're wound tight with sexual tension?' I shouldn't tease her. I'm not doing myself any favours, but I can't help it.

The way her voice hitches sends my heart rate soaring higher.

She pauses for a long beat. Is she imagining the same sexy scenario as me?

'As much as I'd love to discuss this further,' sarcasm hangs on her every syllable, 'there's a reason I'm calling the most irritating man on the planet on a Saturday evening.' The slightest flicker of vulnerability inflects her tone.

Worry flares in my chest. For all my teasing and bravado, and pent-up desire for Savannah, I'd do anything in the world for her. And I mean anything.

'Is everything okay? Are the twins okay?' Over the past couple of years, I've come to adore those little girls. At six years old, Eden has more sense than most grown women, and Isla has more balls than most grown men.

'The twins are fine.' Savannah hesitates. 'I need a favour.'

I can't help myself. It's there for the taking. 'Oh, sweetheart, you've come to the right place.' One of these days, she will slap me.

'Not that kind of favour, you ass.' She blows out a long slow breath, like asking me for anything is killing her.

Curiosity curls in my core, along with an intrinsic desire to please her. 'Well, go on then.'

'Do you offer adult lessons?' she asks meekly.

Multiple multicoloured images of the kind of adult lessons I'd like to give her flash through my delinquent brain, but the sheer desperation in her tone prevents me from spouting another suggestive one-liner.

I clear my throat and readjust my dick in my pants. 'I don't, but I could, I suppose.'

Can Savannah Kingsley, the feistiest woman I've ever met, seriously not swim?

'I'll pay you, of course,' she says.

'Oh, sweetheart, spending time with you in a swimsuit is more than enough payment, trust me.' I'm not even joking.

'Are you an asshole to everyone? Or just me?'

If she knew the truth of the situation, she'd know I'm not being an asshole. I'm being brutally honest. To save any awkwardness on both our parts, it's probably best for both of us if she doesn't find out. 'That's a good question. I honestly don't know. You're the only woman who calls me one.'

'Hard to believe,' she mutters.

'Believe it, sweetheart. But this asshole will teach you to swim if that's what you're looking for. I don't want your money, though.'

'What do you want, then?' Her voice is thick with suspicion.

'Go on a date with me,' I blurt before I can bite my tongue.

She exhales again. 'I don't date.'

'Don't or won't?' Why am I pushing this? I know the score.

'Both.' She sighs. 'Does that mean you won't help me?' Panic permeates her words.

'I'll help you. I suppose seeing you in a swimsuit will be payment enough.' I'm not joking.

'Ronan!' she chides, but with less vehemence than usual.

This can only end in trouble. The woman is more volatile

than a volcano and more tempting than Eve's forbidden rosy red apple. But she could ask me for anything, and I'd never say no to her. And the funny thing about it is, she doesn't even have an inkling.

'Thank you.' Relief is audible in her tone. 'When can we start?'

'What's the rush?' I rock back on the couch, cradling the back of my head with my free hand.

'I've been offered an advertising contract with Coral Chic. They want me to be their brand ambassador.' A hint of excitement bites into her voice.

Impressive. Coral is Ireland's most exclusive swimwear brand. To be the model for the female range is a huge deal.

'But the photoshoot is in the water.' The nerves creep back in.

I blow out a breath. 'Can you swim at all?'

'No,' she admits.

'When's the shoot?'

'In a couple of months. Details to be confirmed.'

'Okay, we've got time, but if you're a total novice, we should start asap. When are you free?' The prospect of spending time with the woman I've been fantasising about for two years makes me feel like a giddy schoolboy again.

Especially when it involves seeing her body sculpted in synthetics.

'Tomorrow?' she edges. 'Though it is Sunday.'

Sundays are traditionally a family day. We go to Mam's for a roast. My sister, Rachel, helps with the dinner while Richard and I tear around the garden after our nephews. I've been caught out before by "Ronan, will you change Mark's nappy? It's only a wet one, I promise."

Rachel's husband, Jonathon, usually brings out the board games afterwards. Now and again, we smoke one of Dad's favourite cigars in his memory. Keeping the family tradition going has become a religious routine since he passed.

I never work on Sundays, but for Savannah, I'll make an exception. Hell, if she wanted me to work on Christmas Day, for her I would. Any excuse to spend time with her.

'I could probably squeeze an hour in the morning.' As long as I don't go out with Richard tonight, drink my weight in whiskey, and end up in bed with another random. 'Meet you at St. Jude's at eleven?' I suggest. 'I'll have to run it by the principal, but I'm sure she'll be cool with us using the school pool on a Sunday.'

'No need. Ashley Kearney might be the principal, but she's also my best friend. I'm meeting her tonight. She won't mind.' Savannah sounds certain of it.

'Well, I guess I'll see you tomorrow then, Sassy Sav.' I pick up the TV remote again.

'It's Single Sav, as you well know.' There's less of a protest in her tone than usual.

'More's the pity.' For once, there's no trace of teasing in my tone.

She pauses, like she's waiting for the punchline, but there isn't one. 'See you tomorrow. And Ronan...thank you.'

'I would say it's a pleasure, but given you hate the ground I walk on, I'm not sure it will be.'

'I don't hate the ground you walk on. I hate your ego.'

'Ouch.' Maybe she has a point.

I should rein it in.

But then what will I hide behind when she's so close that the scent of her feminine floral perfume sends my dick into overdrive?

Chapter Four
SAVANNAH

'Girls, we need to leave or we're going to be late.' I whizz round the open-plan country-style kitchen grabbing my purse, phone, and car keys.

Eden is waiting patiently by the front door with her shoes on. Isla is hopping around on one foot in just a pair of pink striped panties.

'Isla, seriously! Go and get dressed, please.' I fling my hands up in despair. I'm jittery and it has nothing to do with three glasses of Sancerre I had with Ashley last night, and everything to do with the fact I'm about to get into waist deep water for the first time in over twenty years.

I concentrate on my breathing. Ronan will not let me drown. The man is a professional. He might have dented my Range Rover, and my ego, but I trust him - in the water at least.

My phone vibrates with a message from Ashley, my best friend. Obviously, she said it was no problem to use the school pool.

> Ashley: Good luck with the hot swimming instructor.

Gah. I'll be too terrified to notice how hot he is today.

Ten minutes later, I load the girls into my brand-new Range Rover, one that neither Ronan nor I have dinged, yet.

Crashing into him was one of the most embarrassing experiences of my life. I blame him, but truthfully, I might have been in the wrong. It's impossible to call it. We were both attempting to park in the same spot from opposite sides. Admittedly, I was distracted, but he must have been too when he didn't see me ploughing in from the other side.

'Everyone got everything?' I check as I start the engine. Isla finally picked a dress from her extensive collection, and both girls are strapped into their car seats.

'Yep,' they chant in unison.

I pull out of my winding gravel driveway and make the journey across the city to my dads' house with *The Greatest Showman* soundtrack blaring through the speakers of the car.

Fear and doubt loop through my brain like a spinning carousel.

What was I thinking, asking Ronan Rivers to teach me how to swim?

The man has the filthiest mouth I've ever come across. *Or not, as the case may be.*

His suggestive remarks and one-liners don't offend me, quite the opposite, in fact. The reason they infuriate me is because my mind refuses to stop playing them back each night after I put the girls to bed. It's not helpful.

But he is the best swimmer in the country. I've seen his teaching methods first-hand. He's kind and gentle, to the girls, at least. I'll have to suck it up if I want to fulfil my role for the Coral Chic contract. Which I do, badly.

And if I learnt to swim, I'd be able to bring the twins to the beach without the fear of drowning hanging over me. It's a stone's throw from the house. I can see it from my sitting room window, yet I make every excuse under the sun why we can't go. A wave of guilt ripples through me.

Being a mother is the hardest job in the world. No matter how much of myself I give, it never feels like enough. I wrote an entire book on how to parent as a single mam, but sometimes I think I'm none the wiser. As the book title suggests, I really am winging it.

I swing into the driveway of my childhood home. April in Ireland can be a beautiful month, especially if you have access to a garden like this one. As usual, the lawn looks like a golf course, the boxwood bushes are perfectly preened, and pink and purple tulips line the perimeter.

Both of my dads are obsessed with gardening. They even grow their own herbs and vegetables in raised boxes at the back of the sandstone house. Thankfully, they take pity on me and work their magic on mine once or twice a month, too.

A warmth expands in my chest as the red front door swings open and both dads rush out. I'm under no illusion it's to greet me. No, it's the twins. They're obsessed with them.

Stuart and Steve Kingsley are both lean, athletic, and well able to lift my daughters and swing them in the air like dolls. Of course, the girls love it. They might not have a dad, but they have the best two grandads in the world.

Stuart is more playful than Steve. He loves to tease me about getting married, despite being famous for my single status. I'm sick of telling him that "Married Sav" just doesn't have the same ring to it. Even if I spent my childhood parading around the house with a pillowcase on my head as a veil singing *'Here comes the bride.'* Doesn't every little girl dream of a big white wedding? It's just that life had different plans for me.

I pull to a stop next to their matching ebony-coloured Audis. 'Thank you so much for taking the girls.' I let down the window but don't get out of the car. If these two start talking, I'll be late, and I'm cutting it fine as it is.

Stuart goes to Eden's door to get her, while Steve goes to Isla's.

'No problem. Take your time,' Steve says, over the girls shrieking their greetings. 'Where are you going again?'

'I've decided to take swimming lessons,' I admit, like it's nothing.

My dads eyes lock. Steve's mouth falls open. Stuart arches his eyebrows, all too aware of the origin of my fear of the water.

'I got offered a contract as the ambassador for Coral Chic and the promotional shoot is in the sea.'

'That's amazing, honey.' Stuart leans in through the open car window to grip my shoulder and squeeze. 'I'm so proud of you.'

'Me too, baby,' Steve says, ushering Isla and Eden up the semi-circular front steps.

'We'll have a glass of wine ready for you when you're finished,' Steve promises.

'Steve bought fresh salmon from the guy at the pier for dinner and we've got new potatoes, carrots and kale from the garden.' Stuart gives one more squeeze before removing his hand from my shoulder.

'Sounds delicious.' The nausea swirling in my stomach has prevented me from eating anything since my conversation with Ronan last night.

Steve approaches again, peering in the window. 'Just an afterthought, but who exactly is teaching you to swim?' His silver eyes gleam. 'Please tell me it's the ultra-hot former Olympic champion who teaches the twins!'

I put the gearstick in reverse and deliberately ignore the question. 'Bye dads. See you later.'

'Good luck,' Steve calls, stepping back.

'Behave!' Stuart shouts, wiggling his eyebrows suggestively.

Ronan never replaced the Aston Martin. He bought a Tesla instead. When I reach the car park at St Jude's, it's already there. It's safe enough today. The car park is empty and there's ample parking.

I suck in a huge breath as I enter the building and strut through to the female changing rooms, exuding way more confidence than I feel.

The silence is eerie.

Ronan must already be in the water.

I slip out of my denim dress and change into a lemon-yellow bikini. Thank God for laser hair removal.

Oh God. As if not being able to swim wasn't humiliating enough, being almost naked with Mr Ego himself is kind of mortifying.

'I suppose seeing you in a swimsuit will be payment enough.'

His teasing knows no bounds.

I'm not ashamed of my body, despite its stripes and scars. Quite the opposite, in fact. It grew, nurtured and carried my beautiful daughters, and it's in good enough shape to run five miles three times a week, but it has a habit of betraying my baser needs.

I leave my belongings scattered across the wooden slated benches. No one will touch them. No one else is coming.

It's just me and Ronan today.

I swallow thickly and pad over the ivory tiled flooring towards the pool, wondering if I'll sink or swim.

Chapter Five
RONAN

Holy fuck.

Savannah steps out of the changing rooms and my cock lurches to full mast.

The woman is trying to kill me.

A bikini? Seriously. Did she come to torment me or to be taught how to swim?

Her perfect tits are pushed up by the flimsiest scrap of yellow, the outline of her pebbled nipples protruding like twin peaks.

Her softly curving hips are all woman.

Her stomach is smooth and flat and practically begging for me to roll my tongue over. Begging me to roll it lower than her belly button, begging me to explore what she's hiding beneath the tiny scrap of yellow between her legs.

Oh. My. God.

If I was wearing more than a thin pair of swimming shorts myself, I'd happily soak up every inch of creamy satin skin. To eye-fuck every morsel of flesh before committing it to memory.

But I'm not.

I drop further into the water. Over the past two years, I've imagined what Savannah would look like in her underwear many times, but none of my shower fantasies ever came close to the reality. The word stunning simply doesn't do her justice.

She angles her face upwards, tilts her chin out defiantly, and those brilliant blue eyes lock on mine.

'Looking good, Savannah.' I shoot her a lascivious wink, praying she might once again miss the fact I'm obsessed with her.

'Hilarious.' Her hostile tone cannot hide her nerves. From the way her voice cracks, she sounds genuinely terrified. Time to stop being a cock or thinking with it, at least.

I glide through the water towards her, ensuring my delinquent dick stays well below the surface. I curl my legs beneath me and bob by the edge of the pool, using my index finger to beckon her in.

She nips her lower lip, clenched fists hanging by the side of her body. Perfectly pedicured feet take a tentative step towards the pool.

'Did you have a bad experience in the water?' She's so confident in every other aspect of life. It's the only explanation I can think of.

She nods but doesn't elaborate.

Why would she? We're not friends. She's made it clear she can't stand me, even though her eyes are once again roving over my ripped torso.

I place the flat of my hands on the white edge of the pool and stare up at her. Half-naked, with the sun slanting through the Velux windows illuminating her caramel-coloured hair, she looks like a goddess.

A lost one.

The urge to comfort her surges in my chest.

'I won't let anything happen to you, Savannah. I promise.'

My voice is low and sincere. 'Whatever you think of me, or whatever differences we've had in the past, I need you to trust me, or this isn't going to work.'

I pat the side of the pool and motion for her to sit.

Her head bobs in a reluctant nod and she closes the distance between us, dropping to a crouching position.

When I thought I couldn't be any more obsessed, her vulnerability proves how very wrong I was. The urge to comfort and protect her roars like a caveman in my chest. 'Don't worry. By the time I've finished with you, you'll be a pro, I promise.'

'Who are you and what did you do with the arrogant alphahole?' She attempts a shaky smile as she perches on the edge of the pool and drops her toes into the water.

It takes everything I have not to stare at the shapely curve of her calf, the way her toned thighs seem to go on forever. 'I know you have a somewhat low opinion of me, but I'm not all bad.'

'I don't have a low opinion of you. I just think you have a high one of yourself.'

'Fake it til you make it, right?' She has no idea that I bury my biggest insecurities behind that outward confidence.

That I worry I'm a has-been.

That my best days are behind me.

That I have no idea how to fill the Olympic-sized void in my life, bar drinking whiskey and sleeping around.

She shoots me a quizzical look before returning her attention to the water.

'Are you ready?' I take a step back and motion to the clear, inviting water around me.

She swallows hard again and squeezes her eyes shut for a long beat before nodding. 'As I'll ever be.'

'It's not deep.' I stand tall, the water lapping at my waist. Thankfully, the full mast has subsided to half-mast now.

'Can we take this really slowly?' She grips the side of the pool so tightly her knuckles are white.

'Yes.' Instinctively, I reach out to touch her hand and a million volts of electricity surge across my skin. Ignoring the fire sparking in my fingers, I peel her trembling hands from the mosaic tiles and place them in mine. 'I've got you.'

I pull her forwards until her ass is right on the edge of the ledge.

She peeps out from under thick lash-framed eyelids, a look of sheer terror pinching her features.

'Savannah, you're getting into the shallow end of a swimming pool with an Olympic swimmer. You're safe. You can touch the floor. And I'm holding your hands.'

'There's that ego again, Mr I'm-An-Olympic-Swimmer,' she mutters, eyeing the water like it might magically swirl into a tsunami and swallow her whole.

'Stating facts is not egotistical. But glad to see the man-hater is still in there somewhere.' My lips roll into a smile.

She clings onto my hands tightly enough to turn them white. I should be in agony, but I'm in ecstasy because every nerve in my body is on high alert from her sheer proximity.

'Excuse me if my fear of drowning warps my personality,' she says, inching herself into the water.

It's not Savannah who's in danger of drowning... it's me.

Drowning in those beautiful blue eyes.

From the way they're lingering on my torso again, she doesn't find me as repulsive as she makes out.

But that doesn't change the fact she doesn't date.

Ever.

Chapter Six
SAVANNAH

I squeeze my eyes tightly shut as my ass hits the water with a not entirely unpleasant slap.

I'm in and it's not nearly as bad as I feared.

The water is just slightly above my waist.

My feet are firmly on the floor.

My hands are still in Ronan's.

My pulse roars, and I'm not convinced it's purely because of the pool.

When I finally dare to open my eyes, I'm greeted by Ronan's perfect pecs.

The air zings between us, crackling like a live wire.

I suck in a breath and blow it out slowly.

'You're okay.' He gives my hands a gentle squeeze. 'I've got you. I know what it's like to be afraid, but I promise I won't let anything happen to you.'

Oh. My. God. He's always been infuriatingly hot, but now he's being infuriatingly nice too. It's easier when he's being a douche.

'Thank you.' I swallow hard. 'What now?' I tilt my head upwards and meet his encouraging eyes. All trace of his usual teasing's evaporated.

Funnily enough, so has my usual disdain for him.

He releases my hands and drops his torso beneath the water, his knees pushing between us. 'Do you think you can go down?' He shoots me a wink.

Okay, I take it back. Not all his teasing has evaporated.

'Funny fucker, aren't you?' I inch myself lower until my breasts touch the water. He watches them sink beneath the surface with an approving look.

'Good girl,' he says, when my shoulders are under.

A hot jolt strikes between my legs.

"Good girl"? Seriously?

I should be horrified. Patronised. Put out. But nope, my core clenches with long pent-up lust.

For fuck's sake.

I suppose this is the first time in years that I've been nearly naked with a hot man.

Okay, technically, I've never been nearly naked with a man as hot as Ronan Rivers.

My ex might have been a personal trainer, but he has absolutely nothing on the professional athlete in front of me.

'You okay?' Ronan checks but makes no move to take my hand again. I feel oddly bereft without it.

'I think so.' I take slow, deep breaths, revelling in the way the water soothes my skin. Or maybe it's being in the water with him that's soothing. 'It's not so bad in the shallow end.'

'Do you think you'll have to go deep for the shoot?' Ronan's velvety voice harbours a hint of humour.

Is that another innuendo or have I just got a filthy brain?

I haven't been with a man in seven years. Being this close to one is sending my ovaries into overdrive. Funnily enough, being abandoned and pregnant with twins was enough to put me off for a very long time. I hadn't intended to be single for life, but, when my Single Sav brand took off, I couldn't very well start dating.

I decide to give Ronan the benefit of the doubt with the "go deep" remark. 'I don't think so. They want shots of the swimwear, not my shoulders, so hopefully not.'

'That makes sense.' Ronan stands again, his powerful body slicing through the water. A devilish smirk lifts his lips. 'How do you feel about doggy?'

Yep. My doubt was misplaced.

Heat pools between my legs. 'Paddle or style?'

What am I doing?

Flirting with Major Manwhore?

My only excuse is that it's a great distraction from my fear of drowning. It's a good job my bikini bottoms have a legitimate excuse to be wet because the images he's forcing to the forefront of my mind are downright pornographic.

And decadent.

And fucking delicious.

I need a hot minute with one of my many vibrators. Just because I don't date, it doesn't mean I don't have needs.

His eyes snap to mine. 'I meant the former, but I would be more than happy to hear your thoughts on the latter, too.'

'I bet you would.' Am I imagining it, or is there something bulging in those swim shorts? 'Perhaps we should stick to the paddle?'

Ronan shrugs. 'You're the boss.'

We both know that's not true. Here in the water, he's the teacher and I'm the student. He's the expert and I'm the novice. I'm at his mercy and he knows it.

And the worst thing about the entire scenario?

It's hot as fuck.

Surrendering control is almost as emancipating as surrendering my body to the buoyancy of the water. All day, every day, I'm constantly thinking about the things I need to do. Work. Homework. Dinner. Laundry.

Here, all I have to do is what I'm told.

And it's oddly cathartic.

We do some footwork, treading water and kicking. Ronan hauls himself out of the water, returning with a foam float that even my daughters don't need anymore. Heat flashes from my chest all the way to the tips of my ears.

The shame. It's mortifying being so vulnerable.

I feel the weight of his stare as he drops back into the water. 'Look at me,' he demands. 'We all had to start somewhere, okay?'

Through all his teasing and flirting, I never considered he could be so sympathetic, not to me anyway; the woman who totalled his precious car, then blamed him for the accident.

I nod, unable to speak through my shock. This has been a million times easier than I expected.

Then again, as Ronan said, I'm in the shallow end of a pool with an Olympic swimmer. How will I fare when I have to brave unpredictable waves in the freezing cold sea?

His hand brushes my waist as he positions the float around my midsection. Goosebumps fire across my flesh in an alarming display of desire. His blue eyes pin me in a pensive stare. Instead of pulling me up on my obvious reaction to his touch, he reassures me instead.

'You're okay. We'll take it slowly. I won't let anything happen to you.' He repeats the same three phrases until they finally sink in.

I nod. 'Thank you. You're very good at this.'

'It's my job.' He shrugs like it's nothing, but we both know he's going above and beyond for me. It's Sunday after all. Surely, he has somewhere better to be.

Does he have a family?

Friends?

I know nothing about him, other than what the press has printed over the years.

I open my mouth to ask before remembering I'm not supposed to care.

'Look at my hands.' Ronan clasps his fingers together and curls them into a curved hook. 'Fingers tight together make the paddle.' He grabs mine and bends them into the same position as his and drags them through the water.

A tingling sensation surges across my skin, sliding over every vertebra in my spine.

His jaw locks tight.

Does he feel it too?

Or is he simply toying with me with those teasing comments and innuendos?

Either way, it doesn't matter.

I'm Single Sav. I've built a lucrative empire on my relationship status.

And Ronan Rivers is a manwhore.

My single mum followers would feel so betrayed if I started dating again. I've always been so vocal about not needing a man. Not wanting one. Even if it's not entirely true.

My single status is my entire identity. My brand has provided financial security for my girls, but also emotional security for me. It's a rock-solid wall around my heart, one that I've grown exceptionally comfortable with.

Which is precisely why I need to stop salivating over my swimming instructor.

Chapter Seven
RONAN

It's been almost a week since Savannah's first swimming lesson. Almost a week of reliving how her hand felt in mine. How her skin rippled under my touch. And how her tits looked in that bikini top. The low-cut maxi dress hugging her curves today isn't doing anything to take my mind off it either.

She watches from the plastic seats as I instruct Isla and Eden, correcting their breathing technique. Each time I glance around, she glances away, but the burning sensation penetrating my shoulders assures me she's watching.

I saw a different side to her last Sunday.

A softer side.

She projects this hard exterior, but she must have her reasons.

She obviously dated at some point in her life. The twins are living, breathing proof of it. What happened to her to put her off men for life?

Who's the twins' father? I've stalked her online, but as far as I can tell, she's never revealed his identity. Why?

What happened between them?

Where is he?

What kind of man wouldn't play an active role in his children's life?

If I was lucky enough to be a father, I'd ensure I saw my kid every day. Even if I couldn't stand their mother.

'Tilt your head to the right, Isla.' I push my face into the water and turn my head in a demonstration.

Isla rolls her eyes and splashes me. Laughter lurches in my chest. She has all her mother's sass.

'Isla Kingsley, stop messing around and do as you're told.' Savannah attempts to sound stern even as she bites back a smirk.

'Sorry, Mammy.' Isla's features tighten into a contrite expression, but the second Savannah looks away, she splashes me again.

If only her mother was a little more playful, we could have some fun.

She doesn't want you.

She doesn't want any man.

Don't even go there.

Isla's next splashing attempt knocks her off balance. She swallows a mouthful of water, spluttering as she slips beneath the surface. I'm at her side in seconds, hoisting her up before she can sink. 'You okay?'

She nods and clings on to my bicep. I glance at Savannah to make sure she's comfortable with her daughter clinging on to me like a koala, half expecting a scowl, but all I see is relief and gratitude flash through her eyes.

I think Savannah Kingsley might actually be warming to me. And I'm not just talking about the hot flush I usually rise in her cheeks.

Once Isla catches her breath, she splashes me again.

'Right girls, practise your diving technique. Go up to the deep end.' The lesson is almost over and I haven't had the chance to flirt with Savannah once. 'And be careful. Don't rush it. I don't want either of you hitting concrete at the bottom.'

Eden reaches the deep end first and hoists herself out. I haul myself out of the pool and hover next to Savannah. 'You on for another lesson tomorrow?'

Sapphire eyes flick to mine. 'I guess so.'

'It'll be fun.' I grab my towel and run the fluffy cotton across my face.

'Yeah right.' But her usual red-hot hatred for me has mellowed into a wariness.

'Don't tell me you'd rather jump into the Irish Sea,' I tease, lowering the towel over my chest, watching as her eyes unwittingly follow before darting back up to my face.

'Careful what you wish for, right?' Her rosebud lips roll, and she shakes her head with what looks like disbelief. 'That's exactly why I'm in this predicament.'

'We'll make sure you're ready, don't worry.' A huge splash from the deep end steals my attention. 'Well done girls.' I applaud, the thwacking of my palms echoing across the room.

'You're fantastic with them,' Savannah says with what sounds like begrudging respect.

'I love kids. My sister Rachel has three. Her youngest, Mark, is only three-months-old.' I drag my fingers through my wet hair, smoothing it back from my face.

Pristinely plucked eyebrows arch skywards. 'Thought you'd be too busy practising making babies to have any interest in other people's.'

'Think about me a lot, do you?' I toss her own line back in her face.

Her chin juts out defiantly. 'Never when I'm in the shower.'

Now there's a visual.

'See you tomorrow.' She stalks away, ass swaying as she

wraps an arm around of each of her daughters, bringing the term MILF to life.

Tonight, I have no desire to go on the pull or to drink whiskey. For the second week running, I'm more excited about Sunday morning. Though hanging out with the boys beats sitting at home counting down the hours until I get to see Savannah in that tiny yellow bikini again, which is exactly why I stride into Elixir, Dublin's newest, trendiest cocktail bar, to meet my brother, Richard, and a couple of our childhood friends.

Elixir's opulence is undeniable. Crystal chandeliers droop from the ceiling and the walls are a brilliant shade of white, dotted with carefully curated art. The floor is a mat marble speckled with silver granite flecks. Strategically placed mirrors enhance the sense of space.

Plush, comfortable seats are scattered throughout the huge lavish space. The place is full of famous faces and wannabe celebrities.

The bar is packed, obviously. Saturday nights in Dublin are always thronged. My brother is propping up the bar, flanked by Shane and Nick, brothers from the same village where we grew up. Not that I saw much of them. Even as a kid, I had a rigorous training schedule.

Richard spots me and raises a hand in greeting. Where I'm fair-haired and athletic, he's dark-haired and academic. He started referring to himself as Dr Rivers when he graduated with a PhD. in economics from Trinity.

To me, he'll always be Dr Dick. Not because of his PhD, but what he thinks with. Savannah calls me a manwhore but Richard is twice as bad.

I nudge through the jostling bodies towards him.

'Hey, aren't you that hot swimmer?' A curvy blonde in a

white dress drops a hand on my chest, halting my progress. A week ago, I might have entertained her advances, but since spending time with Savannah in the pool on Sunday, my obsession with her has only grown.

'I'm the swimmer,' I confirm, ignoring the hot bit.

Despite what Savannah thinks, I don't have a huge head or an overinflated ego. I'm not bad looking by most standards, I suppose, but I'm not stupid enough to think that's the reason women flock to me.

Everyone these days wants their five minutes of fame.

Everyone except me.

I've had mine. Well, I would have, if the paps would stop photographing me with my conquests and plastering them on sleazy blog sites. I fucking detest cameras. Worst invention ever. I do everything and anything to avoid being caught on them.

'Did I do well to recognise you with your clothes on?' she slurs. Someone started on the cocktails early.

I must have heard that line a hundred times before. I exhale a weary sigh and keep moving.

'I see you've made a friend already.' Richard slaps my back as I reach the bar. He nods towards the blonde, inching closer, stalking me like I'm her next meal.

'It would seem that way.' I turn my back to her and shake hands with Shane and Nick before ordering a Diet Coke from the barman.

'Coke?' Richard splutters. 'What's up? You pregnant?'

'Funny.' I motion to the barman to get another round for the boys. 'I'm working tomorrow.'

'But it's Sunday.' Richard's dark eyebrows crease together in disbelief.

As usual, we're due at Mam's for a huge roast.

'It's a one-to-one lesson.' I shrug, playing it down. 'I'll see you up at Mam's afterwards.'

'Who's the client?' Richard nudges me with his elbow. 'Someone special?'

'No one you know,' I lie. Everyone knows Sassy Sav. She has a million followers on Instagram and even though a lot of them are single women, like her, I'm pretty sure there are a lot of single men following her too, just for very different reasons.

'Incoming.' Richard raises his pint glass to his lips, eyeing the front door.

Instinctively, I turn to see who his beady eyes have landed on.

A familiar, stunning, five-foot-seven blonde struts into the bar and my stomach somersaults. However good Savannah looked in that maxi dress earlier has nothing on what she's wearing tonight. A sculpted black jumpsuit caresses every decadent curve before dipping into a V that plunges almost to her navel, exposing inch after satiny inch of her smooth torso.

Holy fuck.

She's an absolute knockout.

'Fucking hell.' Richard's eyes look like they're about to pop out of his head. 'How is she still single?'

My sentiments exactly, but that doesn't stop the irritation coursing through my veins at the way my brother is leering at the woman I want. A screw tightens in my chest.

Even to have her just once .

To trail my tongue over her full bottom lip. To tease the aggression from her tongue with mine. To trace the taut line over her collarbone and lower.

Fuck, I'm hard again just looking at her.

'Who's she with?' Richard finally drags his jaw from the floor.

'Ashley Kearney, the principal of St Jude's.' Ashley is the

woman who originally approached me to make use of the Olympic pool.

'Let's go buy them a drink.' Richard lurches off the bar.

'Trust me, they don't want us anywhere near them.' I take a sip of Coke just to do something other than stare.

Savannah and Ashley are flanked by two vaguely familiar brunettes.

Nick and Shane halt their conversation, their eyes following our gaze across the room.

'Isn't that Nate Jackson's wife?' Shane squints at the women.

Nate Jackson is a Hollywood movie star who married a teacher from St. Jude last Christmas.

'You're right.' Nick clicks his fingers. 'I knew I recognised her. And the girl next to her is Nate's sister.'

'I don't see any girls there.' Richard wiggles his eyebrows. 'They're all women to me.'

I give him a hard elbow in the ribs, and he coughs. 'What was that for?'

'Pervy men like you are probably the reason women like Savannah don't date.' God, I'm such a hypocrite. I've been perving over her from the first day I met her.

I watch as Savannah shouts something to her friends, clutches her bare chest and tips her head backwards with laughter. Thick lustrous hair cascades across her shoulders in bouncing waves. Her sparkling sapphire eyes radiate a rare playfulness. Those full lips I've dreamed about kissing are painted a bright, fire-engine red. What I wouldn't give to see that red smeared all over my cock.

Yep, I'm officially worse than Dr Dick.

As if Savannah senses she's being watched, her head whips round. Her initial surprise at spotting me is quickly replaced by indignation. Her lips drop into a tight, grim line as she presses them together. As if my mere presence here is an inconvenience.

So much for her warming to me. Her stare is colder than Antarctica. If looks could kill, I'd be taking my last breath right about now.

'You,' she mouths across the sea of faces. Long black eyelashes flutter closed in exasperation a split second before she turns her back on me.

Chapter Eight
SAVANNAH

Of all the gin joints in Dublin, I have to be in the same one as Ronan fucking Rivers. It's bad enough I had to endure him earlier, and tomorrow, but tonight as well while he's out on the pull... that's just cruel.

Watching him today, half-naked, forcing his formidable frame through the water to protect my daughter, was a special kind of torture. The type that makes my ovaries weep. He has a natural knack with the girls. Even Isla listens to him, sort of.

And it seems not only does he have the body of a fallen god, but he has a hidden, inexplicable compassion lingering beneath that teasing façade.

Last week's kindness was unexpected. The way he touched me in the water was tender but firm. Reassuring but pushing for progress. The way he held my hands wasn't in any way inappropriate, but my God did it incite some inappropriate thoughts in my lady parts. Thoughts that have haunted me all damn week.

Ronan was uncannily accurate. I wasn't just frightened, I was embarrassed. He saw me without my clothes on, and without the mask I wear for the rest of the world. The one that conceals every vulnerability I hide behind my flawless make-up and winning smile.

The smile that says, "I've got everything under control."

The smile that says, "I don't need a man."

The smile that says, "I don't need anyone. I'm fine alone."

Want to know a secret?

I don't have everything under control.

Some days I'm winning at life. Others I'm winging it, but either way I have two tiny people relying on me. I have no choice but to put on my big girl pants and get the fuck on with it, no matter how flat I feel.

I don't *need* a man, but truthfully, some days I want one. High speed vibrating silicone can only do so much for a woman. It doesn't hug. It doesn't say, "Hey, you're tired. I'll get up with the girls this morning." And it doesn't keep me warm at night.

I don't *need* anyone, but sometimes when I'm in bed alone at night, when the girls are asleep, and the house is eerily quiet, sometimes I think I might like someone of my own.

But that would ruin everything I've ever worked for.

"Married Sav" doesn't have a blog.

"Married Sav" doesn't have anything.

I guess the vibrating silicone will have to do. Maybe I could get a blow-up doll... a male one, of course. Until then, I'll keep placing a pillow lengthways on the other side of the bed and pretend I'm not alone at night. And avoid spending any unnecessary time with men that are super-hot and unexpectedly kind.

Is it possible I mistook Ronan?

That he's confident, rather than arrogant?

Look what he's achieved. Two Olympic gold medals and the honour of representing his country in a sport he loves. Hell, maybe I'd be shouting about it too.

. . .

'Hey, look, it's your sexy swimming instructor.' Ashley nods towards the bar, her auburn hair brushing the tips of her pale creamy shoulders.

'He's not sexy. He's irritating,' I lie. He's both, though, given the three glasses of Sancerre I've drunk, the scales are significantly tilted towards the sexy side.

What's irritating is his sexual innuendos. Specifically, that I can't act on them, that I can't shut him up by slanting my mouth over his and shocking the shit out of him. That I can't turn them back on him and push his buttons the way he pushes mine.

He must be here on the pull. I've lost count of the number of women he's been photographed with this year. A professional tennis player, a model, and lately, even the beautiful blonde weather girl on the evening news. The days I'm home in time for the six o'clock news, I switch it off before *her* smug face pops up on the screen. Knowing she's been with him twists my stomach with distaste.

Seems like everyone's had a piece of him.

Everyone but me.

My skin prickles with the weight of being watched. The heaviness of someone's attention searing into my skin. I don't need to look around to see who it is. I feel it in my core. There's a growing attraction between the manwhore and me, and it's escalating every time we're near each other. But I can't act on it. I can't. Even if he wasn't a manwhore, I've devoted my life to celibacy.

My stomach twists. Realisation strikes like a blow to the brain.

It wasn't distaste I felt seeing him with the weather girl.

It was jealousy.

Fuck.

My neck yanks round of its own accord. Ronan lifts a drink to his lips and the way he slowly presses them against the glass is nothing short of sexual. His eyes remain on mine over the rim. His usual teasing expression is absent. Yep, this guy across the room looks like he means business. I swallow down the saliva pooling in my mouth, ignore my fluttering heart, and force a glare in his direction.

How dare he turn me on?

How dare he turn up in the very place I'd picked to obliterate all thoughts of him?

The dark-haired guy at his side says something in his ear. Ronan scowls and propels himself off the bar he's leaning against and strides through the crowd in my direction.

A furious hammering in my chest drowns out the sound of the music. The crowd parts to let him pass, the way the Red Sea parted for Moses, and suddenly, the man I've been fantasising about all week is standing in front of me for the second time today.

At least this time he's got clothes on.

Though his fitted white shirt only showcases the sharp lines of his powerful shoulders, the crisp white cotton contrasting those bright cobalt eyes.

Everyone else fades away.

'Savannah.' His lips brush my cheek in a fleeting greeting, leaving a trail of fire in their wake.

Is he trying to kill me?

To make me combust with lust?

The best defence is always offence.

'Don't ever kiss me again. I would say I don't know where those lips have been, but even I scan the gossip blogs sometimes.' I fold my arms across my chest to form a barrier between us, and to hide the frankly visceral reaction his sheer presence has invoked in my nipples.

A quick glance to my right shows my friends have left me

in favour of the bar. Ashley raises her hand and beckons me over, waving the cocktail menu like a flag. I motion with my finger for her to give me a minute.

'Never mind where they've been. Where would you like them to go?' Ronan's gaze skates across the front of my chest and suddenly the jumpsuit I'd earlier felt empowered in now leaves me feeling powerless.

Powerless to deny the display of my carnal needs peaking against the flimsy fabric.

Between the wine and the scent of his woody cologne mixed with his own unique raw masculinity, my armour is wearing thin. For a brief second, I imagine his full lips suctioned against my breast while his fingers skate over my stomach and lower. A tiny sigh slips from my lips. I mask it with a huff.

Our eyes lock in a powerful stare. His pupils are so dilated it's almost as if they've swallowed his irises. I could cheerfully drown in those onyx-like pools.

If I'm not careful, I just might.

I tear my eyes from his and jut my chin out. 'I'd like them, and you, to stay away from me.' My molars clamp together so tightly they're in danger of cracking.

'But only after I've taught you to swim, right?' He tips his face down, inhaling my breath like he's savouring it.

We're toe to toe. Hip to hip. Every cell in my body vibrates, shocked back from a slumber Sleeping Beauty would be proud of.

'Exactly.' I take a step back. 'Don't drink too much tonight. You're working tomorrow.'

'I'm driving.' His tone is low and seductive, and makes me wonder if he's planning on driving a car or a woman.

'Glad to see you're taking our arrangement seriously.' I tried to pay him after last week's lesson, but he point-blank refused to take any cash. His glittering eyes twinkled like I didn't get the memo about the correct currency.

'I'm taking *you* seriously, Savannah.' His thumb brushes under my chin, tilting my gaze up to meet his again. 'Believe it or not, I want to help you.'

Oh. My. God. Those smouldering eyes suggest he wants to devour me. Not helpful. Really not helpful.

'I'll help you out any way I can.' Another innuendo, but with this one, there's no trace of teasing.

'Why?' It's barely more than a whisper.

'Call me a sadist, given the way you insult me, but I really like you.' He brushes a thumb over my lower lip before dropping his hand from my face. 'See you tomorrow.'

I nod, lost for a one-liner for the first time in my life.

I really like you.

It's possibly one of the simplest, most honest compliments I've ever been offered, which is why it heats my heart like a roaring, welcoming fire.

A fire that's rapidly extinguished by an arctic shower half an hour later when he leaves the building with a woman in a white dress. She's draped across him like a fucking scarf.

I didn't have him wrong.

He's a manwhore, and I'd be a fool to forget.

Tell that to my flaming lady parts though.

Chapter Nine
RONAN

I reach the pool early and swim fifty lengths without breaking a sweat. As I slump against the mosaic-tiled pool ledge, Savannah enters the pool area wearing a hot pink bikini and a definitive pout.

'Good morning, sunshine,' I call, hoisting myself out of the water. The mere sight of her smooth, supple curves makes my dick twitch in my shorts, despite the fact I got off twice last night.

Dropping a kiss on her flawless face seemed like an appropriate greeting in the bar, but judging by the rage rolling from her in waves, today it would be dangerous.

I could have almost sworn she was warming to me. Our exchange at Elixir was brief, but there was no missing the heat radiating from her every pore in that revealing jumpsuit. Heat and hunger. I smelt it like a shark smells blood, and if she looks at me with even a hint of the lust I saw in her eyes last night, today I'm going in for the kill, metaphorically speaking, of course.

'What's good about it?' Savannah saunters towards the pool, snapping a hairband from her wrist and twisting her honey-streaked locks into a messy bun on top of her head. Her slender neck is the most elegant thing I've ever seen. The urge to sink my teeth into her skin and mark her as mine surges through my soul.

She's not mine, though.

She's not anyone's.

She belongs to the millions of women following her. Looking up to her as a role model or a symbol that they too can go it alone. It would be easier if she were married to a man instead of her job.

'The company, for a start.' She glares at me.

I extend a hand to help her into the water as she crouches to a sitting position by the edge, but she shakes her head vehemently. Fiercely independent as ever.

Does that keep her warm at night? I doubt it.

'I'd rather spend the day with Adolf Hitler than the next hour with you.'

'Who pissed in your cereal?' I contemplate splashing her with water, but she might actually thump me.

'Nobody,' she spits, her blue eyes blazing with an inexplicably higher level of anger than her usual playful disdain. 'Unlike you, I don't bring strangers home, so that's something I don't have to worry about, along with catching crabs, of course.'

Realisation strikes my stomach.

She thinks I took that woman home last night. The drunk one in the white dress. And she's... angry about it.

No wait, is that jealousy?

A grin splits my face in half. 'I don't take strangers home. Well, not often, and I certainly didn't last night.'

She rolls her eyes like a petulant teenager. 'I watched you walk out the door with her, but whatever. I don't care. It's none of my business. As long as those crabs you caught can't swim.' She eyes my swimming shorts with what looks like hate and hunger.

'I took that woman to *her* home. Not mine.'

Savannah huffs. 'Well, I suppose that's perfectly fine then... as long as you didn't piss in her cereal.' She drops her legs into the water and my gaze is drawn to those shapely thighs. Specifically, the cerise triangle they extend up to.

'I didn't go anywhere near her cereal, or any other item in her house, because I didn't make it past the front door.'

Savannah's shoulders drop an inch and her eyes flash to mine with what looks like relief. Something stupid like hope stirs in my chest.

She *is* jealous!

Which means I'm not imagining the crackling surges of electricity between our bodies. The weight of her stare when she thinks I'm not looking. The way her skin prickled when I took her hands last week.

'Saw sense, did she? Realise your cock's had more rides than a merry-go-round?' Her eyes flit to my shorts again, shrouded beneath the water.

'No. She was drunk. I wanted to see she got home safely, and it provided the perfect excuse to escape my brother, who was trying to force me into doing shots with him. She tried to drag me inside, but I made it clear to her that not only do I not sleep with drunk women, I like someone else.' I pause to allow the last few words to sink in. 'Then I went for a long, hot shower.' I wiggle my eyebrows meaningfully to make her laugh.

It doesn't work.

Fire blazes in her eyes. She sucks in her lower lip. The meaning of my words isn't lost on her.

I wasn't lying.

I like her more than is healthy, given the circumstances.

As I said, I must be a sadist because all she's done is insult me, but her feistiness only makes me more determined to crack her outer shell.

'You like me?' she repeats slowly, a question hanging in her statement.

'Is it so hard to believe?' I extend a hand again and this time she reluctantly accepts it. Her palm slips into mine like it was made for it. I tug her gently into the water. This time, she doesn't close her eyes. They remain firmly locked on mine.

'Why? I'm not exactly nice to you.' She stands waist deep in the water, just inches away. The scent of that enticing floral perfume clouds the air between us. We're still holding hands and I'm pretty sure it's not because she's scared.

'Shall I let you in on a little secret?' I whisper shout, even though we're the only two in the entire building. 'That's part of the appeal.'

'Because I'm a challenge?' She cocks her head. 'Do you think you're the first man who assumes he'll be the one to crack Single Sav?'

'No, not because you're a challenge, because you're beautiful. You emit a class that most women can only dream of. And because beneath that bolshy exterior, there's a vulnerability about you that makes me want to wrap you in cotton wool and take you to bed before unravelling every inch of you.'

A gasp slips from her lips. 'You can't say things like that.'

'Why not? It's true.' I squeeze her hand to reiterate my words.

She exhales heavily. 'It's easier when you torment me.'

'Oh, sweetheart, you have no idea of all the delicious ways I dream of tormenting you – with my tongue.'

'Is that any way to speak to your student?' She adopts an indignant tone, but her lips lift like she's fighting a smirk.

'It's the only way to speak to my student. Now let's get on with this lesson before I do something that will truly scare you away from water for the rest of your life. I said I wanted to help you and I meant it.'

'Okay.' Her tone is uncertain. Like she wants to say something, but she's not sure what.

I guide her to slightly deeper water. 'I've got you. Don't worry, I won't let anything happen to you. You have nothing to fear with me.'

'I know.' Her voice is small but weighted with a trust that only makes her more endearing. Fuck, she's so beautiful when she's vulnerable.

'How about we get you on your back?'

Her huge, hooded eyes blink back at me from beneath thick lustrous eyelashes. She shakes her head, but not with disgust this time. More like wonder.

I place a hand on the small of her back, lift her into a reclined position and watch as goosebumps ripple across her flesh. 'I won't take my hand away until you're ready. Relax back and float. Feel the water supporting you. Your body is made to float.'

It was made to fuck too, but I keep that thought to myself. I'm already at half-mast again. Not helpful.

'Concentrate on your breathing, spread your arms. I won't let anything happen to you.'

'I know,' she murmurs.

'How does that feel?' I slip my hand from beneath her, keeping it just inches away in case she needs it.

'It feels like heaven,' she admits dreamily, staring up at the Velux windows as the sun beats through the glass. Her eyelids flutter blissfully closed.

The weightless sensation of the water is my second favourite sensation in the world. The first one is being inside a woman. What would it feel like to experience both at the same time?

Savannah's eyes fly open, and I wonder for a split second if I said that out loud.

She drops to her feet again. 'I think I'm ready to actually try to swim.'

'Good. Let's start with breaststroke.' My eyes stray to her perfect cleavage, and her gaze follows. She arches a single eyebrow.

'Sorry.' I raise my hands up in an apology. 'I'm only human and you are smoking hot.'

She readjusts her bikini top over her tits, which only draws my attention again. 'Why are you being nice to me? You're scaring me.'

'I'm always nice. You just never take my compliments seriously.'

'I thought you were teasing me.' A wariness creeps into her tone.

'When I'm teasing you, Savannah, you'll know about it.'

'I told you, I don't date.'

'I know. I heard you loud and clear. Which is why I'm not asking you on a date.' I bob beside her in the water, fully aware I'm abusing my position as her swimming instructor, but utterly unable to stop myself.

She swallows thickly. 'What are you asking me, then?' Her voice is low and sultry, and it cracks with a pent-up need.

'I'm asking you to fuck me.'

Chapter Ten
SAVANNAH

Ronan's filthy mouth could be the undoing of me. That and his huge body which is inching towards me like a lion stalking its prey.

'I don't fuck,' I manage to utter.

I don't, but I'd like to.

For the first time in years, I want nothing more. Abstaining from sex goes against every law of nature in the animal kingdom. We're here to reproduce. Mate. Further the species. But I've already done that and look what happened with the last 'mate' I picked. Though even that doesn't stop the broodiness I sometimes feel for another baby. Mother nature is one powerful bitch.

I spent last night fuming in bed. Replaying the image of Ronan leaving the club with the woman in white. I swear my chest hurt so badly I wanted to rip it open and free the demon haunting me.

'I'll do the fucking. You could just lie there and take it.' A wicked grin lifts Ronan's lips.

'How kind of you to offer.' My dismissive tone isn't fooling either of us. My nipples are like bullets and I'm sure the water levels rose at least an inch with the wetness pooling from between my legs. 'But one I'll have to turn down.'

'We'll see about that.' Ronan takes my hands again and arranges my fingers into the cup-like position he demonstrated last week. I'm submerged in water, but I feel like I'm on fire.

He continues the lesson like he didn't just turn my world upside down.

Like he didn't just offer me the very thing I've been fantasising about since the first time I saw him.

Is that why I'm so sharp with him? Have I been trying to make him hate me because deep down I actually really like him?

His fingers skim my hips as he helps me onto my front, supporting me as I stumble clumsily through the first few strokes. The air is thick with humidity, and it has nothing to do with the pool's heating system.

How can he act so normally when the chemistry between us is like a ticking nuclear bomb? One which, if we act on, is liable to cause the same level of destruction to my career and maybe even my heart.

'We'll get the arms right first, then we'll worry about the legs.' His voice is so encouraging, I'd swear he genuinely wants to help me. 'Fingers tight together. Remember the paddle. Push the water out of your way.'

He walks next to me while I practice. 'That's it.' He nods as my technique improves. 'Good girl.'

That God damn praise again. I never realised I had a praise kink until a six-foot-something blond Adonis started telling me I was a good girl. Would he tell me I took his dick like a good girl too? My cheeks flush just thinking about it.

'You okay?' he checks, his hand reaching to steady my belly at the same time as I tilt my pelvis down and drop to a standing position. His hand lands on the pink Lycra triangle directly between my legs and freezes there. Our eyes lock. Seconds feel like minutes as my clit pulses beneath his palm.

All too soon, he drags it away. 'I'm so sorry.' He retracts his hands, crossing them over his chest.

So am I.

Sorry it's over.

Fuck. I need to get out of here before I do something I regret, like undoing six years' worth of hard work. Work that provides a wonderful income for my daughters, allows them to go to the best school in the country, and provides them with everything they could ever need.

What about my needs, though?

'I need to go.' Before he steals the rest of the air from my lungs. Before I grab his hand and shove it right back again.

'It hasn't been the hour yet.' A frown flickers across Ronan's usually sunny face.

'I'll pay you for the hour.' I stalk towards the silver steps. My hands are shaking so badly, I don't think I could drag myself out of the water without help.

'I told you last week, I don't want your money.'

'But it's your Sunday too.'

'I could think of worse ways to spend my Sunday.' He follows me out of the pool, water glistening across his chest. 'Then again, I could think of better ways, too.' His husky tone leaves nothing to the imagination.

We're chest-to-chest, just an inch between us. Silver fire dances around his irises. His face dips until his mouth captures mine and my entire world bursts into flames. Flames that lick my lips all the way into my soul.

My mouth parts, allowing his probing tongue access, revelling in the wet heat and the dizzying sensation of submitting to this. My greedy fingers thread through his damp hair, dragging his lips harder against mine, devouring him with a hunger I didn't know I possessed. White hot lust lances through every single cell in my body.

Huge hands find my hips, dragging them flush with his, pressing my pelvis against something hot and hard, intriguing and terrifying in equal measure.

A moan seeps from my soul straight into his mouth, and his hands reach to the curve of my ass, cupping and squeezing. Suddenly my toes are no longer touching the ground and my lady parts are pressed deliciously against his masculine parts and, holy fuck, I swear if he grinds against me once more I'll explode.

Then suddenly he tears his lips from mine and sets me back on the floor. Fire still lights his stare, but he steps back, a reluctant expression etched on to his face.

'If I don't stop now, I'll take you here and now by the side of the pool, and I want to be in a bed the first time I'm inside you.' His voice is low and guttural, masculine and primal.

'The first time?' I repeat with a squeak. My fingers thrum over my lips.

'Think about what I said, Sav. It could be our secret.' He saunters into the changing rooms, leaving me with my mouth on the floor.

It takes every inch of willpower I possess not to follow him.

Chapter Eleven
SAVANNAH

After the most decadent, debilitating kiss of my life, I'm too worked up to go straight to my dads. Steve has a habit of sniffing out secrets and the fact I want to have – no NEED – to have sex with Ronan Rivers is something I don't wish to discuss with him. I mean, they're liberal, but perhaps not that liberal.

Why him?

Why now?

Until a couple of weeks ago, I thought the man was a plague. Okay, I didn't really. He's always been infuriating, but there's no denying he's sexy as fuck, but still. One smoking hot kiss, a few kind words, oh, and a couple of hundred dirty ones to go with those fleeting touches, and I'm desperate for him to contaminate me.

My self-control snapped like a cord.

What if someone had seen us?

My brand would have been obliterated in mere seconds.

While mindlessly replaying the best kiss of my life over and over in my head, I somehow end up outside Ashley's place, a three-story Victorian house in Ranelagh, an affluent Dublin suburb.

Her black Lexus is parked in the driveway. I pull up on the curb outside and suck in a few huge breaths, revelling in the spring sunshine on my cheeks as it beats through my open sunroof.

'Are you coming in or are you just going to sit in the car all day?' Ashley calls from an open upstairs window.

'Stick the kettle on,' I shout, angling my face upwards.

I drag myself out of the car, lock it, and saunter up Ashley's cobbled pathway. She opens the front door as I approach, her cheeks slightly rosy. Jees, I hope I'm not interrupting anything.

'Sorry for just dropping in like this.' I plant a kiss on her cheek and accept the hug she offers.

'Don't be. Your timing is perfect. I've just finished a "Get Fit With Finn" workout online.' She points to her Lycra running shorts as proof. 'Do you follow him on Instagram? He's running this intense new abs program. It's a killer,' she runs a palm over her flat stomach, 'but it works.'

Once again, I'm catapulted seven years back.

'I'm pregnant.'

'I'm actually married.'

'He and his wife have opened a new chain of gyms in the UK. Wouldn't it be cool if they opened one in Ireland?' Ashley continues, oblivious to the blood draining from my face.

No, it would not be cool. It would be horrific.

I follow her along the corridor, willing the rage simmering inside me to subside. Ashley nods towards a closed doorway off the hall. 'Matt is locked away in his man cave writing.'

I have no interest in Matt's manuscript, but I'd rather pull my own fingernails off than talk about Finn Reilly, his wife, or his abs program. 'Is he any closer to finishing yet?'

She shrugs, and a brief flicker of frustration flits across her face before she catches herself. 'Hopefully.'

Ashley's boyfriend of almost eleven years has been working on the same sci-fi novel for eight years. *Eight years*. Seriously. Real life cities have been built quicker than his fictional world.

I don't like Matt. Neither does our other best friend, Holly, and there's not many people she can't warm to. He lives in Ashley's house rent free, promising he'll pay her when his novel sells millions of copies. Which wouldn't be so awful if he was good to her in other ways, but he's not. Ashley would love to get married, but Matt has shown absolutely no sign of that becoming a possibility anytime soon either.

None of us are getting any younger and Ashley's made no secret of the fact she wants kids.

I have mine, obviously.

Holly had baby Harriet last year.

Ashley has two cats and a boyfriend who refuses to entertain the idea of anything more.

She deserves better.

I hope one day she gets it.

'How did the swimming lesson go?' she asks, closing the maple wood kitchen door behind us. Brilliant sunshine illuminates the kitchen. The back patio doors are open and the scent of freshly mowed grass wafts in, along with sun cream and lavender. A million summer memories slowly soothe the rage rippling inside of me.

'Okay, I guess.' I take a seat at one of the high-backed stools at the island.

'Only okay?' Ashley flicks the kettle on and turns to face me. 'Is it because of what happened when you were a kid? Are you afraid?'

'No.' I slump forwards and press my forehead against the

cool granite counter. 'The only thing I'm afraid of is shagging Ronan "I'm asking you to fuck me" Rivers.'

'Shut the front door!' Ashley's green eyes sparkle. 'I knew you guys had the hots for each other!'

'Don't be ridiculous.' My reply is automatic, defensive, and utterly obvious to my best friend.

Laughter bursts from Ashley's cherry-coloured lips. She suppresses it with a hand, but not nearly quickly enough. 'Me thinks the lady doth protest.'

I groan. 'Okay, okay, the man is a fucking ride.' It pains me to admit it aloud, but not nearly as much as I thought it would.

'You want to kiss him, you want to touch him...' Ashley sings, dancing on the spot, glee dripping from her every word.

A heavy sigh escapes my lips. 'I did kiss him. And now I want to touch him.'

'No freaking way!' Ashley squeals, her parted mouth hanging open.

'Yep. Fuck. My. Life.'

'Why? What's wrong with that? You're both single consenting adults. The sex would be electric. I've seen the way he looks at you.' The kettle hisses to the boiling.

'I think we need something stronger than tea for this conversation.' And because she unintentionally poked my Finn-shaped wound. I point at the wine rack mounted above the sink.

'Will your dads collect you?' Ashley is the sensible friend. Always has been, always will be.

'Yep. They'd love the excuse to come and see you.' It's true. My dads love my friends. They consider them second daughters.

They'd have adopted more kids if they could, but sadly the way things were in Ireland thirty years ago, two gay men adopting children simply wasn't an option. The only reason they could adopt me is because my mother signed over sole care of me to Stuart in a legal document.

Stuart is my uncle. My mother's brother. I'm not religious but every day I thank God or whoever is out there for that fact. Without Stuart and Steve, there's no telling where I might have ended up.

'Great, I have a nice bottle of Gavi in the fridge. Let's take it out to the garden.' Ashley sashays across the kitchen, swinging her hips.

A swell of guilt flickers through me. The twins.

'Don't even think about feeling guilty for taking some time for yourself.' Ashley is a mind reader. 'You're no good to them if your cup is empty.' She thrusts an empty wine glass into the air. 'But don't worry, Sav, I'm going to fill it up for you.'

I follow her through to the L-shaped white wicker couch in her garden and slump onto the plush baby blue cushions.

'So, explain why you can't have sex with Mr So-Hot-I'm-On-Fire-Under-Water.' Ashley fills the wine glasses as I fire off a quick text to Stuart asking him to collect me in a couple of hours. My dads are heading off on a month-long cruise next week, so they'll probably be only too happy to get some extra time with the twins today.

'Hello... he's a manwhore and I'm Single Sav, author of *Single Sav's Guide To Winging Parenthood Alone.*'

'Well, maybe it's time you wrote the next book, *Single Sav's Guide To Shagging Her Swimming Instructor.*' Ashley hands me a glass of wine and I take a huge slug.

'If I start dating, it will destroy my brand, everything I've ever worked for. It could alienate the millions of single women who relate to me. And especially a player like Ronan.'

'You underestimate the power of a good, old-fashioned happy ending. They'd probably love to see you settled. And the man has a past. So what? At least he's had enough practice that he'll know what to do with it.' Ashley's upturned palm swats the air. 'Do you think, given half the chance, those same single women wouldn't ride off on Ronan Rivers' giant cock into the sunset?'

I snort. 'I take it you've seen the footage of his last race? Those budgie smugglers...'

'Were smuggling something significant.' Ashley nestles into the couch beside me. 'Why do you think I invited him to teach at St. Jude's?' She snorts, slapping the couch beside her.

'You are so bad.' I shake my head and take a sip of cool, crisp wine.

'Let's cut to the crux of it. You're scared of letting anyone in.'

'Wow.' Slice me open with a razor-sharp accuracy, why don't you? 'Straight for the jugular.'

'You were hurt by the last man who you let in. So much so that you've never even told us his name.' Ashley eyes me over her glass. 'I think deep down, you're terrified of it happening again.'

I take another huge mouthful of Gavi. She's right. There's no point even trying to deny it. 'Okay, that's a part of it.'

'A huge part,' Ashley insists, using her hand to shield her eyes from the sun.

'But even if that were true, and I'm not saying it is.' I tug my sunglasses from where they're tucked into the front of my dress and slip them on. Not to shield my eyes from the sun, but to shield them from Ashley's scrutiny. 'It doesn't take away my branding issue. I can't just do a complete one-eighty. The reason I've snagged so many advertising deals for baby ranges is because I'm a single mother.'

'Yes, but that doesn't mean you have to be single forever.' Ashley thrusts a hand into the air to emphasise her point.

'Hmm.' I can't agree.

Dating now seems hypocritical, given support for my situation as a single mother elevated my career to where it is today.

'Besides, who says anyone has to know?' Ashley's green eyes glint with mischief. 'Have sex with the swimming instructor. See how it goes. You don't have to announce it to the world. It's not like you're getting married. You don't even have to date him, just shag him.'

Funnily enough... that's exactly what Ronan said.

Maybe, just maybe, I should.

If I can only ignore the voice in my head screaming, 'hypocrite.'

Chapter Twelve
RONAN

Moonlight spills through the open window, casting a warm light on the queen-sized bed, plush furnishings and sixty-inch television mounted on the wall in my bedroom. I have everything a man could want, yet sometimes I feel like I have nothing.

My mind wonders to Savannah yet again.

Is she reliving our kiss, like I am?

Is she thinking about what I said to her today?

Is she replaying the filthy words that spilled from my tongue?

I've never spoken to a woman like that before.

I've never been so blunt about what I want. So carnal. But then again, I've never wanted someone so carnally before either.

Her unavailability is kind of sexy. Who wouldn't want to be her man when she could have her pick of millions? But it's so much more than that. It's her stunning face, her stellar body, and her sharp tongue.

A woman like her doesn't *need* a man.

But to be the man she *wants*, well, that makes me hard even thinking about it.

The chemistry between us earlier was painful, especially to my poor strangled dick in those shorts. When my hand brushed over her pussy and I felt the heat radiating from it, I thought I was going to blow there and then.

Is she still awake?

Is she staring at the moon, picturing me like I'm picturing her?

I snatch my phone from the glass-topped table beside my bed. It's 1.05 a.m. and I'm no closer to falling asleep than I was two hours ago.

My finger hovers over the Instagram app for a few seconds before I succumb to the inevitable; cyberstalking Savannah. I only joined the damn site so I could spy on her.

From her updates, it looks as though she went straight from our lesson to meet Ashley. A picture of the two women clutching wine glasses and beaming into the camera with the sun beating off their faces fills my screen.

Savannah's eyes are covered by oversized designer sunglasses which rest on her delicate cheekbones. Her button nose is dusted with a few light freckles, which only add to her appeal. Her full, rose-coloured lips are stretched to expose her perfect white teeth.

The way the camera is angled, I have a perfect view of Savannah's tanned cleavage peeping from the top of her summer dress.

The caption below is #girlpower.

It has thirty-seven thousand likes and over three thousand comments.

Bookishmama *Well deserved, you're an inspiration*.

Mammy_bear_98 *Mams medicine ;)*

Mammasmessyhouse. *Knee deep in nappies - have one for me*.

Shona.S *If I'm lucky enough to be a mother I hope I'm half as good at it as you are.*
Rachel_Rivers *You're a legend.*

I pause. Rachel Rivers? My sister follows Single Sav?

Of course she does. Does Sav have any idea that she isn't just an inspiration to single mothers, but to all mothers, and to women everywhere?

Would it make a difference if she did?

I scroll further down the comments.

Dave_Duggan. *Nice tits.*
ShellyB *You're so pretty.*
CarlyCoggins *Have fun mama!*
Brucethebodybuilder *You're too stunning to be single forever. Marry me.*

Even though Brucethebodybuilder's comments send a surge of irritation through my veins, I'd have to agree with him. Savannah is too stunning to be single forever. But the three hundred replies below his comment vehemently disagree.

Pinkandperfect *feck off Bruce.*
Mamasgotthis *Do one Bruce, she's our Queen, not yours.*
Singleandsurving *Dude, it's a bit like Ronseal Woodstain - does what it says on the tin.*

I can see why she'd be cautious.

Her whole career is built on her single status. But does it

mean she has to remain single forever? For all her success, it seems to me she's been handed a life sentence too.

Did she tell Ashley about our kiss? About my indecent proposal?

Probably.

Do I care?

Not in the slightest.

The only thing I care about is if she'll go for it.

I close the app and open iMessage, clicking on Savannah's name.

I text her each week to let her know what time I have available for the twins. It changes because my extracurricular swimming lessons are sought after by almost every parent with a daughter in St. Jude's. Even if I were to work every afternoon and all day Saturday and Sunday, which I don't because we already established Sunday is traditionally a day of rest, I still couldn't squeeze them all in. So, I organise the lessons on a rotating basis to fit everyone in every second or third week.

Savannah's daughters are the only two children I squeeze in every week without fail. I adore Isla and Eden, but I accommodate them without fail because it's the only opportunity I get to flirt with Savannah.

I'm thumbing through the last few weeks of our insignificant text messages when I notice three dots bouncing on the screen.

It's the middle of the night and Savannah Kingsley is texting me.

A jolt of electricity sparks in my chest.

Is her pussy still pulsing?

What I wouldn't do to find out.

All she'd have to do is say the word and I would jump out of bed, drive to her house, and take care of every single one of her primal needs.

My heart races. Anticipation eats me alive. Hope floods through every single cell in my body.

The dots keep bouncing.

Minutes pass.

What's she writing?

A fucking novel?

And then they disappear, along with all my foolish expectations.

Chapter Thirteen
SAVANNAH

It's Saturday again and my ass is once again numb from the cheap plastic poolside seats. Ronan's in the water with my daughters. Isla is trying to jump on his back, while Eden is listening attentively as he explains something I can't quite hear.

He'll make a brilliant father one day.

Where the fuck did that thought come from?

Who am I kidding? I've been thinking carnal thoughts about Ronan all damn week, and my daughters are living proof of where carnal thoughts lead to.

Seriously though, the sight of him with the twins makes my ovaries want to combust with lust.

He glances around and I drop my gaze to the contract from Coral I've been skim-reading on my lap. I know what it says. I've read it multiple times this week. I pull out a pen from my handbag and sign my name on the dotted line.

I've been holding off just in case I couldn't hack the water. In case when it came down to it, I couldn't do it. But I can do it, with the help of a certain sexy swimming instructor who I can't take my eyes off.

It's almost like I dreamt up that smoking hot kiss last week, and the conversation that followed. I thought he might text or call but the only contact from him after that was his perfunctory text with the time for today's lesson.

But I didn't dream it because I can still feel where his lips touched mine. The heat burning where his hand grazed my bikini bottoms.

Can still feel heat exuding from his liquid molten eyes.

Feel his hot breath skimming my skin.

After the wine on Sunday, I almost caved.

I even typed out the text. But when it came down to it, I just couldn't do it.

No matter how much I want to.

Even contemplating starting something with Ronan feels like cheating on my followers. Like I'm a fraud. Like I'm claiming to be something I'm not.

I glance at my watch. The lesson's almost up. That's my Ronan fix over for another day, sadly.

My phone rings in my pocket just as Ronan hauls himself out of the pool and stands directly in front of me. The girls have gone to the deep end to have their five minutes of fun before the next students arrive.

I fumble in my bag and pull out the phone, tearing my eyes from Ronan, half naked, dripping, and gorgeous, to the screen which says number withheld.

'Sorry, I need to take this. It's work.' I swipe to answer, shooting him an apologetic glance.

'Hello?'

'Hi Savannah, it's Susie here from Coral.'

'Susie, how are you?' I thumb the contract on my lap.

'Fine, thanks. Just checking everything is okay. We didn't receive the contract back yet.' Concern taints her tone.

'Everything is fine.' My eyes lock with Ronan's. He's hovering. Probably to arrange a time for tomorrow. 'I've signed it. I'll drop it in the post first thing Monday morning. Or I can scan and email it if you need it before then?'

'Actually, I know it's short notice, but I was wondering if you're free tonight? Lucas Beechwood is in the city this evening and wants to meet you.'

Lucas Beechwood. As in the CEO of Coral? My mouth dries and my lips part.

'I, err...' My heart quickens. Why does he want to meet me? Does he meet all his brand ambassadors?

'Savannah, are you still there?'

'Yes, sorry, I'm just thinking. I don't have any childcare.' Typical.

My dads left for their cruise at five o'clock this morning. It's a major drawback of being a single parent. If I had a husband or a partner, popping into the city to meet my new boss for a couple of hours wouldn't be a problem.

I could ask Ashley to take the girls, but she's already agreed to take them tomorrow so I can have my swimming lesson. She might be their godmother, but I don't want to take the piss.

Though, if I don't go, will Lucas assume I'm not committed to the contract or to Coral as a company?

I'd hate to lose this opportunity.

'Oh, that's a shame.' Susie's tone falters. 'Lucas likes to meet all of his brand ambassadors in person.'

Ronan's thick fingers tap my knee and a surge of electricity shoots up my thigh. 'I can help you out with the twins if you're stuck,' he mouths.

I roll my lips, eyeing the curves of Ronan's topless torso. 'Sorry, Susie, can you just give me a second, please?' I place a palm over the speaker and tilt my face up to meet Ronan's.

'Are you crazy? You're seriously offering to babysit my girls?' A tiny sliver of hope unfurls in my chest.

'Yes. They know me. I'm vetted to work with kids. If you

trust me to take care of them, I'll do it.' He grabs a towel from a nearby chair and my eyes follow as he rubs it over his muscular chest and lower.

Not only do they know him, but they love him. Eden stares at him like he's some sort of god. Isla clambers all over him any chance she gets, the lucky duck.

I hesitate, weighing up my options.

Basically, without Ronan, I don't have any.

'Why are you being so nice to me?' I whisper, eyeing him warily.

'I told you last week, I'm actually a nice guy.' His gaze falls to my lips. 'I also told you I want to f–'

Yep, I definitely didn't dream up that conversation. A hot flush of longing crawls across my skin. That filthy mouth. I wonder if he knows what else to do with it...

Fuck. He's driving me loopy with lust.

I thrust a hand up to silence him, eyeing my daughters at the top end of the pool. Isla seems to have convinced Eden to take a few risks for once in her life, because they're dive bombing into the water holding hands.

Maybe I should take a leaf out of her book and take a risk or two myself.

'It's to meet my new boss,' I explain. 'I can't imagine it'll take more than a couple of hours.'

'No problem.' Ronan's lips part into a sexy smile.

I peel my palm from the phone and raise it to my ear. 'Sorry, Susie, are you still there?'

'I'm here,' she says.

'A friend just offered to help, so I will be free to attend a meeting.'

A friend? More like the guy I've been imaging riding like a unicycle all week, balancing on one long, strong upright pole.

I cross my legs and hope my lace bra is thick enough to

hide my pebbled nipples. If Ronan's darting, dilating pupils are anything to go by, it's not doing its job very well at all.

'I'll make a reservation and email you the details. Mr Beechwood will be pleased.' A hint of relief seeps into Susie's voice.

'Great, thanks. I'll see you tonight.'

Susie chuckles. 'Oh no dear, I'm not going. It'll just be you and Mr Beechwood.'

She hangs up before I can ask any further questions.

'Are you one hundred per cent sure about this?' I stand, clasping the contract in my hand like it's a ticket to Charlie's chocolate factory.

'The chance to hang out with my two favourite students, and snoop in their mother's knicker drawer when they go to bed…' He winks. 'Abso-fucking-lutely.'

My jaw drops. 'You wouldn't.'

'Relax, I'm kidding.' His fingers brush over the back of my tricep and my skin pricks to attention. 'The only time I want to see your lingerie is when it's damp and discarded on the floor.'

My core clenches. He's going to be the death of me.

'What time do you want me tonight?' The corners of his eyes crinkle as he smirks.

'I'm not sure yet. I'll text you when Susie emails me the details.' The next family enters the pool area and Ronan and I jump apart guiltily.

'I guess I'll see you later then.' Ronan adjusts the waistband of his shorts, and I force my eyes away. The memory of something impressive pressed against me is seared in my mind forever. Will I ever be bold enough to feel it again?

Bold enough and brave enough.

'Let's go girls.' I signal to the twins.

Mammy has to get ready for a hot date.

And not necessarily the one in the city.

Chapter Fourteen
RONAN

How hard can it be babysitting six-year-old twin girls? Minding the kids is the perfect excuse to get close to Savannah.

I'm at my local store picking up confectionary when my brother, Richard, rams me with his trolley. 'Evening, brother.'

It's not unusual to run into him here. Richard bought one of the apartments in the same block as mine just along the street. Thankfully, it's not the one directly below because it has had a few high heels traipsing across the wooden floorboards.

Though there's been no one in weeks. I want Savannah more than ever and it's an itch no one else can scratch. I know because I spent the last two years trying.

'The boys are meeting in the new club in forty minutes. Don't even think about driving tonight.' Richard gives me a pointed stare.

'I'm not going out tonight.' I shake my head to reinforce my point.

'What?' He nods at the popcorn tucked under my arm.

'Oh, I see... Netflix and chill.' He uses his fingers to make quotation signs in the air. 'Who's the lucky lady?'

'No one you know.' My molars clamp together. I'd prefer not to have to explain myself, for Savannah's sake.

'Oh, don't hold out on me now, Ronan!' Richard's black eyes gleam as he rubs his palms together.

'I told you, you don't know her.' I inhale a deep breath and blow it out slowly. I swear to God he's worse than a gossiping granny. 'And don't even think of turning up at the apartment because I won't be there.'

'Oh, now I'm really intrigued.' He rams my thighs with his trolly, which is when I notice it's filled with wine and whiskey.

'Someone's having a party.'

'Nah, just like to keep stocked up. Nick and Shane brought a couple of girls back last night after you left with the woman in the white dress. They made a good dent in my drinks' cupboard.'

'Yeah, well.' I shift from foot to foot. 'Enjoy your night.'

He raises his hand in a sarcastic wave. 'I expect all the gory details over Sunday lunch at Mam's tomorrow.'

'Yeah, Mam would love that.' Not. Sarcasm seems to be a family trait.

I grab a packet of Kinder bars and a couple of Barbie magazines with the plastic accessories attached to the front. 'See you tomorrow.'

Richard's beady eyes linger on the confectionary and magazines, but I stride away before he has the chance to bombard me with any more questions.

Outside, I slide into my Tesla and type in Savannah's address. Her house is in Dalkey, one of the nicer suburbs. I wonder if she's near the beach. I'm about to find out.

Twenty minutes later, I swing into an asphalt driveway. A large white, two-storey modern house comes into view. It's set well back from the road. The generous sized garden is surrounded by high trees. The driveway is lined with stunning rose bushes, bursting with colour. I'd never have pegged Savannah as the green-fingered type, but a garden like this takes maintenance.

A wooden treehouse with swings and a slide sits to the left of the house along with a wooden Wendy house and sandpit overflowing with brightly coloured toys.

The property itself is symmetrical in appearance. Huge corner windows flank either side of the house. I glance at the beach in my rear-view mirror. She must have one hell of a sea view. Thank God she's learning how to swim. When the twins get older, they're going to want to be at that beach any time the sun shines.

Something squeezes in my chest at the thought.

A huge summer wreath, painted a deep shade of pink, hangs on Savannah's front door.. Did I expect anything less?

Probably not.

I step out of the car with the treats clutched to my chest like a shield.

'Ronan!' Isla cannonballs out of the door and lands surprisingly on her feet while Eden hangs back a little shyly in the doorframe.

'Hi girls. I brought treats. I thought maybe we could watch a movie...' I trail off as Savannah appears in the door.

My greeting lodges in my throat as my jaw hits the floor.

Pale pink silk sculpts her every curve, showcasing her stunning cleavage and clinging to her womanly hips. Her blonde hair bounces over her shoulders in huge curls that I've dreamt about wrapping round my hand. Her stunning blue eyes appear twice their normal size with whatever make-up she's applied, and I swear to God her skin is glowing like a fucking angel.

And those lips.

They're outlined with a slightly darker shade of pink and all I can think about is having them wrapped around my....

'We're not watching a movie, Ronan.' Isla's high-pitched voice drags my mind back from the gutter.

'We're not?' I tear my eyes from Savannah and focus on the two little girls.. Carbon copies of their mother, apart from their colouring. 'What are we doing, then?'

'We're going to make up a dance routine,' Isla announces. Eden nods enthusiastically.

'A dance routine?' I repeat, dumbly. Rachel's boys are so much easier pleased. Snacks, magazines, and a movie usually ensure my babysitting duties are effortless.

I'm beginning to realise I'm not going to get off nearly as lightly tonight.

'Come in.' Savannah beckons me in.

I step forwards, still salivating over her figure in that dress. Every caveman instinct lurking inside demands I sweep her up into my arms and claim every inch of her body with every inch of mine.

Eventually, I find my tongue. 'You look stunning.'

'Thank you.' A subtle blush lights her delicate cheekbones.

Cheekbones which I feel brave enough to brush a kiss over as I step into the hallway. She inhales sharply as her fingers mindlessly trace the spot my lips just left. 'Are you any good at dancing?'

A quick glance behind me shows the twins temporarily engrossed in their magazines. 'Oh, honey, I've got all the moves.' I pump my hips subtly against hers.

'Ronan, I...' She grabs my arm. 'I really appreciate you helping me out tonight. I never thought I'd hear these words coming out of my mouth, but you're a good friend.'

A good friend.

Who knew three little words could be so damning?

My face must betray me because she grabs my arm again. 'You're teaching me to swim, but truthfully, you're the only person who can sink me.'

I get what she means.

I do.

Her entire image.

Her branding.

Would it be any better if I hadn't been papped with so many women over the last couple of years?

Maybe.

I don't know.

I'm probably everything her followers wouldn't want for her.

Our eyes lock and something powerful passes between us. A fire flickers in the silver flames rimming her irises.

If I could only get her to trust me, it could just be the beginning of something beautiful.

If I could find a way to persuade her to let me in behind her carefully curated wall, then she'd understand how I feel about her. She'd understand I've been obsessed with her for years.

Now I know she's not as repulsed by me as she pretends to be, there's no way I'm giving up.

Single celebrity status or not.

I'll be her friend.

I'll be anything she needs me to be.

There's only one thing that I won't be – deterred.

Chapter Fifteen
SAVANNAH

I stride into Azure, the most exclusive restaurant in Dublin, with butterflies fluttering in my stomach. It's impossible to get a table here. I've been once before with my best friend, Holly. Holly can demand a table anywhere, anytime, because she's married to a Hollywood movie star, the same guy whose poster she had pinned to her bedroom wall for years. True story, seriously. There's an entire book in it. One where they live happily ever after.

My mind wanders to Ronan for the millionth time.

Is he okay with the girls?

A shred of guilt rips through me, but I force it away. I know technically I'm here for work, but I don't get called to many meetings in a restaurant like Azure. It feels like an indulgence I don't deserve.

How many times have I longed for a night out somewhere like this? A night where I can wear something other than my pyjamas and have a real adult conversation?

So why is every cell inside me screaming I should be at home with the girls?

Or more specifically, Ronan and the girls.

I wish I had cameras set up in the house to record their dance routine. I can only imagine. If Ronan's one thing, it's game for a challenge. I don't doubt he's prancing around with them now, indulging their every whim.

I hover waiting to be shown to the table, soaking up the opulent ambience, high ceilings, intricate chandeliers, and more candles than a Yankee Candle factory. The tables are set with crisp linens, delicate tableware and sparkling silverware that catches the light of the evening sun shimmering through huge sash windows.

I smooth down my dress and smile as the Maitre d' asks for my reservation details before leading me to a private booth.

Lucas Beechwood is already waiting, menu in one hand, glass of champagne in the other. His jaw is square and strong, his cheekbones chiselled, and his long straight nose one the Romans would have been proud of.

He stands when I arrive, his frame athletically lean and lithe. Chocolate brown hair flops into his hazel eyes. He rakes it back with thick fingers before extending his hand to shake mine.

'Savannah, it's a pleasure to meet you in person.' He flashes a killer smile, a testament to years of expensive orthodontics. 'Please sit. I took the liberty of ordering champagne.'

'Thank you.' I slip into the velvet trimmed booth and pick up a crystal flute that's waiting for me.

'When Susie told me you accepted our offer, I was desperate to meet you.' He sucks in his lower lip as his eyes roam over my face like he can't quite figure me out.

'Thank you... I guess.' I raise my glass to his in a toast. 'I'm excited to represent Coral Chic. I'm a huge fan of the range,' I admit, placing my glass on the table and running a finger up its stem.

'I think you're the perfect fit.' His gaze flicks to my dress, then up again. 'You're a fantastic role model for women. Wholesome. Hard working. The fact you're raising twin girls on your own is admirable.' His lips slant upwards in a smile. 'And if you don't mind me saying, the fact you're absolutely stunning is really going to further the brand.'

Is he hitting on me?

Or just being nice?

Now I'm almost thirty, am I emitting some sort of weird pheromones that attract gorgeous, successful men? Or maybe I'm just noticing them more because my biological clock is ticking.

It's true. "*A baby would be nice...*"

No matter how many times I try to quieten it, to tell it we're done, that I have two beautiful girls and I doubt I could cope with any more, the thought leaps up like a Pop-Tart.

Mother Nature seems to have erased the memory of the traumatic sleepless nights.

The teething.

The ear infections.

The reflux.

Yep – she's one hell of a force to be reckoned with.

I flash Lucas my most professional smile, taking in his expensive tailored suit, crisp white shirt, and chunky Swiss watch. 'Thank you.'

'Did you bring the contract?' His upturned palm reaches across the table.

I pull out the paperwork from my cream, oversized Mulberry handbag. 'I did. Sorry I didn't sign it quicker.'

'No problem. The male ambassador we've chosen has yet to return his either.' He shrugs, like it's no big deal.

'Male counterpart?' It's the first I've heard of it.

'Yes, it made sense to film the 'his 'n' hers' range simultaneously. We'll get footage of you individually for the two different campaigns, then film you together before we wrap up.'

'Oh.' It makes sense, I guess. 'Who is the male model?'

'Until he signs, I'm afraid I'm not at liberty to discuss that. He's driving a hard bargain.' He frowns for a second, then sits up straighter. 'Oh, gosh, that came out wrong. I don't mean financially. His contract is identical to yours. Coral is firmly committed to equality.'

My skin pricks, but I say nothing. Seeming to take my silence as disbelief, Lucas blurts out, 'Your male counterpart wants me to invest in his business as he starts up in Dublin. A partnership could be mutually beneficial but to be honest,' he lowers his voice, 'I'm not one hundred percent convinced about him. On paper, he's squeaky clean, the perfect role model, but he gives off this vibe.' Lucas shakes his head, more to himself than me. 'I shouldn't be telling you all this.'

'Don't worry, I won't say a word.' I take another sip of champagne, my mind wandering. As a former competitive swimmer, Ronan would be the perfect choice, but I don't know if I'd like to work with him or if it would be yet another temptation that could land me in trouble.

'Did you consider Ronan Rivers?' The words tumble out of my mouth before I can stop them. I hope I'm not overstepping.

'I did.' Lucas sits back, clasping his fingers together on the table. 'His success at the Olympics is unrivalled but his weekend rendezvous don't do him any favours. I don't want Dublin's biggest player associated with my campaign.' His head snaps up. 'Do you know him?'

'He's teaching my children to swim.' I deliberate adding 'and me,' but before I can decide, my phone vibrates in my bag. 'I'm so sorry,' I say to Lucas. 'I've left the girls with a... friend tonight. I'm keeping an eye on the phone to make sure they're okay.'

It feels weird to admit Ronan is the friend who's minding the girls tonight. Especially given I just suggested him as the ambassador for Coral Chic's male range. It would give Lucas the wrong impression.

Lucas motions at my mobile, encouraging me to check it.

I tap the screen to open a message from Ronan. Instead of the SOS I half expected, it's a video of him standing between the girls, arms folded, studious expressions on each of their faces. Beyonce's '*Who Rules the World'* blares out and the three of them burst into uncannily symmetrical dance moves.

Eden is beaming from ear to ear, Isla is crying with laughter, and Ronan... what can I say? His torso ripples as his hips gyrate to the music and instead of looking ridiculous, he looks ridiculously hot. Especially when he looks so overtly masculine, wedged between my two tiny princesses.

Laughter bursts from my mouth.

'Everything okay?' Lucas arches an eyebrow.

'Yes, sorry, it's the girls and my, err.. friend.' There's nothing platonic about the way I feel for Ronan Rivers, the man who Lucas rightly reminded me is Dublin's biggest player, and not on the pitch.

Which is exactly why, even though I want to ride Ronan like a wild stallion, I shouldn't.

Lucas is easy company. In other circumstances, I might be attracted to him, but all I can think about is getting out of here and getting home. And not necessarily because of the twins.

When our dinner meeting finally draws to a close, Lucas rises, leans across the table, and presses a kiss to my cheek. His lips linger slightly longer than necessary. 'Are you sure I can't persuade you to come for a drink with me?'

'I'd better get back to the girls.' And my hot manny.

'Well, thanks for joining me tonight.' The scent of his citrus cologne brushes my nose.

'Thanks for inviting me.' I stand, grabbing my bag.

His huge eyes fall to my lips. 'I hope this isn't too forward, but I wondered if you fancied coming out for a drink with me some other time. For pleasure, not for business, obviously.'

I shake my head. 'Oh, no, I'm afraid I don't do dates...'

But I have been seriously considering having sex with my swimming instructor.

'Never?' He persists, pinning me in a stare with espresso-coloured eyes.

'No.' A mild flicker of shame stirs in my stomach, but technically it's the truth, no matter what I've been fantasising.

'Pity.' His gaze lingers on my face for a beat. 'If you ever change your mind...' He whips out a black business card embellished with gold italics, and slips it into my hand.

Oh god.

I have not one but two gorgeous guys propositioning me.

Someone, somewhere, is seriously testing my commitment to celibacy.

But the biggest test will be if I let Ronan out of my house again tonight, because after a couple of drinks with dinner, and watching his torso rippling to Beyonce, my resolve is considerably weaker than it was four hours ago.

I flag a taxi outside the restaurant and spend the entire ride home, repeating the same phrase over and over in my head.

Ronan Rivers is in my house.

There's something sublimely satisfying about knowing he's minding my girls, instead of out on the pull on a Saturday night.

Jesus, the man deserves a shag for that alone. Though that doesn't necessarily mean I should give it to him. It's all very well for Mr-I-Don't-Want-To-Date-You-I-Just-Want-To-Fuck-You, but that's easier said than done.

He might be a pro when it comes to casual sex, but I've never had a one-night stand in my life. In principle, I like the idea of it, but for me, sex and feelings have always been interwoven.

The bedroom lights are off upstairs, which is a good sign. Light flickers from the living room windows. Ronan must be watching TV. I pay the driver and step out of the car.

Will Ronan stay for a drink?

Will he try to kiss me again?

Am I brave enough to let him?

I creep into the wide hallway, a forbidden sense of excitement racing through my veins.

My heart warns me to tread carefully, but my vagina... she's like a metal detector in search of a steel pole.

What if I *could* find a way to separate sex and feelings? What if I gave into him just once? Just to get it out of my system?

It's been so long since I experienced any intimacy.

I kick off my heels and pad barefoot towards the living area with my pulse racing and heat pooling in my core.

A familiar masculine scent fills the air as I tiptoe into the lounge.

The TV is on. Ronan is sprawled deliciously on my couch, with his shoes off and his t-shirt riding just high enough over his jeans for me to appreciate the distinctive V of his hips, the fine hair that trails beneath his waistband, promising untold treasure.

Unfortunately, my two beautiful daughters, who are draped across his chest, their golden hair spilling over his shoulders, put paid to my filthy 'what ifs?'

It might be for the best, but the vision in front of me is

only fuelling my delinquent desires, because there is nothing sexier than a man who's good with children.

Especially *my* children.

I exhale a sigh of relief and frustration. At least I don't have to make any hard and fast decision tonight.

Instead, I head in search of my vibrator.

Chapter Sixteen
RONAN

A movement on my chest rouses me from slumber. I blink hard and rub my eyes, wondering why it feels like I have six stone on top of my body.

Oh wait, I do.

Isla and Eden finally crashed out on my chest, watching the new Paw Patrol movie. If I ever see another animated dog in a cape, it'll be too soon.

A quick glance at the huge, Shabby Chic clock mounted on Savannah's wall shows it's just past midnight. She should be home soon. A million hummingbirds swirl in my stomach at the prospect. Being in her house, surrounded by her possessions, and the floral scent of her perfume, does things to me.

I place a hand on each of the twins' backs and rock forwards slowly into a sitting position. Isla is draped across the right side of my torso. I wiggle closer beneath her and slide Eden onto the couch.

Lifting Isla in a fireman's carry, I tiptoe through the hallway lined with portrait after portrait of the girls. Christenings, birthdays, Christmases, and holidays. My heart swells in my chest at the smiling faces staring back at me.

I creep up the stairs, holding the rail for support, and steal into Isla's bedroom. She took great pleasure in showing it to me earlier, even if it looked like the Tasmanian devil had whizzed through the wardrobe and flung every item she owned onto the floor.

Placing her gently on her plush pink bedsheets, I drop a kiss on her forehead and pull the blanket around her waist. Thank God I'd insisted they put their pjs on earlier. I close the bedroom door and go down to collect Eden.

Eden's room is immaculate. Her books are colour-coordinated in her bookcase, her stuffed animals are lined up in order of size from largest to smallest, and she hasn't left a stray shoe or dress anywhere, unlike her sister.

Is Savannah's room tidy like Eden's?

Or is she as chaotic as Isla?

The urge to find out pricks my skin like an itch.

Would it be so bad if I peeked? It's not like I'm really going to rifle through her knicker drawer, even if the prospect sends blood pulsing below. I have too much respect for Savannah to violate her privacy. Besides, I wasn't joking when I said the only place I want to see her lingerie is on the floor.

A pulse throbs in my neck as I saunter along the corridor to the master bedroom, justifying my curiosity under the ruse of checking for intruders.

The familiar sexy scent of Savannah's perfume is stronger on this side of the house. No wonder. An image of her in that decadent dress springs to the forefront of my mind. I'm only praying she's going to need help to get out of it.

I know her body craves mine the way I crave hers. I wish to God she'd just give in to it.

I approach her bedroom door. Soft, warm light spills from a

small crack where it's not properly closed. Was that lamp on earlier? I don't remember, but it was still light outside, so maybe I just didn't notice. A soft buzzing hum is coming from the room.

A toothbrush?

A fan?

I step closer and push open the door to investigate. My jaw hits the floor.

A white lace thong is discarded on the floor.

I had envisioned I'd be the one to fling it there, but still, I'm not complaining. Not when Savannah is sprawled across her bed, blonde hair mussed sexily across her pillow. The strap of her dress has slipped down over her shoulder, offering a clear view of one pert round breast , its nipple pointing so far upwards it's practically praying to be sucked.

That sexy little dress looked good on her earlier, but it looks way hotter hauled up around her waist. Her long, toned legs are spread wide, offering me the perfect view of her sweet pink pussy. Her fingers are deftly working a vibrator over her clit, and, oh my God, I think I've died and gone to heaven.

I've never seen her looking so beautiful.

So turned on.

So fucking tempting.

Her eyes are squeezed shut, her full lips open, her chest rising and falling as her breath quickens. She's close.

Her tongue darts out to wet her lower lip and a single breathy word tumbles from her mouth and I am done.

'Ronan.'

I hiss out a breath and push the door open, my cock straining so hard in my pants it might fucking explode.

'Savannah.' My voice is low and husky and overflowing with fucking awe.

Her eyelids fly open. She bolts upright in the bed,

crossing her legs and tugging her dress down. Her cheeks flush a deep crimson, her gaze a mix of horror and hunger.

'Don't stop, please.' I stride across the thick blush-coloured carpet. 'Please, Savannah, you're so fucking beautiful. Please let me see you.'

A deep doubt flits across her face along with unmistakable mortification. 'You want to see me?' Her tone is incredulous.

'More than anything else in the world. I need to watch you come. Just let me watch.' Something flickers in her eyes as I drop to my knees by the side of her bed. 'You whispered my name.'

'I was imagining I was with you.' Her onyx eyes burn at her confession.

'Well, do us both a favour and make that fantasy a reality. I want to see your pretty pussy pulse. I want to watch as pleasure rips through every limb of your body. I want to watch you buck and scream and hear my name from your lips while you do it.'

She winces. 'You're never going to let me live this down.'

'More like I'm never going to get it down.' I grab my rock-solid cock through my jeans. 'Touching yourself is fucking natural. You're a red-blooded woman.' I swallow back the saliva pooling in my mouth. 'Your body needs the release. Show me what you like.'

Her eyes darken as her throat bobs. She wants to. I know she does. But will she give in?

She wets her lips, contemplating for a second before uncrossing her legs. 'You can watch, but don't touch.'

What I wouldn't do to swipe my tongue through her glistening centre, but I won't. Not tonight. Not unless she begs me.

'I promise I won't touch, but the second I leave here, I'm heading straight for my shower.' If I even make it that far. My poor dick is weeping.

She grabs a pillow from the other side of the bed and shoves it behind her head so she can watch me watching her. My dirty girl doesn't like being watched; she loves it. If there was even a sliver of a chance she'd let me, I'd watch her touch herself every damn day for the rest of my life.

She lifts her dress again and I almost come there and then. 'Open your legs wider,' I demand, and she obeys, reaching for her toy again and coasting it across her centre. My greedy eyes dart between her pussy and her face, committing every decadent detail to memory.

Her pupils almost swallow her irises. 'Do you like what you see?' she asks tentatively.

'I don't like it. I fucking love it.' I run a palm over my crotch, and the bulge that's threatening to rip open my jeans at the seams. 'You drive me fucking wild, Savannah. Do you know how many times I've beat myself off in the shower imagining your wet pussy?'

'Tell me,' she whimpers, circling her clit with the vibrator.

'Every damn day since the second I laid eyes on you. You crashed into my car and into my head, and I can't for the life of me get you out of there. I've been obsessed with you for years.'

'You? Obsessed with me?' She says slowly, her voice loaded with disbelief. She drags her head off the bed until she's in a semi-reclined position. Her hand stills, and she lifts the vibrator from herself as she waits for clarity.

'Every compliment, innuendo, every filthy suggestion – I meant every damn word,' I confess in a rough gritty tone, memorising the image before me.

'Fuck, that's enough to get me off alone.' She lowers the vibrator back onto herself and resumes those circular movements, her glassy eyes never leaving mine, until she's on the brink of blowing.

When her legs go taut and rigid, I'm so not ready for this

to be over. 'Stop,' I demand in a ragged voice. 'Take your dress off, please. I need to see all of you.'

She discards the toy, leaving it buzzing on the bedsheets and tugs the dress upwards. It catches and she sighs impatiently.

'Can I help you with that? I won't touch you, just the dress.' It's the truth. Because if I touch her, even once, I won't be able to stop.

'Okay.' Her voice cracks as she slides down the bed towards where I'm on my knees for her. Because that's what she does. The woman literally brings me to my knees with need.

She twists onto her front, positioning her peachy ass just inches from my face. Fuck, what I wouldn't do to sink my teeth into her skin. To sink my fingers into her centre and suck her clit until she screamed my name.

My fingers skim up the middle of her spine, tracing the zip until I find the top. She whimpers. 'You said you wouldn't touch.'

'I'm touching the dress, not you.' I'm not fooling either of us.

I pull the metal and it releases with a satisfying swish. She hoists herself onto her knees, thighs spread, ass still in my face, and yanks the material over her head before tossing it on the floor.

Her head twists over her shoulder and her eyes lock with mine, a seductive smirk curving her lips upwards. 'Happy now?'

'Nowhere near, sweetheart.'

She crawls up the bed slowly on her knees, giving me the perfect view of her pussy, but she's too far away.

'Grab that toy and bring it back down here to me.' My desire is making me demand things I have no right to demand, but from the way she complies, I think she relishes relinquishing control.

I'd bet my last euro she wants to be bossed around in the bedroom.

She grabs the dildo and crawls backwards in a feline motion until her feet reach the end of the bed.

'Turn over. Let me see your perfect tits,' I beg.

She obliges, lifting one leg high into the air, over my head and down past my shoulder, until I'm between her thighs with a front-row seat to the most exquisite show of my life.

Chapter Seventeen
SAVANNAH

Ronan Rivers is obsessed with me.

Me.

That's going to take some time to process.

And that time isn't now.

The brief flicker of horror that washed over me when he walked into my bedroom has well and truly left the building.

This is what I wanted.

This is what I needed.

A man lavishing his undivided attention on me, looking at me with lust and longing, telling me how much he wants me, because it's something that's been missing my entire life. I've never been wanted. Not like this, anyway. Not so viscerally.

This is what I've been missing.

This is what I gave up when my entire identity became Single Sav.

And for the first time in six years, I'm beginning to see exactly what I've been missing, and Ronan hasn't even laid a finger on me.

What I wouldn't do to feel his thick cock sliding between my legs, filling me so deeply that he plugs the void, not just in body, but in my soul, too. But he's a manwhore, even with his confession of obsession, and I'd do well to remember it. Even if he is drinking me in with the thirst of a man who's been crawling across the Sahara for days. Huge, liquid navy eyes carnally caress every inch of my skin.

'So fucking beautiful.' His voice oozes awe, like he's never seen a naked woman before. We both know how far that is from the truth, which only makes his primal appreciation for mine so much more satisfying.

'Touch your tits for me, please, Savannah.' I'll do anything he says right now, give him anything he needs. Almost, anyway, because he's meeting needs in me I didn't even know I had.

The fingers of my left hand trace my collar bone before dipping lower over the curve of my breast, while the fingers of my right grip the dildo like it's real. The urge to pump myself with it is feral, but I don't want this to be over.

I skim over my nipples, nipping my lower lip.

'Good girl, Savannah. Look what you're doing to me.' His hand grabs his crotch again. 'You are the sexiest woman I've ever met.' His face is so close to my centre, his breath ignites every sensitive nerve ending down there.

That good girl comment was my undoing in the pool last week. So fucking hot. With his blond hair and blue eyes, the man looks like a fallen angel, but he has the devil's dirty tongue and I fucking love it.

My needy clit pulses for attention. I glance down between my thighs and like a mind reader, he says, 'Touch it.'

I lift the vibrator, but he prises it from my fingers. 'Use your hand.'

I skim the skin of my stomach until my fingers reach their destination, working small circles around my clit, but it's not enough. 'I want more,' I admit.

'What do you want?' he growls.

'What I want, and what I can have, are two entirely different things,' I rasp, heat pooling between my legs.

'You can have everything. Just say the word.' His lips lift in a smirk as he blows a long, slow teasing breath over my pussy.

'I shouldn't. We shouldn't,' I pant.

'I told you, Savannah, I'm not asking you to date me.' His cobalt eyes gleam. 'I want to fuck you.'

I want him so badly, but is the physical pleasure worth the emotional trauma that will inevitably follow?

What if I catch feelings?

It's a chance I can't take.

He seems oddly in tune with my senses as he backs off and opts for a different path. 'How about I fuck you with this?' He takes the vibrator. From the way his jeans are bulging, it's got nothing on what he's got stashed away down there. 'Technically, I'm not touching you. A piece of silicone is.'

I think about it for an entire millisecond before inching myself further off the bed, accepting his proposal.

'Good girl,' he purrs.

Every cell in my body tingles.

My eyes widen as he places the silicone to his lips and wets it with his tongue. Our eyes meet with a longing so intense it strips me right back, and I swear he can see my soul.

He lowers the toy, nudging it against my entrance, sliding it in, inch by glorious inch. The sensation is exhilarating. It's exquisite. It's fucking everything, and it's all down to the man driving it into me.

Back and forth, he works me in a delicious, decadent rhythm, watching as my body unfurls before him. I can't focus on anything other than where the next thrust is coming from. That and the huge twin pools I'm drowning in.

My limbs tremble, my vision blurs, and wave after wave of hedonistic pleasure winds from my head to my toes and every inch between. 'Ronan, I'm going to come.'

'Come for me, baby,' he demands, in a voice that's thick with a lust that matches my own.

He pumps me harder, pushing the precise point I need pressure, and I whimper as I'm catapulted into the most intense climax I've ever experienced. My pelvis arches off the bed, chasing every drop of the endorphin-charged high I've been so fucking deprived of.

Because I have.

Nothing has ever felt so intense.

And it probably never will again.

My body eventually stills, but my heart continues to hammer in my chest. Hammering because I crossed the line. Hammering because I want to do it again. And hammering because it's wrong, but it feels so fucking right.

Ronan rocks back from his knees to balance his ass on his calves. That's it. He got his show. Now he's leaving. Panic rips through me.

He-Who-Has-Never-Been-Named left.

Everyone leaves.

I cover my eyes with my hands, waiting to hear the soft padding of his feet across the carpet, but it doesn't come.

'Are you seriously hiding from me now?' His voice is mystified and mocking.

'Are you still here?' I part my fingers to peep through the cracks. 'Show's over. You got what you wanted.' It comes out harsher than I intended, my defence mechanism kicking in in full force.

'Wow.' Ronan discards the dildo on the bed and appraises me with huge, soulful eyes. 'I know you're probably a little out of practice, Savannah, but when someone hand-delivers the best orgasm of your life, it's polite to say thank you, not ask if they've left yet.'

He's right. I am out of practice, but even when I was 'in practice' my ex never hung around after we'd finished fooling around. Probably because he had to rush home to his wife.

'What makes you think it was the best orgasm of my life?' I pout, peeping through my fingers.

'Because that's what you screamed when I made you come harder than a freight train.' His eyes rove unashamedly over my body again. 'I don't know what you were used to before you became who you are, but let me tell you this, Savannah. If you were my woman, and I were allowed to touch you, just know that right now I'd be cleaning you up with my tongue, worshipping every millimetre of your satiny skin and working you into another fantastic fuckfest.'

My greedy clit pulses at his filthy, alluring description.

'But given I promised not to touch you, I'm going to get you a hot washcloth, and then I'm going to tuck you into your bed and wish I could get into it with you. Instead, I'll go home and wank myself senseless over what we did tonight.'

'You'd do that for me?' Surprise colours my tone.

'You have no idea what I'd do for you, Savannah Kingsley.' He stands with the protuberance in his trousers still putting a painful amount of pressure on his Levis. 'But yeah, I'll wank myself senseless for you, like I have done almost every other night since I laid eyes on you.' He cranes his neck over his shoulder and winks as he disappears into my ensuite, presumably in search of a cloth.

I slide up the bed, my limbs weighted with the exhaustion that only sublime sex brings. He returns a minute later and drops onto the bed beside me. 'If I wash you with a cloth, I'm still not technically touching you, okay?' He gently nudges my legs open and I marvel at how tender he is. How hot this aftercare is. And how much I never knew I needed someone like him in my life.

When he's finished, he pats me dry with a towel and stands to leave.

'Wait.' I bolt up in the bed. The thought of him leaving sets my heart plummeting to my toes.

'Yes?' He perches on the edge of the bed.

I try to summon the right words without sounding super needy. 'Don't go' dances on the tip of my tongue, but I can't bring myself to say the words out loud.

It turns out I don't need to. 'Want me to stay for a while?' he offers. 'I'll stay on top of the bed covers. If the duvet's between us, it doesn't count, right?'

'Yes, please. Stay a while…' I exhale a breath I'd been holding. 'But make sure you're gone before the twins wake up. I don't want to confuse them.'

The bed dips as he curls his strong muscular body around mine. I want to ask how he coped with the twins tonight. I want to ask him if they were good. If they missed me. But most of all, I want to revel in the forbidden comfort of having a man here beside me. One who I feel uncannily at ease around.

But seconds after he drops an arm over my cotton-covered body, I drift into a blissfully satiated slumber.

Chapter Eighteen
RONAN

If I was obsessed with Savannah Kingsley before last night, I'm enamoured with her this morning. How is it possible to miss someone I only just left? To miss someone who I technically barely touched.

I'm pacing my kitchen, counting the hours until our swimming lesson, praying she won't freak out and cancel on me. Praying that she enjoyed last night as much as I did. Praying that it was so fucking good for her she's going to need a repeat.

My phone chimes with an incoming text message.

> Savannah: I'm so sorry, I won't make it today.

My thumbs fly over the keypad.

> Me: The hell you won't. Don't let last night get in the way of your contract with Coral.

Three dots appear.

Then disappear.

Then appear again.

I wait with bated breath, thrumming a finger over my lips before firing out another message.

> Me: I swear not to bring up last night. If you're freaking out, we don't have to talk about it. You don't have to be embarrassed.

> Savannah: I'm not embarrassed.

> Me: So what's the problem?

> Savannah: I'm horny. Again.

> Me: I can be at yours in half an hour for a repeat.

> Savannah: Do you have water in your ears or something? I told you, I can't start something with you, even if I wanted to.

Even if I wanted to.

There might be hope yet, if I can only find a way to persuade her she doesn't have to be 'Single Sav' forever.

> Me: In that case, stop telling me you're horny and get your ass down to the pool to do some work.

> Savannah: Fine. But don't even think about touching me.

> Me: Don't worry Sassy Sav, you're in safe hands.

> Savannah: It's not you I don't trust.

Boom. This thing burning up between is real. The way she cried my name last night was real. The way the void in my previously empty life is plugged when I spend time with her and her adorable kids is real.

But how do I make her mine, when she's committed to leading the single mothers of the country? And why do I have a feeling there's more to it than that? Like it's a convenient front she's hiding behind.

Once again, my mind strays to the twins' dad. Obviously, he fucked her over big time. No wonder she's cautious, but I'm not him. Given half the chance, I'd give her everything she needs and more. I just need her to let me in.

I inhale a breath and let it out slowly.

One day at a time.

I grab my keys and head to the pool to burn off the restless energy that's crusading through my veins.

I don't need to raise my face from the water to know when Savannah arrives. I feel it in the whisper of every molecule I'm made of. I cut through the water gracefully and effortlessly, only lifting my head when I reach the shallow end.

Savannah's wearing that damn pink bikini again. Her golden hair, piled high on her head bar a few loose tendrils framing her face, gleams in the light. She's as stunning this morning without a scrap of make-up as she was last night.

A low groan of appreciations slips from my lips.

'Behave,' she warns, lowering herself into the water without a moment's hesitation. Her confidence has improved immeasurably in only a few weeks.

Instead of the awkwardness I feared, there's a newfound closeness between us. Like a deeper layer of friendship or something. That's not to say the air isn't crackling like a live wire, because it is.

'Yes, ma'am.' I raise a hand to salute her. 'You're getting brave.'

'You make me brave.' Whether she's referring to the water, or the way she let me watch her get off last night, the rawness of her admission is almost as intimate as the display she gave me last night.

A surge of pride swells in my chest. 'Let's get started then.'

True to my word, I don't touch her. Well, barely, anyway. I've waited too long to rush things now. If something's going to happen between us, it needs to be at her initiation.

With a little coaxing, she manages to swim an entire length of the pool using breaststroke. It's not graceful by any standards, but she manages.

'Do you want to try putting your face into the water?' I bob next to her as she clings onto the ledge in the deep end.

She shakes her head vehemently. Is her reluctance simply because she doesn't want to get her glossy hair wet? Or something else?

'Do you want to talk about what's been putting you off the water? It might help dispel the fear. Sometimes the things we're afraid of grow into monsters in our head and the only way to get rid of them is to free them from your mind.'

'My monster is real.' A bitter laugh leaves her lips. 'She goes by the name of Mother.'

There are so many layers to this woman. She shows up online every day with a smile and words of encouragement for her followers, but who shows up for her, if it isn't her family?

Without my family, and our Sunday gatherings, I'd be lost.

I tread water, literally and metaphorically, keeping my mouth shut while silently willing her to open up to me.

'I'm adopted,' Savannah admits, eyeing me with trepidation, like I'm going to judge her for it or something.

'I think I read that somewhere online.' Whoops. Did I just admit to cyberstalking her?

She lets it slide. 'My mother got knocked up on a one-night stand and didn't want to be a single mother, so she signed over sole custody of me to my uncle. He and his partner, Steve, have raised me since I was a tiny baby.'

Another piece of the Single Sav puzzle slides into place. Is she determined to be the best single mother that ever was, the champion of all mothers as a silent fuck you to her own mother for not stepping up?

Is her past holding her back from her future?

'So, you have two dads?' I thought winning one over would be hard. After all, what father is genuinely happy to meet their daughter's boyfriend? But knowing that the boyfriend is sliding his cock into their daughter…

Boyfriend?

Fuck. I'm getting ahead of myself and there hasn't even been any sliding or riding.

'Yep, Stuart and Steve.' Her eyes soften at the mention of their names. 'I'm lucky in so many ways. I dread to think what would have happened if she hadn't handed me over to them. She couldn't take care of a cat, let alone a baby. The only time she spent any time with me, I almost drowned.'

No wonder she never learnt to swim.

'What happened?' My hand hovers over hers where she clings white-knuckled to the ledge of the deep end.

'I was four years old. It was a beautiful summer's day. She convinced my dads to let her take me for the day, and that she wanted to spend some time with me. We took a train to the countryside. She took me to a lake with a picnic area. It's a gorgeous spot in Meath, with a waterfall and everything.'

I know the spot. I've been a couple of times. It's secluded and stunning.

She continues, staring blankly ahead like she's seeing it play out in her mind. 'We packed a picnic. Took bathing suits. I remember feeling so special, so wanted. I was at the age where I was beginning to realise most people had a mother and a father, and I was so happy that mine had finally come back for me.

'She took a million pictures of us with one of those Polaroid cameras, probably for the child benefit I later found out she was claiming, then drank a bottle of wine she'd packed and fell asleep in the sun. I was so disappointed that I'd waited to spend time with her, and instead of playing with me she fell asleep, pissed.'

I nod sympathetically but don't interrupt her flow.

Savannah swallows thickly. 'I went into the water on my own. It looked so inviting, but it was deeper than I thought. I got into difficulty, but when I screamed for help, she was in a Chianti coma and wouldn't wake up. There was nobody else around, and I was petrified. I thought I was going to drown until a dog-walker heard the commotion and pulled me out of the water.

'My dads collected me from the train station and that was the last time I saw my mother.' She arches her eyebrows and shrugs.

'I'm so sorry, Sav.' I squeeze her hand, but there's nothing sexual about it.

'It's not something many people know,' she confesses. 'I'd hate them to pity me.'

'I don't pity you, Savannah. I pity your mother. Look what she lost.'

Savannah flinches. She puts on a brave face, but I bet it still rips her apart that her mother abandoned her, especially now she's a mother herself.

'This hot mess?' She motions to her make-up free face and forces a smile that doesn't quite reach her eyes.

I sweep a hand across her face. 'You're amazing.'

'You know you're not too bad yourself.' Her lips lift into a rare smile. 'For a cocky manwhore.'

Chapter Nineteen
SAVANNAH

I'm obsessed with you. I'm obsessed with you.

It's been playing in a loop around and around my mind for a full week.

If I was smart, I'd forget about it, but I can't.

I thought Ronan might have called but I've heard nothing, apart from a text saying he can squeeze the girls in for a lesson at eleven am.

Then again, he is a manwhore, so what did I expect?

I didn't even get him off, or tell him to get himself off while I watched, something I've regretted a million times this week.

What was I thinking?

Clearly, I wasn't.

I shove the girls' bag into the changing room lockers and head out to the pool to take my seat for the weekly perving session – oops, I mean swimming lesson.

Ronan greets the girls enthusiastically, taking Eden's hands to help her into the water, but his navy eyes are locked on me. There's a chemistry in the air and not just the clawing smell of chlorine from the pool

Those full, plump lips.

That chiselled chest.

The way those fucking shorts hug his granite glutes.

My mind is made up.

I'm going to fuck Ronan Rivers.

And the sooner the better.

The buzzing of my phone steals my attention. I tut at the interruption, fumbling in my handbag to silence it, but one look at the screen has me swiping to answer instead.

My agent, Cassandra Steele, never calls unless it's urgent. And given it's the weekend, I assume it's something serious.

I stand, moving towards the changing rooms and away from my kids who are squealing at Ronan, in his smoking scarlet shorts.

'Savannah,' Cassandra rasps with the voice of a woman who smokes forty fags a day. 'I've got some big news. Inkwell Imprints have reached out. They want you to write another book on parenting solo, especially with divorce rates higher than they've ever been.,'

'They do?' You couldn't make it up. The second I decide to end my celibacy, in rolls an offer I can't refuse.

'Think *Single Sav's Guide to Winging Working and Whining Kids,*' Cassandra booms. I imagine her hand gesticulating wildly, like the title is written in the stars in the sky.

'So, they want me to write a book about work life balance for parents?' I clarify.

'No, they want you to write a guide specifically for single mothers like you.' I flinch. 'How to work without feeling guilty. How to decide on a creche versus a childminder at home. How to make these decisions solo. Throw in some practical tips, maybe mindfulness or journaling or something, that shit is really popular these days, although why, I have no idea. I barely have time to work, let alone parent, and I don't see that changing anytime soon,' she cackles.

'I guess I could do it...' My heart isn't in it. My heart is somewhere else.

I told you I can't differentiate between sex and emotions, and there hasn't even been any sex.

'You *guess?*' Cassandra's tone is incredulous. 'Inkwell is offering a huge advance, generous royalties, and a country-wide book tour.'

I sigh.

The universe is conspiring against me.

How can I write, let alone promote, a book about being a single parent if I'm not one?

But then again, Ronan doesn't want to date me. He wants to fuck me, apparently. Obsessed or not, he's a player and I'd be a fool to forget it.

It's not even midday and I could do with a drink.

By the time Cassandra runs through the brief, the stipulations, and the contract offer, the twins' lesson is almost over.

I glance at the clock as I rush back to take my seat, hoping for even a couple of minutes alone with Ronan but his next pupil and her parents arrived before Isla and Eden were even out of the pool.

Ronan bids my daughters goodbye with high fives before turning to me. 'I'll text you a time for tomorrow.'

'Thanks.' I bolt out of the door before I do something stupid like beg him to come over tonight. Then again, I couldn't, even if I wanted to. I have somewhere else I need to be.

Tonight marks the official opening of my friend Holly's Dublin-based art gallery. She already has two galleries in the States, but given how much time she and her movie star husband, Nate Jackson, spend on Irish soil, it made sense that they have somewhere this side of the Atlantic to showcase her paintings.

I knew it was going to be a lavish affair, but the old, refurbished church is a work of art itself. A high vaulted ceiling soars above my head, and evening sunlight streams through the stained glass windows, casting a kaleidoscope of colours across the polished concrete floors.

Huge oil-based portraits have been carefully suspended from the exposed brick walls, many of which capture the image of Holly's handsome husband. It's not hard to work out why the Hollywood movie star is her muse. I can't paint the wall, let alone a portrait, but with dark hair, startling green eyes, and a jaw that could cut glass, I'd be inspired to paint Nate too.

In a red, backless, full-length Gabriela Hearst dress and with a glass of champagne in my hand, I look and feel more like Single Sav than I have done all week. The publishing contract is a gift horse. I'd be a fool to turn it down. I've worked too hard to fuck things up for a flash in the pan. If it got out that I'd had sex with Ronan Rivers, Dublin's magnetic manwhore, it would ruin my brand.

Ashley is my date tonight. Matt is once again 'working on his novel' and I, for one, am delighted not to be the only one here flying solo.

I've hardly seen or spoken to my friends this week, primarily because I can't lie for toffee and I'm not ready to admit what I did with Ronan the other night. It's hard enough to process without those two hopeless romantics wading in with their ten cents' worth. It was what it was, and now it's over.

Ashley links her arm through mine as we stroll across the polished concrete floor, admiring the work of our super talented friend and celeb spotting. The place is crawling with them. Real celebs, not bloggers like me. Actors, models, singers, you name it, they're here.

'Who is minding the girls tonight?' Ashley knows my dads are away. She also understands that I could write the names of people I trust to mind them on a piece of paper the size of a stamp.

'I asked the neighbours' teenage daughter if she'd do it. Shona's only sixteen, but she's really mature. The kids love her because she's a "big girl".' And my only option, given my dads are still sunning themselves cruising around the Mediterranean.

My core clenches as I recall last week's babysitter.

I've never come so hard in my life, nor am ever likely to again.

Unless...

No, Savannah.

Just NO.

Think of the book deal. Think of the blog subscribers. Think of the brand.

Besides, Ronan's probably out in Elixir or some other fancy bar right now, looking for his next conquest and I can't blame him. I can't give him what he wants, no matter how badly I want to.

I should be proud of my restraint, my commitment to my brand.

Instead, I'm kicking myself. If it was only going to be that one time, I should have gone hell for leather on him. I'm such an idiot. I might not be able to start something, but if I ever find myself in a similar situation with him, alone and away from prying eyes, it would be hard to let the opportunity slip by a second time.

But no matter how hard I try, I can't erase the image of him between my legs, watching like a horny teenager.

'Touch your tits for me.'

'Good girl.'

Why, oh why, do I have to choose between my career and my carnality?

'Are you okay?' Ashley arches a quizzical eyebrow.

'Yeah, why?' I take a sip from my glass, hoping the chilled bubbles will cool me down.

They don't.

Concern touches Ashley's tone. 'You spaced out for a minute there.'

'Sorry, I'm tired.' It's the truth.

I'm emotionally wrecked from fantasising about Ronan all week and physically wrecked because I've been sneaking into the gym every morning to use the pool.

Not just because of the shoot. Stupidly, a part of me wants to impress Ronan. Craves his approval. His compliments and his praise. I despise how clumsy I am in the water next to him. Clumsy and helpless isn't my style.

My technique is improving with each day.

I can't wait to show him what I can do tomorrow. I need to hear those two little words fall from his lips again, even if it's for all the wrong reasons. *Good girl.*

'Sexy Olympic swimmer at four o'clock.' Ashley whispers gleefully, squeezing my arm.

My head whips round to see the man I've been fantasising about all week. Okay, all year, truthfully, even if I thought he was an asshole.

Ronan clutches a glass of champagne, his sharp oceanic eyes scanning the room. He's wearing tailored navy suit trousers and a crisp white shirt, the sleeves rolled up to reveal tanned powerful forearms. It's a far cry from his usual sexy swim shorts, but he looks good enough to eat.

His presence here shouldn't be such a surprise. Anyone who's anyone was invited. I don't know why it didn't occur to me.

Finally, his gaze lands on mine, pinning me in a stare so intimate it strips me bare. He strides over, sucking the inside of his cheek like he's biting back a grin.

'Good evening, ladies,' he purrs to both of us, but his eyes remain fixed on me.

'It was...' I mutter, making a production of rolling my eyes. Ashley is going to take one look at me and know I've been keeping a secret from her.

'Ouch.' He holds a huge hand over his heart mockingly. 'And there was me thinking we bonded last weekend.'

'Ronan.' The warning is clear in my tone.

'Is that any way to talk to your new babysitter?' A smile splits his mouth wide enough to reveal his straight, naturally white teeth.

'You let him babysit the twins?' Ashley shrieks.

I shrug like it meant nothing. 'I was desperate.'

'Yes, you were.' Ronan's cobalt eyes twinkle.

I shoot him a warning look.

Ashley's beady eyes bounce between the two of us. 'Shut. The. Front. Door! You two had sex.'

'We didn't,' Ronan and I say simultaneously.

Ashley's eyes narrow. 'You so did.'

'I would've, given half the chance,' Ronan admits, torrid pupils boring into mine with an intensity that melts my underwear.

'Yes, but I'm a good girl,' I fire back. Laughter tumbles from his lips.

The air is heavy with hormones, mostly mine. Ronan's raw masculine scent surrounds me, and I can't think straight, dizzy with lust.

'If it's any consolation, I told her she should bone you.' Ashley sweeps her auburn hair behind her ear, her voice as solemn as a judge's. How this woman is the principal of the most prestigious Catholic school in Ireland, I will never know.

'Thanks for your support, Ashley. Nice to know you've got my back.' Ronan's lips twist into a smile.

'Hello, I'm standing right here, you know.' I roll my eyes and pretend I'm not secretly enjoying their exchange.

From my periphery, a familiar flash of dark hair catches my eye. Lucas Beechwood.

Ashley spots him a second later. 'Isn't that Lucas Beechwood, AKA your new boss, sort of?'

Ronan turns, following Ashley's shameless stare.

'That's him.' I raise my hand in a greeting as he turns towards us. 'We went for dinner at Azure on Saturday to discuss my contract.'

'That's who you went for dinner with last Saturday night?' Ronan growls.

'He is paying me a million euro to model his swimwear range.' I roll my lips, watching as Ronan's jaw locks. 'He wanted to check my "vibe" personally, apparently.'

Ronan's face dips forwards, his lips brushing over my earlobe as he whispers, 'The only man checking your vibe is me. If I hadn't caught you moaning *my* name after that dinner, you'd be in big trouble tonight.'

'Is that right?' I rock back on my heels to stare up at him.

Is that jealousy I detect? A surge of satisfaction that I have no right to feel runs straight down my spine.

Before we have the chance to discuss it further, Lucas swaggers towards us, every bit as smooth as he was the other night.

'Savannah.' He presses a kiss to both my cheeks. 'Such a pleasure to see you here tonight.' His perusing stare roams over my dress. 'You look stunning.'

His flattery is sincere, but it doesn't have even a fraction of the effect of Ronan's basic praise.

'I'd have to agree.' Ronan steps forwards and extends his right hand to Lucas. 'Ronan Rivers.'

'Lucas Beechwood. Founder of Coral. It's a pleasure to meet you.' Lucas's eyes dart between us several times before he focuses on me. 'Perhaps we might get to have that drink after all?'

A definite growl rumbles in Ronan's throat, but he masks it with a cough.

My phone rings in my clutch handbag. My immediate thought is that it must be Shona and the girls. 'Sorry, I need to get this.'

It's not the babysitter. It's the woman I employ to clean one of my rental properties, a luxury villa in Ballybowen.

'Liz, is everything okay?' Stupid question. She wouldn't be calling me on a Saturday night if it were.

'No Savannah, sorry, it's not. I went to clean up the villa tonight and get ready for Monday's guests, but there's been a leak. The main bathroom is flooded. I don't know what to do. Water is pumping out from one of the pipes. I'm frightened it'll go through the ceiling and into the kitchen.'

Fuck. My. Life.

Why do these things always happen when my dads are away?

'Is it bad?' I exhale heavily, watching as Lucas turns his attention to Ashley, while Ronan stares expectantly at me.

'Bad enough. I called the plumber, but he can't come out until Monday. He said as long as no one uses the upstairs bathroom it won't get any worse, but it's not rentable until it's fixed.'

The rental income isn't the issue. Monday's guest is a British soccer player who is planning to propose to his girlfriend. 'Okay. I'm on my way.'

I hang up with a sigh. I'm not sure what I'll be able to do when I get there, but I have to at least try.

'What's up?' Ronan catches my elbow, drawing me closer.

'It's the villa I rent out in Ballybowen. There's been a leak. I need to go.' I toss my phone into my purse and reluctantly eye my half-empty champagne glass. It's my third drink, so I'm not fit to drive for at least a couple of hours.

What will I do with the twins?

This single parent craic is fine until there's a crisis.

'What's up?' Ashley shifts towards us.

'I need to go and sort out my new swimming pool in Ballybowen. The one that's currently filling up in my bathroom.' I roll my eyes.

'You can't drive. You've been drinking. And what about the girls?' Ashley is, as ever, the sensible friend.

'Can't someone else go instead?' Lucas steps forwards.

'There is no one else.' I shrug. Part and parcel of being single.

'I'll drive you,' Ronan offers, dumping his champagne flute on the nearest table. 'I barely touched that, and it was my first.'

'It's on the west coast.' I eye him dubiously. 'It's almost a three-hour drive.'

'I know where Ballybowen is. My best friend lives in the neighbouring village, Ballyshanway. Jake Nolan, you might have heard of him?'

I feel my eyebrows arch upwards. 'I heard he lived in the area, but I've never come across him.'

'He's a recluse. Doesn't drink. Doesn't party. All he does is swim in the Atlantic every day and spend time with his wife. We all handle our retirement differently.' Ronan shrugs.

'Well, if you're sure...' The prospect of a night in Ballybowen with Ronan is too tempting to pass up, whatever the excuse.

'I'm sure.' Ronan's thick, fair eyebrows knit together in concern. 'But what are we going to do about the girls?'

We.

How can one tiny, two-letter word sound so incredible rolling from his tongue?

'I'll take care of the girls. I'll get a taxi there in an hour. I don't want to bomb out on Holly's big night any earlier than necessary,' Ashley offers. 'Matt won't even notice if I don't come home. I'll stay at your place.'

'Sorted.' Ronan's tone is almost gloating as he eyes Lucas like he's won some sort of silent battle. 'Looks like we're going on a road trip.' His deep velvety voice echoes the thrills shivering down my spine.

It's a perfect excuse to spend another Saturday night with the man who I can no longer even pretend to hate.

Chapter Twenty
RONAN

We step out of the gallery into the evening sun, scanning the street for pesky paps. Pulling the only woman no one has in years would do wonders for my reputation, but even I can appreciate it wouldn't be good for Savannah's.

'Ronan, are you sure about this?' Savannah shoots me a sidewards glance as we stride along the pavement, three feet apart.

Am I sure about spending some alone time with the woman I've been obsessed with for two years and three months and about three days in one of the quietest villages in the country?

I've never been surer of anything in my life.

'Yes. I haven't even had a drink. Let's swing by your house, get what you need, and we'll be on the road in less than an hour. I have my gym bag in the boot with spare clothes, so that'll save me having to go home.'

She twists her head and offers me a playful smile. 'Sure you don't want to hang around here and see if you give the paps something to snap?'

'What part of "I'm obsessed with you" did you not understand?' I brush my hand against hers in an apparent innocent gesture, but there's nothing innocent about the memories of those hands touching herself for my viewing pleasure. 'I thought I made my desire for you pretty clear.' I glance over my shoulder to glare at the art gallery. 'Though if I'd known I had competition, I might have made it even clearer...'

She snorts and waves her hand dismissively. 'Lucas? Don't be silly, it's business. What did you think of the exhibition?'

'Oh, Savannah,' I sigh. Is she really that clueless? 'The only reason I went was because I knew you'd be there.'

She slows to almost a stop and sweeps her gorgeous glossy hair back from her face before turning to me. 'Why?'

'Because I've been thinking about you all damn week. Reliving Saturday night over in my head, and in my shower every damn day, multiple times.' I grab her elbow gently and steer her down a side street towards where my car is parked, before I really do give the paps something to snap. 'I picked up the phone a million times to call you this week.'

'Then why didn't you?'

'Because you're Single Sav and you've made it clear you don't want to date me.' *And because I've been biding my time for an opportunity like this.* 'What did you expect?' We reach my car and I place my hand on the base of her spine, guiding her to the passenger side, and open the door for her.

She shrugs, slipping in and sinking into the black plush leather. 'I've learnt not to expect anything from anyone.'

I think that might be the saddest thing I've ever heard.

But it doesn't surprise me.

Someone hurt her enough to deter her from dating men for over half a decade.

We drive to her house in silence.

. . .

By the time I crush up her driveway, the sun's set, painting the sky a vivid shade of pink. I hop out of the car and stride to the passenger side to open the door for her.

'Do you want me to come in?' I offer her a hand, helping her out. A charge of electricity scorches the skin where our fingers meet.

She hisses, like she feels the burn as sharply as I do. 'No, just give me ten minutes to check the girls and throw a few things into a bag.'

'Are you packing your favourite toy?' It's out before I can stop myself.

'Do you want me to?' Startling blue eyes fall to my lips.

'You know what I want, Savannah.' My eyes bore into hers. 'I want to fuck you. And it seems the universe is conspiring to help me.'

She stalks towards the house, but not before I catch the smirk stretching her lips. 'That filthy mouth will get you in trouble one of these days,' she calls over her shoulder, her ass swaying sultrily.

'Here's hoping.' Another idea springs to mind. I'm full of them tonight.

'You know we're going down on a clean-up mission,' she calls from the doorway.

'Sweetheart, I'll go down for you on any mission.' Savannah Kingsley brings out the filthiest thoughts in me. I can't help it.

She shakes her head in exasperation, but I don't miss the pink tinge to her cheeks.

'I'll be back for you shortly. I just need to pick up a few things.' And make a phone call, because there's no way I'm going to waste the entire night on a clean-up mission. Not when I can call in reinforcements.

She nods, gripping the door frame like she's holding on for dear life.

We might have a job to do, but we also have the rest of the night together and presumably, we'll be sleeping under the same roof. A roof far, far, far away from here and the prying eyes of the paps and her children. I, for one, plan to make the most of that opportunity.

I head to the nearest convenience store and pull up my best friend's phone number on the handsfree system. Jake answers on the second ring.

'Well, if it isn't Dublin's biggest Don Juan. What are you doing calling on a Saturday night? I thought you'd be on the prowl with your brother.' Jake's voice echoes like he's somewhere spacious, but given the size of his house, he's probably at home.

'Funny. Very funny. We aren't all lucky enough to be smug and happily married like you,' I tease, but even as the words leave my mouth, I catch the envy in them.

Marriage is not something I've given much consideration to before, but honestly, it's not something I'd shy away from if the circumstances were right.

I haven't even admitted to Savannah that I want to date her for fear of scaring her off, let alone entertained the M word. Maybe it's time to change all that. Maybe instead of treading carefully and not scaring her off, I should be paving the path for both of us, beating back any obstacles that might stand in our way.

'So, how's things?' Jake interrupts my thoughts.

'Good.' What else can I say? I'm obsessed with a woman who's more unavailable than a nun, but I'm working on wearing her down. 'How are you?'

'Great thanks, just chilling here on the couch with Jess. Is everything okay?'

'Everything is fine, but I need your help,' I admit.

'Course you do,' he sniggers. 'Let me guess... girl trouble?'

'No. Plumbing trouble.'

'Oh shit. Is there something up with your junk? All jokes aside, you should be careful if you're having casual sex.' Genuine concern weighs on my friend's warning.

'Not my junk! Actual plumbing trouble. I have a friend who owns a house in Ballybowen. There's been a leak. We're on our way to fix it right now, but I wondered if you'd be free to help. I know how much you love the water,' I tease. 'And many hands make light work.'

'For fuck's sake, you want me to leave my comfortable sofa and my stunning wife for a clean-up mission?' he grumbles, but I can tell he's already on the move.

Jake's one of those guys I could call on at any time of the night or day for anything, and if he can help, he will. That's why he's my best friend. I only hope I get to return the favour one day.

'Yep…' I thrum my fingers on the steering wheel as I negotiate the car into the only space outside the store. 'Bring your wife. She's not afraid of getting wet either.'

'Careful,' Jake warns, but his chuckle assures me he appreciates my joke. 'There better be at least beer and pizza involved.'

'Of course.' I slide out of the car and enter the store, grabbing a trolley. I'm going to need it for all this beer and pizza, apparently. 'And thank you. I'll text you the address. We're on our way. The key is under the mat at the front door if you get there first.'

'Huh, you'll probably arrive when all the work is done,' he huffs.

'I'll get there as fast as I can.'

'Who is this friend? Do I know him?' Jake adds, like it's an afterthought.

I clear my throat. 'It's a her, actually.'

His guffaw nearly deafens me. 'Course it is.'

'She's different…' I clear my throat. 'She's special to me.'

'Special as in you're together?' His tone is filled with wonder. It's not surprising. I've never had a serious girlfriend before. I've never found anyone special enough to want to settle with, not until Savannah, anyway.

'Special as in I'd like to be, but it's complicated. You'll understand when you meet her.' I pause. 'And one more thing, Jake, please be discreet, okay? I don't want to scare her off, or to make this into something it isn't.'

'Oh shit,' his voice drops to a whisper. 'She's not married, is she?'

'No! What do you take me for? She's currently not in line for dating, but I'm working on it.' Starting by dropping the "I just want to fuck you bullshit."

The truth is, I don't want to just fuck her. I want to fuck her forever.

And maybe it's time I told her that.

'I'm intrigued,' Jake muses. 'I'll see you when you get here. Jessica's brother is a plumber. I'll give him a call now.'

I fist pump the air. 'You are a legend, my friend.'

'I'll see if I can get it sorted. If this girl is as special as you say she is, you might want to score some brownie points.'

'I owe you big time.'

'You owe me nothing.' Jake's tone is sincere. 'See you in a couple of hours. I've got news too. It'll be great to tell you in person.'

'News? Like a new job or something?' I rub a thumb over the stubble dotting my jaw.

'Something like that,' he chuckles.

In the store, I fill the trolley with pizza, olives, and every other antipasti I can find.

The condoms I throw in are a prayer to the universe that I might get lucky enough to need them.

Chapter Twenty-One
SAVANNAH

It's not a date.

It's not a date.

It's not a date.

So why am I lashing on extra mascara and another three squirts of Jo Malone perfume?

Because Savannah Kingsley, you know, you will never get a better excuse to be alone with Ronan "Ride Me" Rivers.

I slip out of the Gabriela Hearst number and pull on a casual denim dress. It has spaghetti straps and stops mid-thigh. It's casual, but there's no denying it's cute. I stuff two more summer dresses into an oversized Mulberry handbag with a few cosmetics and with the sexiest lingerie I own, you know, just in case.

I'm sailing dangerously close to the wind, and I know it.

I want to have sex with Ronan Rivers.

I want it more than I've wanted anything in years.

I spend so much time running around after the girls, driving them to after-school activities, and then posting about it online so every mother in the country knows she isn't alone, but truthfully, it's me who feels alone. And I'm sick of it.

Tonight, I'd like to share my bed with someone. Fall asleep in a man's arms. Again.

Not just any man.

Ronan.

I'll get it out of my system once and for all and then be on my merry way, with my merry new single mother book and no one will ever know. Child free, in a remote setting, with stunning scenery. I couldn't have planned it better if I'd tried.

I'm starting to wonder if I've had Ronan all wrong.

He didn't hesitate to help. He's great with the girls. Great with me. He's as close to Mr Right as they get. Which is precisely why he is wrong for me.

I'm not looking for Mr Anything, let alone a relationship.

I don't want to date you. I want to fuck you.

That, Ronan, I might just be able to do.

Though it's been a while. I hope I remember how.

I grab a white cardigan, sling my bag over my shoulder, and creep into Isla's room. She's sprawled width ways across the bed, her glossy hair splayed across her purple bedspread. Her dark eyelashes flutter in her sleep. I know I'm biased, but my God, she's beautiful. There's no love like my love for my daughter in the world.

'I love you, princess. I'll be home tomorrow,' I promise, even though she can't hear me.

I tiptoe into Eden's room to check on her. She's nestled below her duvet with her favourite stuffed animal tucked into her chest. She's just as stunning as her sister, but even in sleep, her features are set in a much more solemn expression, but her breathing is deep and even and peaceful.

Out of both my daughters, I worry more about Eden.

Is her desire to be good all the time because of something I've done? Or is she naturally a rule abider, where Isla is naturally a rebel? It's a relief that Eden is so easy to manage, but maybe she's not expressing herself the way a six-year-old should.

Sometimes, just sometimes, I wish I had a partner to bounce these things off.

The sound of a car engine outside alerts me to Ronan's return.

'Are you sure you're okay?' I double-check with Shona, who's watching reruns of Friends on my couch, and sipping from a can of Diet Coke. 'Ashley won't be long, I promise.'

'It's fine, Savannah. Don't worry,' she assures me. At least if there is a problem, her mother is only down the road.

It's hard to relinquish control when I'm used to doing everything myself, but walking out of the door is also selfishly liberating.

Ronan opens the passenger door for me, the scent of his cologne stealing my senses.

'You all set?' His dark blue eyes are dazzling, even in the dusk.

'As I'll ever be.' I hope the flooding isn't too serious. The one in my panties is bad enough.

'I got some supplies.' His lips curl, but he keeps his gaze on the road ahead.

'Hmm. Do I even want to know?' I mutter, but a thrill rips down my spine.

'Just covering all the bases. These Saturday nights are becoming a regular occurrence,' he muses, changing lanes as we hit the motorway.

'They are, aren't they...'

His hand falls from the steering wheel to my bare thigh. Feather-light fingers brush over my skin and I gasp. 'Am I allowed to touch you tonight, Savannah?' His voice is deep and gritty, weighted with the same need that curls around my core.

'We'll see.' I glance pointedly at where his fingers continue to tease me, but I don't ask him to remove them.

'How are the girls?' he asks.

'Fast asleep. They'll be over the moon when they see Ashley there in the morning. They adore her.'

'As much as they adore me?' he teases.

'It's close,' I admit. 'They must have asked me a hundred times this week when you are going to babysit again.'

'Yeah?' His tone hitches, like he's surprised and delighted. 'What did you tell them?'

'I used the same two words every mother uses when she has no idea. "We'll see".'

Ronan chuckles. 'They're beautiful girls, just like their mama.' His fingers slip a little higher up my thigh.

An image of Ronan cradling a newborn baby to his chest makes my ovaries somersault. I can't think about him in that capacity.

I'm Single Sav.

But I can't think about that either. In fact, I can't think about anything except those damn fingers drawing maddening circles on my skin. Goosebumps rip across my flesh.

'Cold?' he asks with a smirk.

'Quite the opposite.'

'Care to elaborate?' His fingers steal higher again until he's a mere inch away from my lingerie.

I pinch the bridge of my nose and exhale heavily. 'You do things to me.'

A low chuckle rumbles from the back of his throat. 'You do things to me too, Savannah.' He grabs my hand and rubs it over his crotch for a fleeting second before releasing it and resuming those slow, sensual strokes on my skin.

'I'm going to ask you one more time, Savannah. Can I

touch you?' His voice is low and guttural. I bet he's an animal in bed.

I roll my lips together, pausing for a beat before giving into the inevitable. 'Tonight, and tonight only. When we get back to Dublin, things have to go back to the way they were.'

A low moan of satisfaction rumbles from his mouth. 'In that case, open your legs and let me stroke that pretty pussy. I've been fantasising about it all damn week.'

'But...' I motion to the steering wheel.

'Cruise control.' He shrugs. 'This thing pretty much drives itself. Now open your legs like a good girl. I want to see if you're wet for me.'

Years of pent-up need bursts like a dam and I allow my legs to fall open against the leather. Deft fingers inch upwards until he reaches the lace of my lingerie and rips it clean off me with one sharp tug.

'That's better.' His voice is smooth, satisfied, almost melodic.

Thick fingers slide through my slickness, and my pelvis arches upwards of its own accord. I've been starved of a man's touch for way too long.

'Soaking. I fucking knew it.' He pulls his fingers away and I whimper in protest, watching as he brings his hand to his mouth and slowly sucks them.

'You taste like heaven, Savannah.' Blood pulses furiously below. He's barely touched me and I'm embarrassingly close to coming all over his car seat.

His hand returns to where I need it, sliding through my slippery folds and I swear the relief is like nothing I've ever experienced before.

'Talk to me, Savannah,' he urges in a low, gritty tone. 'Do you like that?'

I love his filthy mouth. I love his filthy fingers, and I can't wait to find out how filthy he can be with his cock.

'No, I don't like it,' I tell him through the darkness. His fingers pause and I cry out like a wild animal. 'I fucking love it.'

'That's my girl.' He slips a finger inside me and pumps while his thumb continues to circle my clit.

My girl.

I wish.

It's so good.

He's so good.

He knows exactly where to touch me. How much pressure. Speed. Tempo. The man is gifted. I'm moaning and undulating and writhing around his expert fingers.

My limbs shake, my thighs tighten, and hot, white delirious oblivion devastates every cell in my body. Wave after wave of pleasure tears through my core. I clench around his fingers, wringing out every last drop, crying his name like a blessing and a curse.

His fingers still and slide out. I watch in fascination as he puts them into his mouth again. 'You taste utterly tantalising. I'm going to need so much more.'

Remind me again why I've been abstaining from men for all these years?

Oh wait, because I've never had one ruin me the way Ronan just did.

Twice he's made me come so hard I can't remember my name.

It's high time I repaid the favour.

Chapter Twenty-Two
RONAN

'Pull in.' Savannah's voice is low and demanding.

'I'm not fucking you on the side of the road.' I refuse our first time to be anywhere but in a bed. It has to be perfect. So perfect that she'll drop the "just one night" bullshit. She was made for me. I feel it with every fibre in my body.

Every day I wake up thinking about her, wondering if she's okay. Wondering if she's thinking of me. And I fall asleep with her face at the forefront of my mind and usually on the screen of my phone.

'I said pull in,' Savannah insists.

I glance at the clock. We're still over an hour away from Ballybowen and if I don't let her at least touch me, I might explode before we reach the town border. I indicate off at the next exit and drive until I find an isolated spot overlooking the sea lapping at the beach below.

'Can I help you?' I take my foot off the pedal and the car cuts out automatically.

'I'm about to help you.' The moonlight spills through the window, casting a dim light on Savannah's gleaming turquoise eyes. I don't recognise this playful, girlish version of her, but I love it. I should get her out of Dublin more often.

She unclips her seatbelt with a definitive click. Dainty fingers reach across the car and tug at the top button of my jeans until they pop open. My cock is rock hard and weeping already, crying for her touch.

'I've been wondering for a while what you've been hiding down here.' Her tone is weighted with want.

I watch as she wraps her hands around my length, gazing down with palpable awe.

Her eyes snap to mine. 'I always thought you were arrogant, but maybe I would be too if I was walking around with something this size in my pants.'

'I'm not arrogant. Confident? Yeah, sometimes, but don't be fooled. We all hide behind the mask we wear for the rest of the world.'

A flicker of understanding ripples across her even features.

'You know what I think you are, beneath the mask you wear?' Her tongue darts out to wet her lips, and her eyes fall to my crotch again.

'What?' My breath hitches and not just because Savannah Kingsley has my cock in her hands, something I've thought about for the past two years, but because what she thinks about me is just as significant.

'I think you are one of the nicest guys I've ever met. You're kind and considerate and caring.'

I laugh. 'Nice guys finish last, though, right?'

'This nice guy's going to finish in my mouth.' Her face lowers as she inches full red lips over my crown and sucks. Fucking hell, it's the most transcendent experience of my life.

I've had a lot of women, but none of them stirred anything in me like Savannah stirs.

If I won fifty gold medals, it wouldn't hold a candle to the sensation of her tongue flicking across my cock.

A moan sounds from her mouth as she takes me deeper.

I've died and gone to dick heaven.

Her blonde hair spills across my lap as she digs her scarlet painted fingernails into my thighs. 'Your mouth feels so fucking good, Savannah.'

She murmurs something incomprehensible. She works me well. Takes her time. Lavishes so much attention on my cock and it is utter utopia.

I writhe beneath her, trying to buck back, but she pins me in position.

'I'm close,' I warn, giving her the chance to stop before I spill everything I've got into her mouth.

She ups the pace, swirling her tongue around my tip before taking me deep again.

My legs go rigid as heat builds in my core. Electricity crackles across my skin. My body is on fire. The cords in my neck are wound so tightly they're liable to snap. My teeth clamp down as I battle my orgasm and the subsequent end to the most decadent experience of my life.

I thread my fingers through her silky hair, staring in awe as it bobs over my lap, driving me over the edge. She milks me with her mercurial mouth, sending a million stars shooting through every inch of my skin.

When she's swallowed every last drop, she raises her head and licks her lips slowly and deliberately, those stunning eyes wide and full of want.

'Who knew you could get drunk on dick?' she laughs, sounding as dazed as I feel. Her lips plant a final kiss on my still thick cock.

'Savannah, that was transcendent.' I reach for her across the car, cupping her chin and dragging her face towards mine.

'It was, wasn't it?' Our eyes lock for a beat and something passes between us.

I said I wanted to fuck her, but after that, I think I might actually want to marry her. One night, my ass. When I get her spread out on a bed and to properly worship every inch of her beautiful body, one lifetime won't be enough for her.

I trace my thumb over her perfect cupid's bow, wiping off the remnants of her lipstick.

Savannah's hand falls to my thick thigh. 'But now we've dealt with the leak in both our pants, we really need to go deal with the leak at my villa.'

'And then?' I lean forwards, touching her lips with mine.

'And then, we'll see.' Which by her own admission means she hasn't got a clue how we navigate this thing between us.

Which makes two of us.

'I hope you don't mind, but I called in reinforcements.' I lean across her and pull the seatbelt tightly across her body, clipping it into position. God forbid anything should happen to her now she's finally mine.

Because she is mine, she just doesn't know it yet.

'Reinforcements?' Her tone sharpens suspiciously. 'Who?'

'My best friend and his wife. I told you, they live nearby.' I start the car and put it into reverse. The quicker we sort out her villa, the quicker we can get back to sorting each other out.

'Jake Nolan?' Savannah screeches. 'Can we count on his discretion about the fact we're here together?'

'Absolutely. I told him we're friends. We are friends, Savannah, aren't we?' My hand falls to rest on top of hers as we speed through the dark night.

'As much as it pains me to admit it, you're probably one of the best friends I have at the minute.' Sincerity rings in her tone. 'It's actually lovely having a boy friend.' Her hand flies to her mouth. 'A friend that's a boy. You know what I mean.'

'I know what you mean,' I repeat. I also know that I'm going to do everything in my power to lose the space between those two words as soon as physically possible. 'But just to clarify, I'm the only boy friend you give head to, right?'

She slaps my bicep playfully. 'Yes. And only for tonight.'

'Well, in that case.' I hit the indicator again and pretend I'm looking for the first available turn off.

Her laughter seeps through the air and straight into my soul, lighting me up from the inside out. This is what I've been craving, this connection. Someone to laugh with. Someone to love.

Her happiness is my happiness.

I'm totally fucked.

Savannah's villa is impressive, to say the least. Nestled almost on the edge of a cliff, it's perched directly above the wild Atlantic Ocean, crashing against the rocks below.

My headlights illuminate the driveway where Jake's jeep is already parked. Low warm lighting radiates from behind glass panels on either side of the duck-egg coloured front door. The scent of salt and seaweed hangs in the air, tickling my nostrils, and I feel like I'm a million miles away from Dublin.

I stride up the steps with Savannah, my palm caressing the small of her back. From the second she said I could touch her, I haven't stopped.

It's impossible to tear my hands from her. I feel bereft anytime they leave her body.

She reaches for the brass door handle, stepping just slightly out of my reach and whispers, 'Hands off until we get this mess sorted, okay?'

'Fine, but just know I'm going to spend however long it takes sorting this mess, imagining exactly where I'm going to put my hands later.'

'Believe me. So am I. But please, respect my wishes.'

'Of course.' I'd never not respect her wishes, even if they're in direct contrast with my own. It's imperative that we take this thing at her pace.

Because we are a thing. Or we're going to be.

Even if she doesn't know it yet.

'Hello?' Savannah calls, strutting down a wide corridor through to a spacious living area and a bright, opulent open-plan kitchen.

A huge open fireplace punctuates an exposed brick wall in the centre of the room. A wraparound terrace flanks the side of the house. I can only imagine the views from there in the daylight.

Jake's familiar voice resounds from upstairs. 'We're up here.'

We pad back through the house, my feet sinking into the plush lavish carpet lining the stairs. 'This place is absolutely fabulous, Sav.'

'Isn't it?' She leads the way, taking the second door on the left.

Jake's lying on the floor in a couple of inches of water pooling beneath a clawfoot freestanding bath big enough to accommodate eight adults. His t-shirt is rumpled and riding high, revealing a neat even six-pack and the tan of a man who is retired. Another man lies on the other side of him, wielding some sort of wrench and barking orders at Jake. Jessica's brother.

Jessica hovers in the corner watching her man with fascination. She's tall and lean with long copper hair and cat-shaped eyes winged with black eyeliner. Her head whips up as we enter. She stares like a rabbit caught in the headlights, eyeing Savannah like she's some sort of goddess, which I can fully attest she is.

One hand cups her mouth, the ring that Jake put there

only a year ago glinting and twinkling beneath the bathrooms spotlights. Her other hand cups her protruding belly.

Jakes certainly does have news.

'Oh my god, Single Sav!' Jessica squeals. 'I'm a huge fan. I just subscribed to your blog last week.' Jessica's palm sweeps over her stomach in a circular motion. 'We just had our twenty-week scan and I'm looking for all the advice on motherhood I can get.'

Savannah hovers in the doorway. 'I, err, thank you.' She's clearly eyeing the rings, or should I say rock, glittering on Jessica's finger.

Does Savannah really have no idea that married woman adore her too?

There's an entire market out there and it's not just single women she can help, but that's not a conversation for right now.

'Nice of you to turn up,' Jake grunts, standing up. He shakes his head, but a grin lights his face all the way to his eyes.

My gaze strays to Jessica's stomach. 'Congratulations, man. You're going to make an awesome dad.' I grab his hand and shake it vigorously.

'Thanks. And you're going to make an awesome godfather.' His head cocks in question for a split second. He watches as his words sink in, and I crush him into my chest in a man hug.

'Seriously?' I look at Jessica over Jake's shoulder and she nods enthusiastically.

'Huh, what about me?' The guy holding the wrench huffs, pulling himself up. His t-shirt is wringing wet and clinging to his torso.

'You're already going to be its uncle, don't be greedy.' Jessica sticks her tongue out at him playfully. 'You remember my brother Bobby from our wedding?'

'Sure, I do.' Bobby was the last man standing at the bar. Ten pints in and he looked as sober as a judge. It probably helps that he's built like a lumberjack.

'Bobby is a plumber. We picked him up on the way,' Jake explains to Savannah, as he extends a hand to shake hers. 'It's great to meet you.'

'And you. Thank you so, so much. I can't tell you how grateful I am. Please, let me know how much I owe you,' Savannah says, glancing between Jake and Bobby.

'The only thing you owe us is a pizza, a beer, and an explanation of what a good girl like you is doing, hanging out with a bad boy like Ronan here.'

'I keep wondering the same thing myself.' Girlish laughter peels from her chest. 'But in fairness, he's proving to be a very good friend.'

There's that word again. Friend.

We'll see if she considers me her friend when my head is buried between her legs.

Chapter Twenty-Three

SAVANNAH

The leak isn't nearly as bad as Liz said. Well, I suppose it's easy to say that now an actual plumber has fixed it, thus limiting any further damage, and further cause for panic.

It's one o'clock in the morning. I should be wrecked, but I'm not. I'm buzzing. I haven't felt as alive in years. Like one almighty orgasm from Ronan shocked every sleepy cell in my body back to life.

I find some towels and hand them to the lads, motioning them to shower in one of the en suites off the villa's seven bedrooms. Ronan starts with a mop and a bucket on the bathroom's varnished original wooden flooring. Hopefully, it'll dry out okay.

'Have you got a portable heater we can put in here overnight?' Sweat glistens above his brow line and dots the space between his nose and upper lip. The temptation to run my tongue over it is real. Given where else my mouth's already been tonight, I'm fairly sure he wouldn't mind.

The car sex (is it sex if it's not penetrative? I have no idea) was the hottest thing that ever happened to me. Ronan is ridiculously talented.

He's had a lot of practice, a niggling inner voice reminds me. I swat that thought away and replace it with the memory of my mouth around his length. It's been years since I've been with any man. I'm surprised I remembered what do to.

Scratch that. If I'd have done anything like that before, it would have been emblazoned on my brain like a tattoo. I've never had sex like it; so carnal, so shameless, so right. If I had, there's no way I would have abstained for almost seven years.

'If you keep looking at me like that Savannah, I'll have to pull your dress up around your waist, bend you over that bathtub and fuck you until you can't walk.' Dilating pupils fall to my chest. My pebbled nipples demonstrating exactly how much his filthy mouth turns me on.

'If you keep looking at me like that, I might just let you.' My eyes drop to his crotch. You'd think now I know what he's got stashed down there, it would have quelled some of the curiosity.

Nope.

It's blazing brighter than ever before.

I want to feel him inside me.

I want to know what he looks like when he cascades over the edge of oblivion.

'Savannah.' His voice is a low growl and there's a definite bulge in those trousers again. I slam the bathroom door shut and he pounces on me like a predatory lion. Lips, tongues, and teeth clash with an urgency I didn't realise I was capable of. Huge palms cup my swollen breasts, his hips pinning me against the door like I might try to run.

As if.

I arch my pelvis against that delicious thickness pressing into me, an animalistic moan rushing from my mouth directly into his.

I pull back, my head lolling against the thick oak door. 'I want you,' I tell him in a breathy tone.

His lips trail a line of sensual fluttering kisses along the column of my throat, dipping lower until his tongue is between my breasts, and my chest is physically heaving with want.

'Pizza's ready,' Jessica calls from downstairs. She took it upon herself to play chef while we finished tidying up.

'Coming,' Ronan shouts. He steps back and rakes his fingers through his dirty blond hair with a groan.

It's been a mere three seconds, but I already miss the weight of his body flush with mine. 'Thank you, by the way.'

'What for?' His face angles down towards mine.

'For organising your friends to help. I really am grateful. The only men that have ever gone out of their way for me before are my dads.'

'You still don't get it, do you, Sav?' Amusement tinged with something else twinkles in his eyes. 'I'd do pretty much anything for you.'

His words are so sincere, I almost believe him.

'It's getting cold down here,' Jessica calls up again.

I open the bathroom door, blinking back the hearts I'm pretty sure are swimming in my eyes.

'Don't make her use her "mom" voice already,' Jake says, loitering in the door of one of the guest bedrooms with a towel wrapped round his middle and his clothes tucked under his arms. His taut tanned chest isn't nearly as appealing as Ronan's but still, I'd be lying if I said he wasn't easy on the eye.

Surrounded by men who look like that, is it any wonder my self-control has left the building?

Ronan shrugs, like he can read my mind. 'Naughty girl,' he mouths and my stomach somersaults. He eyes the bathtub again, a reminder of his earlier threat.

'I was only looking,' I whisper when Jake turns back into the room, presumably to dress.

'The only thing you're going to be looking at is my cock sliding in and out of that perfect pussy of yours. Now, go downstairs before I make you scream so hard, they'll be able to hear you in Dublin.' His palm connects with my ass, and I yelp.

'Yes, sir.'

How someone can be so good, so kind and so caring on one hand, and yet so deliciously dirty in other ways? It's like pineapple on a meat pizza. I didn't think that combination would be so damn delicious, yet just like Ronan, it's a combination I'd devour all day, every day.

I back out of the room, following the enticing scent of mozzarella all the way to the kitchen. Jessica's made herself at home in my kitchen and is slicing pizza into segments of eight, piling them onto a huge tray in the middle of the island. Her brother, Bobby, swipes a slice and loads up his plate.

'Beer or wine?' I offer, opening the fridge.

'Beer,' Bobby says, as Jake and Ronan strut down the stairs, Jake now dressed in a fresh t-shirt and shorts.

'I'll have a beer too, please.' Jake slides into one of the high-backed chairs circling the island and drops a kiss on Jessica's cheek. She turns to him and smiles. My heart flutters.

What would it be like to have a husband?

Someone to share my life with?

Someone to kiss me on the cheek just for the sake of it?

You'll never find out, Single Sav.

I grab Bobby, Jake, and Ronan a beer and pour myself a generous glass of Sancerre.

'Guys, I can't thank you enough for all your help tonight, seriously. I owe you big time.' I grab a slice of pizza and slip onto the bar stool next to Ronan.

Even though I own the villa, I haven't stepped foot in it in well over a year. Now I'm here, I'm wondering why not. It's so tranquil. So plush. I should make more of an effort to get out of the city. Bring the girls here, they'd love it.

I've been busy working to ensure they have everything they might need. I've forgotten what they might really need – downtime with me. A week or two where we're not rushing out of the door to piano lessons or dancing or swimming. A week where it doesn't matter if Isla's standing around in just her panties, because there's nowhere else we need to be.

Jake swallows the pizza in his mouth and turns to me. 'You owe us nothing, but if you feel like keeping an eye on Ronan, that'd be a great help,' Jake says, covering his smirk with his beer can.

'Does he need a babysitter?' I grab a slice of ham and pineapple and glance at Ronan. He picks up a slice of pepperoni and side-eyes me with a smirk and a shrug.

Jake and Jessica exchange a look.

'It would appear he's had one, for the past few weeks, at least.' Jake arches his thick dark eyebrows.

'What do you mean?' Genuine curiosity fizzles in my stomach.

'Well, how long have you and Ronan been *friends*?' Jake emphasises the word 'friends' heavily.

'A few weeks, I guess. Though technically, we've known each other for a couple of years,' I admit, before taking a sip of my wine. It's crisp and cold and utterly delicious.

'And when was the last time you saw an image printed of Ronan staggering out of a nightclub with a stray wannabe on his arm and an unflattering caption below?'

As I think about it, my jaws pause mid chew.

No, Savannah.

Just no.

One night, that was the arrangement.

The minute this becomes something more, the minute you start to expect something, it'll all come crashing down...along with the empire you've built.

No.

'I.. err... we're not... um...'

'You're Single Sav.' Jessica states the obvious. 'But man, why would you knock back the chance of something even bigger?'

Bigger? Has she seen Ronan's enormous cock, too?

'Like what?' It comes out as a squeak.

'Like one half of a power couple who've both proven they're successful alone, but choose to be together instead.' Jessica shrugs like it's simple. Her eyes fall to Jake and I'm sensing there's a story there, but neither of them elaborates, too engrossed in their shared dreamy-eyed stare.

Single Sav isn't just a blog handle or a brand name. It's my entire identity. Without it, what am I?

But is it the identity I want forever?

I'm beginning to wonder, but now is not the right time to jeopardise everything I've worked for. Not with the Coral Chic contract. And not with a second book deal hovering on the horizon.

Ronan is oddly quiet for once, seemingly engrossed in his pizza.

Silence descends upon the room.

I drop my slice of pizza and reach for my wine glass.

Ronan rests his left hand on my thigh beneath the island where my denim dress has ridden up. A jolt of electricity shoots through my skin and I feel like I could burst into flames. But what's worse is, as well as the excitement and the burning yearning swirling inside me, is the deep sense of comfort from his touch.

Even though it's impossible anyone can see Ronan's hand, Jessica glances at Jake again. Clearly, they're having some sort of private conversation conducted purely via eye contact. Three guesses about what . Or who, I should say.

I'm not put out. No, if anything, I'm envious.

What are the chances of me ever letting someone close enough to decipher my crazy silences and fluttering eyelashes?

Bobby finally breaks the silence, nodding towards Jessica's tiny bump. 'If it's a boy, you'll have to name him Bobby after his favourite uncle.'

While Jessica and Jake erupt with laughter, Ronan leans towards me to murmur in my ear.

'You okay?'

I nod. We might not be capable of an entire unspoken conversation, but it's like he can see I'm drowning in my own thoughts.

He turns his face to mine. 'Don't panic. I've got you,' he whispers. The same words he said in the pool when my nerves were eating me alive.

Our eyes meet and the smile that he offers lights the room like the morning sun. He emits a warmth, a radiance that I hadn't fully appreciated until lately. Now I've seen it, it's hard to unsee it.

Is it any wonder my daughters adore him?

Hell, I do too.

Oh god. I've got a feeling this weekend is going to get me into more trouble than I can even comprehend.

Given what happened in the car, it already has.

'I'm exhausted,' Jessica announces, palming her bump.

'Let's get you to bed.' Jake wraps his arms around his wife, pulling her back flush with his chest and reaching a hand around her body to stroke her stomach.

Another pang shoots through me. My own pregnancy springs to mind. No one touched my bump. No one.

He-Who-Has-Never-Been-Named had ghosted me, and

the only attention my fathers gave my stomach were matching looks of sympathy.

'Thanks so much, guys.' Ronan leaps to his feet. He's probably counting down the seconds until we're alone.

'Are you guys staying the night?' Jake asks, his tone not entirely devoid of teasing.

'I'd say so.' How Ronan manages to keep a straight face is beyond me.

As if he didn't bomb down here with the sole purpose of getting me out of the city and to himself for the night.

His dirty words flash through my mind again and I press my thighs together, the anticipation building in my core.

'At least you won't be plastered, drunk and disorderly, all over tomorrow's papers.' Jake nods towards me. 'She's a good influence on you.'

The question is, is Ronan a good influence on me?

I'm about to find out.

Chapter Twenty-Four
RONAN

'Your friends seem nice,' Savannah says, as she tidies the remnants of our midnight feast away.

'They are nice.' I grab a cloth and wipe the crumbs from the counter. 'I can count my friends on one hand, but those I do have are my ride or dies.'

'And am I included in those "ride or dies"?' Savannah turns to me, swallowing hard.

'You, my "friend", are the top of my ride list.' I grab her waist and tug her towards me, tossing the cloth on the counter. Her dress matches the deep denim of her sparkling eyes.

Her teeth sink into her lower lip like she's biting back a smile. I'm on her in seconds. Lips capturing hers, parting them, exploring the moist, wet, wine-flavoured softness with a hungry fervour.

She presses every perfect curve of her killer body against my frame, tight enough that I can feel the pounding of her heart as her chest presses against mine. 'Where do you want me?'

'Everywhere I can get you.' I swing her around until she's backed against the island, and cup the smooth globes of her ass cheek, hoisting her onto the cold granite surface. Her thighs part to accommodate my hips. I wanted a bed for our first time, but this island is big enough to spread her out on and worship her beautiful body. It's better than a sacrificial altar and I'm pretty certain devouring Savannah on it will be a religious ritual in itself.

My hands slide between her legs, and I hiss as I find her soft, wet centre.

'Ronan,' she mumbles into my mouth.

'Yes, baby.' I nudge her backwards until her back is flush with the cool counter, but judging by the heat blazing between her legs, she doesn't feel the cold.

'I need to feel you inside me.' Her admission is a simple one, but it sets my soul alight. I've imagined those words falling from her lips a million times. Imagined her opening herself to me. Imagined how it would feel to touch her, to take her, to make her mine.

'You will, baby. But not yet.' I slide the straps of denim down her shoulders and tug the material low enough to expose a lustrous lace bra the same shade as the panties I tore off in my car. I watch as twin peaks harden on the centre of each of her breasts, the same way I've witnessed in the pool, only this time, I get to touch them.

Savannah's hands slide from her sides to the bra. I watch as she unhooks a tiny clip between her breasts and the material falls away.

'Fuck, Savannah, you're so perfect.' My greedy hands reach upwards, cupping her perfect tits in each hand. I arch my torso lower to lick one of those rosy buds and it's her turn to gasp. Her lungs empty and fill as my tongue swirls and dances over those perfect peaks.

Her body wriggles impatiently beneath mine and I chuckle, dragging the dress lower and lower until both of us are wiggling it over her hips. It slithers to the floor.

There on the kitchen island, with her glossy golden hair fanned out, naked and spread out for me, Savannah has never looked so beautiful.

Hooded eyes communicate her lust and longing. My tongue trails across the silky soft skin of her stomach, inching lower and lower until I'm between her legs. I bury my face in her centre and her hips jolt upwards, her fingers dragging across my scalp as she writhes and moans while I explore every inch of her with my greedy tongue.

Feeling her buck and squirm and arch in pleasure is a more satisfying prize than any Olympic medal. Hearing her panting my name over and over again is the most cathartic experience of my life.

I want her.

Not just her body.

I want all of her.

My palms push her thighs wider and her heels dig into the base of my spine while she unfurls for me like a fucking flower. I slip a finger into her centre and stroke that sensitive spot on her inside wall again, sucking her clit until she screams my name like a plea or a prayer, her body shuddering around me. I don't stop until her limbs go limp and the shudders turn to subtle shivers.

Wordlessly, I scoop her into my arms. Her legs bracket my torso as she rests a cheek on my chest, her ragged breaths the only sound for miles around.

I carry her upstairs like a precious doll, kicking the door to the master bedroom open. It's huge, opulent and boasts a stunning double balcony. Placing Savannah gently on the bed, I brush my lips lightly against hers.

'Ronan, please,' she whispers.

I don't need to ask what she wants. It's the same thing I want. The same thing I've wanted for as long as I've known her.

I nod and pull a square foiled packet from my trouser pocket before unbuttoning my shirt and tossing it to the floor. Her pupils rove hungrily over the ripples of my torso before lingering on my crotch.

In one swift motion, she rocks upwards from the bed and yanks at my trousers, popping the button with a satisfied smirk.

'Patience, princess,' I tease her, kicking off the remainder of my clothes until I'm naked.

'It's been seven years, and you want me to be patient?' Her throaty laugh floats between us as I nudge on top of her, knees sinking into the mattress between her legs.

I capture her mouth with my lips, unable to quite believe this beauty is all mine to do with as I please.

For tonight, at least.

I push that thought away for now.

Her fingers skim my back, caressing the curve of my ass, piercing the skin as she tugs me up towards her. I wanted to take my time with her. To ravage her slowly, but that's not an option. Not for the first time, at least.

I lower my lips to her neck, nipping the skin over her jugular as my hand scrambles for the condom I tossed onto the bed.

'You're massive.' Savannah's hips roll as she grinds against me.

'Don't act surprised. You've been staring at my crotch for the best part of two years, you dirty girl. You knew what you were signing up for.' I tear the square and roll the latex on, peppering kisses across her collar bone before dipping to take her needy nipple into my mouth again.

'Was not,' Savannah lies, parting her legs and exhaling a breathy moan as I nudge my tip at her entrance.

'Was too. Say it, Sav.' I inch myself into her tight walls, slowly, taking care not to hurt her.

She's so tight. So wet. So fucking perfect. She's everything I fantasised about, and so much more. My hips pin her in place, but so does my stare. I can't tear my eyes from her. Can't bear to miss a single second of pleasure that twists her lips.

Her tongue darts out to wet her lower lip as she shifts and adjusts beneath me. I withdraw an inch before sliding back in, deeper this time. Her eyes roll back in her head.

'Say you've been staring at my cock. Wondering what it would feel like inside you.' I give her another inch and her fingers grip the cotton sheet.

'I've been staring at your cock, wondering what it would feel like inside of me. Wondering if I could take it.' Her lips lift in a smirk. 'Wondering if you knew what to do with it.'

I pull back slowly and thrust into her again.

'You take it perfectly.' I grab her right wrist and pin it above her head, grinding into her as deep as her body will allow, our pelvises melding as one. 'And don't worry baby, I know exactly what to do with it.'

'So I see.' She gasps as I slip my thumb between us and circle her swollen clit, slamming into her again and again and again.

'You're so tight. So wet. So fucking perfect.' I wanted her for so long and now she's here, giving herself to me. It's taking every ounce of willpower I have to hold it together.

'Ronan, I...' Her chest rises and falls as she shatters around me, her core clenching my cock in a vice-like grip, dragging me into the most decadent devastation known to man.

'I've got you,' I murmur, kissing her breasts as her chest expels ragged heaves in the aftermath of our fun.

But who's got me?

Because I've fallen so hard for Savannah, one lifetime won't be long enough, let alone one night.

Chapter Twenty-Five
SAVANNAH

Waking up in a man's arms is one of the most underrated pleasures of all time. Waking up in Ronan's arms is practically a religious experience. With his chest pressed against my back, his strong muscular arm slung around my waist in a protective and possessive position, I've never felt so desired, so cherished, and he hasn't even so much as muttered good morning.

Everything he did to me last night, the magnitude of pleasure his body offered mine, pales in comparison to this simple, sublime moment.

Slow, deep, even breaths brushing my neck suggest he's still deep in dreamland.

What does he see behind those closed eyes?

Me?

Or is that just wishful thinking on my part?

In our haste to get to bed, neither of us drew the blinds. Sunlight streams in through the balcony doors. The golden rays cast a luminous glow on every inch of the room, including my soul, which flickers with an unfamiliar warmth from the inside out.

A hundred words flit through my mind while I try to find the right one that justifies this one moment in time.

Finally, I settle on one. Contentment.

The sound of the sea slapping the shore and the gentle rhythmic rolling of rocks dragged out with the tide would be enough of a lullaby to send me to sleep again if I wasn't determined to make the most of these last few hours before we both have to go back to the real world.

I wriggle my hips, deliberately grinding myself against Ronan's morning glory, and how glorious it is. He's as hard as steel.

'Good morning, Sassy Sav,' he murmurs, nipping my ear playfully with his teeth. 'Did you sleep well?'

I let that one slide, given the satisfaction he bestowed on my body. 'Too well,' I admit. Satisfied and secure in Ronan's arms, I've never slept as well in my life. It doesn't bode well for "Single Sav", but I shove that thought to the back of my mind. No point ruining the moment when we only have a precious few.

His hand reaches beneath the covers, cupping my breasts before slowly sliding down over my stomach like he's committing every inch of skin to memory. 'I know you said one night, but how about one for the road?'

As if I could say no.

This time when we move together, it's gentle, tender, less frantic, as if both of us are savouring it. Our last time.

And when it's over and the ragged beating of hearts finally slow, he pulls me into his chest and locks those arms so tightly around me again and whispers, 'I wish we could stay here forever.'

'So do I.' I inhale his skin, savouring his unique scent, a hint of cologne tinged with his raw masculinity.

'Let's send for the girls.' Ronan's fingers languidly thread through my hair. He stares at the ceiling, a wistful look winding onto his face. 'We could stay here for the summer, swim in the sea, sit on the terrace, sunbathe all day and have sex all night.'

Would he seriously want that?

To spend the summer not just with me, but with my girls too? It never occurred to me that there might be a man mad enough to take on all three of us. It's not a notion I allowed myself to entertain before.

But why would I? We've always been fine on our own.

Though, here in this beautiful bubble, I can't deny that 'fine' is a far cry from 'content'.

'If only,' I sigh. 'But you're forgetting one major thing.'

His head cocks to the side, his huge baby blues tersely gazing into mine. 'That you said this was only for one night?'

'Well, there is that...' I trail off, squeezing his bicep playfully. 'But more importantly, this is Ireland.' I point at the balcony door where the sun is blazing through the glass. 'That big ball in the sky won't last until next week, let alone all summer.' I force a giggle, even if it sounds strangled.

It's far safer to focus on the weather than fathom the future of our relationship. Because as safe and content as I feel this morning, wrapped around Ronan, I'm in serious risk of losing everything I ever worked for if I don't walk away from this. And apart from the fact my legs are still quivering like jelly and my vagina feels like I've ridden a horse bareback across a mountain range, even if I *could* physically walk away from this thing between us, mentally it's going to be a hell of a lot harder. As ever, I still can't separate sex from feelings.

Which leaves me in an awful predicament. But I refuse to waste this glorious morning thinking about it.

'You're right.' Something like relief flits across Ronan's features. 'Which is why I propose we hold today's swimming lesson out there.' He swirls his pointer finger in a dramatic circle before angling it at the ocean.

'You want me to swim in the sea?' I repeat, like a moron.

'You need to do it before the shoot.' His hand falls back to my body. 'When is that, by the way?'

'Four weeks.' I received an email with the details from Susie yesterday.

I said I'd rather jump into the sea than into bed with Ronan Rivers, but look at me now, about to tick off both. I'm not sure which is more shocking.

'You won't get a better opportunity and I promise you're in safe hands.' He palms my bare breast to emphasise his point.

I roll my eyes jovially. 'Is this the part where you remind me you won two Olympic gold medals? Again.'

A laugh tumbles from his chest and his fingers dip to my waist, tickling me until I squeal. 'Ha. Funny. Excuse me if I like to relive the best days of my life from time to time.' His fingers halt and his expression turns serious. 'Though truthfully, those days have nothing on last night, or today.'

'Did you pack any swimwear?' Ronan's palms caress my skin.

'Nope.'

'In that case, we'll have to go into the sea in our underwear.' He shrugs.

'I doubt there'll be anyone around, anyway. Ballybowen is like a ghost town until the schools finish up for the summer holidays next month. That's half the appeal of this place. But it doesn't really matter. There are steps that lead from the terrace directly down to a rocky secluded tidal pool.'

'Seriously?' Ronan's eyes light up. 'That's so cool. If this were my place, I'd never rent it out. I'd live in it myself.'

'I've never seen the attraction of the countryside.' Since I had the twins, life has been hectic. I kept it that way deliberately because if in the moments I tried to slow down and allow myself to stop, that's when the loneliness creeps in. The bustle of the city is something I've come to rely on.

'I love the countryside. The peace, the tranquillity, the freedom. Allow me to show you the attraction.'

'Hmm, I think you already did.'

Half an hour later, I'm descending the slippery stone steps towards the rocky shore. The tide is on its way out, which means the rock pool's been freshly filled with sea water and God knows what else. A shudder travels down my spine.

'What if there's fish in there?' I call to Ronan, who is two steps ahead of me and more eager than a beaver.

His resounding laughter echoes off the rocks. 'It's the sea, of course there are fish in there.'

'What about crabs?' I cling on to the salt-rusted handrail, wondering why I ever thought this was a good idea.

'Baby, trust me when I say you don't need to worry about crabs.' Ronan turns and shoots me a wink as I reach the last, slightly larger, moss-covered step.

I slip my palm into his and he offers it a reassuring squeeze.

The air shifts, carrying the tangy scent of salt and the faint fragrance of seaweed. The pool is no more than ten metres wide and more oval shaped than round. The edges are adorned with weathered flat stones, smoothed by the swell of the ocean over time. Barnacles cling to the crevices, while colourful algae paint the scene with hues of green and red.

I eye the water tentatively. Even through my terror, I can appreciate its mesmerising blend of azure and jade. Gentle ripples dance across the surface. Under the sun's gentle caress, the water sparkles and shimmers.

'It's absolutely beautiful.' Ronan tugs me closer to the edge.

'It is. But I still don't know if I can do it.' Nerves gnaw at my stomach.

'Let me go first, then I'll help you, okay?' Ronan drops the towel wrapped around his waist on the flattest part of the largest rock. If the glistening water doesn't entice me in, the glistening sheen on his naked body just might.

'What happened to "we'll go in in our underwear?"'

He arches his eyebrow and smirks. 'You did say there'd be no one else around.'

'It's one way to get me into the water.' I drink him in. The curved rippling torso, the sharp V of his hips. His impressive length. His body is perfection, but the more time I spend with him, the more I see the real appeal. His permanent positivity, his cool confidence and his huge...heart.

He sits and lowers his thick, toned legs into the water.

'Is it cold?' I tentatively drop my own towel and step closer.

'No.' Ronan inches himself in until he's standing, the gentle ripples lapping at his chest. At least it's not too deep. 'Come in. It's fabulous.' He sinks beneath the water, submerging his entire head before leaping up.

The expression of joy on his face appears to be genuine. I lower myself to a seated position and Ronan extends his arms, reaching out for me. 'I've got you, baby. I promise I won't let anything bad happen to you.' His eyes twinkle brighter than the sea. 'I've got you.'

So he keeps saying.

I drop the towel tucked beneath my arm and Ronan pointedly eyes my lingerie. 'Lose it. Fair is fair.'

Our eyes remain locked as I reach to unclip my bra. As it falls to the rocks below, Ronan let's out a low whistle of appreciation. 'Fuck, Savannah, you are so fucking beautiful.'

His praise and the low gritty tones of his voice give me

the courage to drop my panties. They slide downwards across my thighs, and I kick them aside.

Before I can overthink it, I take the hands he's extending and allow him to help me in.

The initial plunge is like a shock therapy session sponsored by the North Atlantic. The water is cold enough to double as a walk-in freezer. My squeal is probably audible in Dublin.

'Ahhh! Liar! It's fucking freezing!' I yell at Ronan, who's laughing so hard he almost chokes on his own tongue.

'It's only freezing for a minute. When you get used to it, it's magnificent.' He reaches for my waist and pulls my body flush against his.

Goosebumps gather at a speed that could break records, then agonisingly slowly, my body begins to acclimatise to the elements. Just when I'm about to retreat, something miraculous happens. The euphoria kicks in.

The shock mellows into an icy embrace that leaves me momentarily breathless.

Ronan's hot body against mine only propels the goosebumps further. My nipples are like bullets.

I'm in the sea!

Okay, it's a salt water tidal pool, but still, Savannah Kingsley, known by her fathers and friends for her fear of water, is in the actual fucking sea!

A colossal sense of achievement erases all my fears. My teeth are chattering to their own jig, but the laughter bubbling in my chest is uncontrollable.

'It's amazing!' I shimmy against Ronan, winding my arms around his powerful shoulders, resting my fingers at the nape of his thick neck.

'*You're* amazing.' He plants a tender kiss on my forehead. 'You did it, baby. You faced your fears and now you can do anything.'

The sunshine beats down on our shoulders like a spotlight shining on this wondrous moment of glory. The water is so inexplicably refreshing. It makes me wonder if I've been sleepwalking through life's lukewarm moments.

One thing is for sure, I have no intention of sleeping through this one. I wrap my legs around Ronan's waist, offering myself up to him.

Chapter Twenty-Six
RONAN

The past fifteen hours have been the single best hours of my entire life. Savannah gave me not only her beautiful body, but her trust, and maybe even a tiny piece of her heart if the fleeting glances she keeps shooting me across the car are anything to go by.

'I wish we could stay.' Her voice is breathy and wistful.

'Me too.' I drop a hand on her bare thigh and leave it there as we pull away from the villa and start the long drive back to Dublin. 'I wasn't joking, though. We could always come back for the summer.'

Barbeques on the beach, leisurely afternoon dips in the tidal pool and complete privacy from the rest of the world sounds like my own personal utopia.

Plus, I need some sort of reassurance that she's not going to shut this thing down the second we get back to Dublin.

'If only.' Savannah's fingers graze over mine. 'The villa is rented out eighteen months in advance. There are rarely any cancellations.' She glances back over her shoulder as it becomes a tiny dot behind us.

'I can see why.' At least she didn't say spending the

summer with me isn't an option. She didn't shut me down. Hope flares like a flickering flame in my chest.

Even this, almost three hours navigating Sunday traffic, seems like a treat, purely because I get to do it with her.

My obsession is growing with every passing minute.

'Tell me something about yourself, Savannah,' I urge. 'We all know "Single Sav" but I want to know the woman behind the public persona, the mask.'

'Thought you might have seen enough last night – and this morning,' she quips.

'Nowhere near enough.' My dick thickens in my pants at the memory.

'Fine.' She juts her chin out defiantly. 'I hate pickles.'

'Doesn't everyone?' I counter with a small shake of my head.

'No. Some people eat them raw or ruin their burgers with them.' She squeezes my hand to show she's messing with me.

'Tell me something no one knows,' I beg.

'Only if you tell me something about you first.' Her head whips round and she shoves her sunglasses on top of her head like a hairband, her deep blue eyes scrutinising my side profile like a laser.

I think about it for a second, desperate to give her something meaningful. 'You weren't the only one who nearly drowned as a kid.'

'Seriously?' She scoops a stray strand of honey-coloured hair and tucks it behind her ear in a feline gesture.

'Yep.' I chance a quick glance across the car to meet her eyes. 'I was at the beach with my parents. My mam was pregnant with my sister, Rebecca, and Rich was just a baby in the pram. I wandered into the sea on my own while Mam was distracted giving him a bottle. Thankfully, my dad spotted me and fished me out. The following day, he enrolled me in lessons. And that's how I got into swimming. Amazing how something that almost killed me turned out to be my salvation. My reason for living at certain points in my life.'

'Wow.' She exhales heavily. 'So, you really did understand my fear.'

'Yes.' I nod. 'Now, your turn.'

'Swimming wasn't the only thing I was afraid of.' Her tongue clicks against the roof of her mouth, and she exhales heavily. 'When I found out I was having twins, I sank into the biggest pit of depression. I hadn't planned one baby, let alone two. Panic plagued me day and night. I had two human beings inside of me and yet I'd never felt so alone in my entire life. Some days, I didn't know how I'd even get through the day. Guilt and shame swirled like a tsunami in my stomach. The only way I could get any relief was to write it down. That's how the Single Savannah blog came about. The truth is, I didn't start writing to help other women. I did it to help myself.'

'The very thing you struggled to survive became your salvation, too.' No wonder she's never considered dating. 'Can I ask, though, why did you feel guilt and shame?'

She arches her eyebrows. 'Are you kidding? Having a baby out of wedlock in this country? In the eyes of the church, I'm a sinner.'

'Fuck that.' Rage rises inside of me at the thought of anyone judging Savannah. Judging women in general. 'Those ideas are outdated and small-minded. Being a single mother isn't as uncommon as it used to be. Not everyone meets the right partner at childbearing age. Some people never meet the right partner. So many women are choosing to have babies alone and that's their choice, their right.'

'I agree with you one hundred per cent, which is why I aim to be the best role model and advocate for single mothers that I can.'

'You're an advocate for *every* woman and mother, single or

not.' It's the truth. 'My sister Rachel loves you. You saw how Jessica reacted to you last night.' I could go on. I could say so much more, but I don't want to push my luck. Don't want her to think the reason I'm saying all women can relate to her, whether they're single or married, is because I don't want her to be single anymore. Even if it's true.

I want her to be mine.

'Maybe.' She offers a shrug, but her tone isn't convincing.

There's one question that keeps forcing its way to the front of my mind, no matter how many times I try to blast it back.

The need to know is killing me.

Not that it's any of my business. Maybe it would be though, onc day, if this thing between us goes the way I hope it will.

I reach for the radio and turn it down to a barely audible beat in the background. 'Can I ask you another question?' My hand drops back to her thigh, the need to touch her stronger than ever.

'You can ask.' A half-smile parts her lips. 'Doesn't mean you'll get an answer.'

'Before I ask, I want you to know that whatever you tell me, whatever we discuss and whatever we do together, will stay between us. You know you can trust me with anything, Savannah.' I sweep my thumb tenderly over her inner thigh.

'Thanks, I appreciate that, but trust is something I struggle with.' Her tongue darts out to wet her lower lip.

'I mean it. I'll be your friend, or more, or whatever you want or need me to be. I just want you to know that you're not alone anymore. Not if you don't want to be.'

'You're a good man, Ronan. I'm sorry I spent the last two years calling you an asshole.'

Her lips roll as she bites back a small smile.

'I'm sure I can think of a few ways you can make it up to me.'

'Because I didn't already...' Her gaze falls to my crotch.

'A bird never flew on one wing,' I tease. She slaps my thigh playfully.

'Go on, what's this question?' Her head falls back against the headrest languidly.

I pause, not wanting to ruin the moment. 'The twins' dad...'

Her lips purse, jaw locks and her entire body stiffens, silently screaming *this topic is off limits*.

'I'm sorry. I shouldn't have opened my big mouth.' I raise my palms like a white flag. 'It's none of my business. I just can't help wondering who the fuck was stupid enough to let you go. Let alone your adorable girls.'

A long beat passes before she slumps forwards in her seat. She blows out a long, heavy exhale. 'I've never told anyone who their father is. . Not Holly. Not Ashley. Not even my dads.' She swallows hard. 'But I will tell you this, he knew I was pregnant. He knows they're his kids. And he's never sent so much as a text to see how they are, let alone a penny towards raising them. Not that I'd take it. I don't need him, or his money.'

'The guy is obviously a complete wanker. I'm sorry, Savannah.' I continue rubbing her thigh, reassuringly.

Silence falls between us. It's not awkward. More like contemplative.

'He was married,' she finally spits out. 'Sorry, I should say, he *is* married.' She folds her arms across her chest and makes a show of inspecting her fingernails. 'I had no idea. He wasn't famous back then.'

My curiosity piques, but I don't push her. 'Like I said, he's a wanker.'

She sighs again. 'Every time I see his smug face on the TV,

I want to punch the screen. Does that make me a bad person?'

Is he an actor?

A news presenter?

A footballer?

'It makes you human. Even if you look like a goddess.' I take her hand and bring it to my lips and kiss it.

'Flattery will get you everywhere, Ronan Rivers.' The seriousness evaporates and we're back to the playful banter in seconds.

'In that case, I'll find somewhere to pull in.' I'm not entirely joking.

Chapter Twenty-Seven
SAVANNAH

Spending time with Ronan has been a total eyeopener. I don't know how I ever thought the man was arrogant. He's like a human golden retriever.

Thanks to the tidal pool shenanigans, we left Ballybowen later than planned. By the time we reach the outskirts of Dublin, it's almost five o'clock. As the saying goes, all good things must come to an end.

I blink hard, forcing back the wetness forming in my eyes. What a baby.

My phone rings from my handbag on the floor.

It's Ashley.

I answer it, putting my finger over my lips to silence Ronan. Ashley might know that's who I'm with, but I don't want the girls overhearing and getting confused.

I'm still trying to wrap my own head around the last twenty-four hours, let alone try to explain it to a couple of six-year-olds.

'I'm so sorry, Ash. We're on our way. I'll be home in less than thirty minutes.' I glance at the clock on the dashboard.

'That's why I'm calling.' Ashley's voice is a hushed whisper. 'Don't come home.'

'What?' Alarm spikes in my stomach. 'Is everything okay?'

'It's more than okay. Matt called. He finally noticed my absence. I told him I was minding the twins and convinced him to come over and help me. Seriously, it's good for him. It might encourage him to get a move on, you know.' Hope hangs on Ashley's every word.

'Well, that's great news, I guess...' Ashley would love her own babies. If playing house with mine helps, then I can work with that.

'It is. Can you stay out a bit longer? Just give us this time. Maybe he'll get a taste for family life. Your girls are so gorgeous. So adorable. Spending time with them might finally make him see we'd make great parents ourselves one day.' There's a pleading in her tone.

Who am I to take this opportunity away from her?

'How long do you need?' My eyes shoot to Ronan. Has he got any plans for the next few hours?

'A couple of hours would be fab,' Ashley says.

'Are the girls behaving? Are they okay?' Isla can be a handful.

'They're perfect. No problems at all. We're just going to take them for a walk on the beach and an ice-cream.' My friend sounds thrilled at the prospect.

'You're a star, Ash. Thanks for everything.' I mean it. I'm truly humbled to have such great friends.

'You're the star, Savannah.' Ashley giggles. 'But tell me, are you still single?'

Ronan remains looking ahead as he concentrates on the road, but his lips twitch. I push the button on the side of my mobile, lowering the volume. I can't be sure he can't hear Ashley's every word already.

'I don't know what I am,' I admit. My gaze falls to my lap

where Ronan's thumb is still caressing my inner thigh with a tenderness I wouldn't have expected from the man who lives to tease me. From the second I said he could touch me, he hasn't stopped.

And I love it.

Love the sensation of being desired.

Cherished.

Even if Ronan didn't hear her words, there's no missing the whooping and shrieking coming from my mobile. I twist my head to look out of the window, hiding the crimson stains flushing my cheeks.

'I'm going to need a full debrief,' Ashley squeals. 'Pun intended.'

'I'll text you when I'm on the way home.' I need to wrap this conversation up sooner rather than later. 'Tell the girls I love them so much and I can't wait to see them.'

'Will do,' Ashley promises. 'Have fun.

I hang up before she can embarrass me further.

'Everything okay?' Ronan asks.

'Everything is fine, but Ashley wants to hang out with the girls for another couple of hours. Do you have somewhere you need to be, or can I take you for dinner to thank you for driving me across the country?'

'You mean driving you into the most decadent oblivion of your life?' Ronan's fingers slip higher for a fleeting second, reminding me exactly what he's capable of.

'Cocky, aren't you? Who said it was the most decadent oblivion I've ever experienced?' I pout.

'You did! When you screamed my name and bucked so hard beneath me, I thought I'd have to tie you down with a rope the next time.'

'Next time?' I pinch his thigh. 'It was supposed to be one night only. Something you're an expert in, if the tabloids are to be believed.'

'Savannah,' he tears his eyes from the road to stare at me for a long beat. 'What part of "I've been obsessed with you since you totalled my car" isn't sinking in? The only reason I spent every Saturday night drinking and fooling around was because the woman I wanted was more off limits than a nun. Believe me when I say I never wanted anyone the way I want you.'

I inhale deeply. 'Dinner?' I deliberately change the subject.

A wince flickers across his face. 'I actually have dinner plans.'

My face falls to the floor as I try to hide my disappointment.

What did I expect? The man's already given me most of his weekend.

'You could join us, if you like, though?' Something like mischief flickers in his bright blue eyes.

'Us?' It's barely more than a squeak.

'My family.' He says it like it's the most natural thing in the world. Like now we've had sex three, no wait, four, (or is it five?) times, I should go to dinner with his family.

Panic stirs in my sternum.

It's too much.

It's too soon.

Being seen with him will ruin everything I've worked for.

I stare out of the windscreen, seeing everything but nothing.

A part of me really wants to meet his family. To learn more about this man who I thought I had sussed but was so wrong about.

But I can't.

I just can't.

'Thanks for the invitation, but it's probably best if I don't.' The regret is unmissable in my voice. 'I'd hate for everyone to get the wrong idea.' Or the right idea, that we can't keep our hands off each other even though I'm sworn to celibacy for the sake of my brand.

'Savannah, please. It's only dinner. I'll introduce you as my friend. You'll love them, I promise. My mother makes the best roast potatoes in the country and her gravy is to die for. You won't want to miss out.'

My stomach rumbles. It's hours since we've eaten.

'They won't think it's weird, you arriving with me?' Code for - *will we be outed if I agree to this?*

'I'll tell them we went to fix the leak at your place. They won't read anything into that.'

I want to meet his family. I do. But more than that, I don't want to leave him. Don't want this day together to be over. Not yet.

With him, life feels different. I feel different. Lighter. More fun. I haven't laughed so much in years.

'You're sure they won't read into this as something it isn't?' Or isn't supposed to be, at least.

'Relax. It's just dinner.'

Half an hour later, we reach Ronan's family home, a huge rustic farmhouse nestled amongst rolling hills on the outskirts of Dublin. The evening sun casts a golden hue across the landscapes, illuminating the lush fields and surrounding gardens. It's not hard to see where his appreciation of the countryside came from.

A gravel pathway leads up to the front porch where two young boys sit on a weathered wooden bench, swapping what looks like football cards.

'My nephews,' Ronan says, lifting his hand in a wave as the engine idles to a stop. 'Joseph's the taller one. John's the cheeky one.'

They leap to their feet at the sight of their uncle, running towards us. He's barely opened the car door before they charge at him, excitement etched in their bright eyes and wide smiles.

'Uncle Ro, can you play football with us?' Joseph begs, tugging Ronan out of the car.

'Uncle Ro, where have you been? We've been waiting hours for you,' John asks, shoving thick-rimmed glasses up on his nose.

'I was busy. Sorry, guys.' Ronan strides around to the passenger side of the car and opens the door. Both boys' mouths drop open in shock. Maybe even horror.

'You brought a girl.' Undisguised disgust drips from Joseph.

'Is she your girlfriend?' John asks, shoving his glasses up the bridge of his nose.

'This is my friend, Savannah.' Ronan offers his hand and helps me out of the car.

Nerves slither over my spine. This was a bad idea.

Both boys eye me with trepidation.

There's only one thing for it. 'Where's the football? Who's going in goal?' Growing up with two fathers has some advantages.

'Really?' Joseph's face lights up like it's Christmas.

'Sure.' I shrug.

A laugh leaps from Ronan's mouth as he places a palm on the small of my back, leading me towards the garden to the left of the house. Two white rusty goals flank each end.

'You should probably go in goal.' Ronan nods towards my metallic gold sandals.

'Is that right?' I kick them off and run after the little guy, John, as he dribbles a football across the lawn. Making a show of trying to tackle him, I let him keep possession and watch as he shoots into an empty goal.

'You go in goal,' I point to Ronan, who's shaking his head, a wide grin splitting his face.

'I never had you down as a soccer queen,' he yells, jogging into position as the older boy takes his place defending the other goal.

'Just like I never had you down as a dance routine queen.' I've watched that video of his rippling torso dancing between my girls way more times than is healthy.

'Dinner's ready.' A plump woman in her sixties shouts from the front of the house. My head whips around and our eyes lock. Her grey, wispy hair is secured on top of her head with a crab clip. She has startling blue eyes, the exact same shade as Ronan's and her cheeks are flushed rosy. The shock on her face is quickly replaced with a warm, welcoming smile.

Her bright eyes seek out her son. 'Ronan! You made it! You didn't say you were bringing a...'

'Friend,' Ronan says firmly.

'Right. A friend.' Ronan's mother turns to me again.

'Mrs Rivers, it's a pleasure to meet you.' I shoot the boys an apologetic look as I cross the lawn and fall into step beside Ronan.

'Please, call me Nancy. Everyone else does.' She takes both of my hands, stares at my face for a long beat, and then drops a kiss on my left cheek.

'Nancy, I'm Savannah.' I glance at Ronan, who's watching with an unreadable expression.

'I know who you are. I've seen you on the TV.' She ushers me inside while she greets her son with a hug that lasts for half a minute.

'Savannah had a leak at the house she rents out, so we were over there trying to fix it,' Ronan explains, straightening himself.

'Is that you, Ro?' another female voice calls from further inside the house.

'It is,' Nancy answers for him.' And he brought his friend Savannah, too.'

Ronan's sister hurtles into the hallway, a gravy-splashed apron covering a polka dot summer dress. 'No fucking way! Single Sav?'

I wince, feeling like the biggest hypocrite in the world. 'The very same.'

But I'm not the same. And I doubt I ever will be, but now isn't the time to analyse that.

'I'm Rachel. Ronan's younger and better-looking sister.' She fires him a wink. 'I'm a huge fan of yours. I say to my husband at least five times a week, "I swear I don't know how that woman does it on her own."' She flings the dishcloth she's holding into the air and up onto her shoulder. 'I can't believe you're actually here.'

A guy saunters out from behind her with a knowing expression on his face. I recognise his dark hair and distinguished features from that night in Elixir. The night I drove myself demented with jealously when I thought Ronan had gone home with that woman in the white dress.

'Savannah Kingsley, in the flesh.' His deep Dublin drawl is as prolonged as his roving appraisal.

He turns to Ronan and clicks his fingers. 'I knew it.' Dark eyes dart between us with delight.

'Savannah and I are friends,' Ronan repeats, taking a step closer to me. I'm not sure if it's protective or possessive but I'm not used to someone else having my back, but I like it.

'Course you are.' Richard sniffs the air, and I swear he can smell the sex hormones radiating from us.

'Inside before dinner gets cold.' Nancy shoos us into the huge country kitchen like a mother hen. A round table punctuates the centre of the room, its top worn and cuffed from years of family dinners and fun. 'Grab another set of cutlery and a placemat,' she instructs Ronan.

A traditional style Aga with exposed brick over the mantle is the centre point of the far wall. I can only imagine what memories this kitchen holds.

Another man enters the room, attempting to soothe a crying baby on his chest, rocking and shushing the bundle in his arms. His silver eyes widen slightly as they land on me, and he nods a greeting before turning to Rachel. 'He must be teething. He won't settle. Won't take a bottle. Won't take a nap.'

'Savannah, this is my husband, Jonathan. And our baby, Mark,' Rachel beams. 'Mark's a pure rascal already.'

'Pleased to meet you, Jonathan. Here, let me take him.' I reach for the baby, offering an encouraging smile, 'if you don't mind.'

Jonathan doesn't hesitate. He hands the baby over quicker than lightning, relief relaxing his shoulders. I position the infant slightly upright, resting his cheek on my breast so he can hear the gentle thudding of my heartbeat. I rock him ever so gently, revelling in the unique baby scent, the smell of his skin and his hair. When a tiny hand curls around my pinkie finger, my ovaries roar.

Yep, still broody.

Not helpful.

Not helpful at all.

Chapter Twenty-Eight
RONAN

If I wasn't already halfway to falling in love with Savannah Kingsley, the sight of her cradling my nephew's tiny body to her breast is enough to ruin me forever.

She might be a celebrity blogger, but she has an innate ability to put everyone around her at ease. By the time dinner is over, my entire family is eating out of the palm of her hand, while baby Mark's deep contented breaths resound around the table.

No wonder. I'd be content too if I were snuggled on Savannah's spectacular breasts.

'I should probably go.' Savannah's lower lip juts out as she preens over the baby in her arms before reluctantly handing him back to Rachel. 'It's almost the twins' bedtime. Also known as 'The Witching Hour."

'The Witching Hour?' I repeat slowly.

'Yeah, that last hour before bed where they're exhausted and fight everything, bath time, bedtime, and especially each other.' Savannah stands up.

'Oh, I remember it well.' Mam's chair legs scrape the wooden floor as she pushes back from the table to see us out.

'Thank you so much for having me.' Savannah hugs my mother with a natural ease that makes me feel stupidly fuzzy inside.

'Anytime,' she says, offering Savannah's arm a parting squeeze.

I brush a kiss over my mother's cheek. 'I'll call you tomorrow.'

'Do,' she says, her blue eyes twinkling.

I was lying when I told Savannah my family wouldn't question me bringing her here. Question that she was simply a friend. I've never brought a woman to meet my mother in my life. Not in any capacity. And tomorrow, there will be a million questions fired in my direction. Despite this, I trust my family implicitly. Trust their discretion.

My hand gravitates to Savannah's thigh once again as I drive her home in silence, both of us lost in our own thoughts.

'Are you okay?' I check finally, as I pull up outside her house.

'Yes.' She nods, staring thoughtfully ahead. I wish I knew what she was thinking. What she was feeling. 'Thank you for everything.' She angles her head to face me and her full lips graze mine for a fleeting second before she hops out of the car with her overnight bag tucked firmly beneath her arm, along with my heart.

'It was a pleasure,' I say, mostly to myself, watching longingly as she strides inside her house without so much as a backwards glance.

She gives me no inclination of when I'll see her again.

Or *if* I'll see her, in an intimate capacity at least.

I'm terrified of pushing her before she's ready, but equally terrified of not pushing for this, for us, when every fibre of my body screams we're meant to be.

. . .

The following day I drive to St Jude's for the swimming lessons, balancing a takeaway double espresso in one hand and the other resting on the steering wheel as I negotiate three lanes of city traffic. Lana Del Ray is crooning about summertime sadness on Ireland AM. Flashbacks of the weekend are driving me demented.

It's only a matter of hours since I saw Savannah, but like an addict, I'm wondering how to get my next fix.

The radio presenter, Abby Connolly, wife of Callum Connolly, a former Ireland rugby player, interrupts my thoughts as she announces her next guest.

'That was Lana Del Ray. Welcome to Ireland Today. If you're just tuning in, you'll be excited to hear this morning's special studio guest is none other than Savannah Kingsley, known to most of you as Single Sav.'

I jolt upright so fast, I almost spill the coffee all over the interior of the car, and myself.

Abby continues, 'It's an honour to have Savannah in the studio with me today. I'm a huge fan. Callum and I have made no secret of our struggles adjusting to parenthood. How she does it alone, balancing her twins with an amazingly successful career all by herself, is a testament to the strength of her character, and to the size of her heart.'

Abby's not wrong.

I reach forwards and whack up the volume. The sweet sound of Savannah's voice floats through the sound system of my car.

'Hi Abby, thank you so much for having me on your show. It's an honour to be here. You don't know it, but you kept me company all through those bleary-eyed baby days. Your familiar voice gave me hope on the mornings I didn't know how I was going to get through the day.'

'Ah, that's so lovely of you to say,' Abby coos.

'The twins both suffered with reflux. They seemed to take

it in turns to wake me each time I dared to close my eyes.' Savannah forces a laugh, though there's nothing funny about reflux. Rachel's boys, Joseph and John, both suffered the same way. It's horrific for both the child and the parents.

And Savannah had to cope with two, alone.

A tsk slides from my lips.

'Oh my goodness. I can't even imagine,' Abby clucks. 'I used to moan if Callum was away for the night. I would have cracked up with two on my own.'

'It was tough.' Savannah pauses. 'But I wouldn't be without the girls for anything in the world.'

'How are you finding things now? You're certainly setting a stellar example to all the single mams of the country.'

'Things are easier in some respects, but every age brings a different set of challenges. At least the girls are at an age where they can tell me what's wrong, if they're in pain or need something. Sometimes I wish there were two of me, so I can shower them both with more attention, but I give everything I can, and I think it's important that they see Mammy following her own dreams too.

'I try to set the example that women can be and do whatever they want to be, whether they're working or a stay-at-home mother, whether they're married or single.'

'You are a wonderful role model, for your daughters, and for women in general,' Abby says.

I like Abby. Specifically, I like the way she didn't limit Savannah's influence to just single mothers.

'Thank you.' Savannah clears her throat.

'You have your blog, and your book, and your fabulous infant clothing range. Your success is inspirational. And now, I believe you have some exciting news to share with us.'

'Yes. Yes, I do.' Savannah clears her throat. 'I'm so excited to announce I've been appointed the role of ambassador for Coral Chic. I absolutely adore their swimwear range. It's so flattering for women of all shapes and sizes. It's elegant. It's durable. And it's more sculpting than a pair of Spanx.'

'Congratulations,' Abby coos and offers a round of applause. 'What a privilege.'

'Thank you. I'm excited to work with them.'

'I'll bet,' Abby says. 'Lucas Beechwood is fairly easy on the eye as far as bosses go. Tell us, Savannah, would you consider dating?'

Eugh. Lucas fucking Beechwood.

There's silence for a long beat.

'I.... err...' Savannah stammers.

My heart pounds like a war drum, every cell in my body willing her to admit that she's mine. That there's something between us.

'Sorry, that was awful of me,' Abby backtracks. 'What a position to put you in! You're Single Sav. Of course, you're not considering dating. I get carried away sometimes, trying to matchmake everyone since I found Callum.' Abby laughs and after a short pause Savannah joins in.

'So, if there's one bit of advice you could give to the women of the country, whether they're mothers or not, what would it be?' Abby gets back to the interview.

Savannah exhales a breathy hum like she's considering her answer carefully. 'I have two pieces of advice. The first being, don't get stuck being the person other people want you to be. Don't put limits on what you want to achieve. Don't let anyone put you in a box and expect you to stay there because that's what they're comfortable with. You can achieve anything you put your mind to. Anything. Test yourself. Push your own boundaries. Reach for the stars. Anything is possible.'

'That's wonderful advice.' Abby's awe-filled tone swamps the car.

Even through my disappointment, I feel like giving

Savannah a standing ovation. She's an amazing role model for women.

'What was the second thing?' Abby asks.

Savannah chuckles, sounding way more comfortable with this line of conversation. 'Always have something prepared for dinner. Hanger is real. When the twins get hangry, all hell breaks loose.'

Abby's laughter mingles with Savannah's.

'So, what's for dinner in your house tonight, Savannah?'

'Hell's wrath, unless I can throw together something really fast.' She snorts. 'I was away this weekend and am still reel– recovering from it, so I'm not as prepared as I usually am.'

Was she about to say reeling from it?

Hope dances through my soul. She might not have declared she's mine, but that one word, that one little sentence is all the encouragement I need.

And now, I have the perfect excuse to show up at her door tonight.

Chapter Twenty-Nine
SAVANNAH

With shaky arms, I dump two bags of groceries onto the kitchen counter, along with the stupid parking ticket I acquired outside the studio today.

My head is splitting.

I need to sign off on the final design of my autumn clothing range, I owe my blog subscribers a newsletter, preferably one that says something useful, and Cassandra is demanding a three-page synopsis of the second parenting book for the Inkwell Imprint.

The house is a mess. It's not dirty, but everything is out of place, upside down. That's what I get for being away all day yesterday. A mountain of laundry glares at me from the overflowing washing basket.

'Mam, she hit me!' Eden squeals, running into the kitchen and darting behind my legs.

'She stole my hairbrush.' Isla lunges for her sister, reaching around my thighs to tug one of her ponytails.

I step forwards, inserting myself as Eden's human shield and exhale a weary sigh. This Single Sav craic isn't nearly as glamorous as it looks on my Instagram page. I should have caved and brought the girls pizza like they asked, but during the week I always try to ensure they eat proper, home-cooked meals. Weekends are another matter entirely.

'I didn't steal it. I borrowed it,' Eden wails.

'Borrowed it and didn't put it back,' Isla screams at her sister, like there aren't fifteen other hairbrushes in the house.

I clear my throat and summon my best mam voice. 'Right girls, here's what's going to happen. You, Eden, go find Isla's hairbrush.' I usher her out from behind my back towards the kitchen door. 'Isla, you can set the table.'

'What's for dinner? I'm starving,' Isla whines.

As predicted, hanger strikes.

'Chicken and grilled broccoli. It'll be ready in ten minutes.' More like fifteen, but if I admit that there will be another meltdown.

'Broccoli? You've got to be kidding me?' Isla flings her small hands dramatically into the air. I should probably enroll her in stage school. She excels at drama.

'Set the table. Please.' I rub my temple and glance around the kitchen for headache tablets. Days like this, I wish I had a partner.

Someone to help share the load.

Someone to step up when I'm feeling down, because after the high of the weekend, I'm experiencing a monumental low.

Isla huffs all the way to the cutlery drawer, slamming it open, then slamming it closed. She bangs the knives and forks onto the kitchen table before bolting out of the kitchen door after her sister. The fighting starts again, but given it's not as extreme as the first round, I heat some oil in a wok and dice three chicken breasts.

While the chicken simmers on the stove, I load the dirty laundry into the machine and switch it on and empty the girls' school bags. The noise begins to escalate from upstairs.

It started off playful, but as the minutes pass, the arguing returns in full force.

'It's my turn,' Eden squeals.

'Give that to me,' Isla yells.

'Mam!' Eden screams from upstairs again, a panicked edge to her voice that sets my hackles rising.

Is five thirty-six on a Monday evening too early for a glass of wine?

Another incoherent scream radiates from upstairs, followed by an almighty smash.

Wine isn't going to cut it. I need whiskey.

I stalk out of the kitchen and jog up the stairs. 'What is going on up there?'

Pitter-pattering feet scurry along the corridor. From *my* room.

'What are you two doing in my bedroom?' My hands fly into the air and my eyelids flutter closed.

Oh shit.

Is this where Isla gets her dramatic streak?

Me?

No. I'll blame Stuart and Steve. The quicker they get back from their Mediterranean cruise, the better. I might only be back from a night away, but I'm in desperate need of another.

Preferably with the hot swimming instructor I've been obsessing about all day. The one whose hands and mouth I've been reliving all over my body. The one who texted me good morning at seven o'clock this morning with a winky face.

Isla jumps, flanking her sister, shoulder to shoulder, both the pictures of innocence, trying to block my view of whatever havoc they're wreaking.

The overpowering stench of my favourite Jo Malone peony perfume assaults my nostrils. 'Why does it smell like a florist's in here?' My gaze narrows, darting between the two of them, both looking guiltier than a monk in a brothel.

Even sweet people-pleasing Eden.

Perhaps I needn't be so worried about her meekness after all.

I scan the room to find my favourite bottle of perfume smashed to smithereens. A million tiny particles of glass are scattered across the floor.

'Seriously?' I exhale a long, weary breath.

'Sorry, Mam.' The two of them perch on the edge of my bed, faces tilted downwards, eyes to the floor. The only positive is that they're clutching hands, fingers entwined. They've clearly put their differences aside to form a united front.

It's not even the fact they've smashed my favourite perfume.

It's the fact I have to clean it up when I have a million other things to do.

'Go and wash your hands, then sit quietly at the table while I hoover this mess up.' My tone is beaten. Not angry, just beaten.

I'm wrecked from the weekend. Wrecked from lying awake last night thinking about Ronan. And wrecked from fighting the urge to call him and invite him over.

When I'm with him, I feel calmer. I feel like I'm part of something bigger than myself. Like he's as invested in the girls as much as he's invested in me.

'What are we going to do about the girls?'
'Let's get the girls and spend the summer here.'
'I'm obsessed with you.'

Could it be true? And if he is seriously obsessed with me, what does that mean for us?

For my career?

Relationships are exhausting and I'm not even in one.

Though I did have sex with the man I'm mutually obsessed with, and I did have dinner with his family yesterday. And if I were to find out he was out with another woman tonight, I'd feel cheated on.

Gah. "Just one night" just got complicated.

The girls traipse down the stairs. The silence is golden for about five seconds before the high-pitched shocking wail of the fire alarm sounds through the house.

Fuck. My. Life.

I've burnt dinner. Again.

I race down the stairs to find the girls huddled by the front door, palms clamped over their ears, and matching looks of horror on their faces.

'It's okay,' I shout over the wailing alarm. 'Open the front door. Let some air in and go play in the garden for a few minutes.' I shoo them away from the thin wispy smoke wafting from the open-plan kitchen, switch off the stove, and open the kitchen windows as wide as they'll go. Crisis averted. Well, apart from the hanger situation, anyway. The alarm will go off in a second or two.

Eden places a hand on the pastel pink front door and flings it open with enough force for to slam against the inside wall.

My mouth drops open.

Not because of the alarm, or the way the house shakes with the weight of the bang, but because the man who's occupied my nearly every waking thought today is standing on the front step wearing a white, tight cut t-shirt, faded jeans, and an expression of concern in his deep navy eyes.

'Ronan,' I mouth. No point even trying to speak over this noise.

'Everything okay?' he shouts, his concerned gaze assessing the twins from head to toe before scanning the house behind me through the thinning smoke.

The breeze coming in the open front door does the trick. The alarm finally cuts out.

Ronan leads the girls out onto the lawn and crouches at their eye level. He says something inaudible before handing them a lollipop from his back pocket. They run off towards the swings and he darts inside, not waiting for an invite.

I grab a tea towel to swat away the lingering smoke smouldering from the pan, its contents charcoal black and still smoking.

Ronan surveys the remnants of dinner with an arched eyebrow. He's standing so close to me that his bulky biceps brush my shoulder and his breath tickles my neck. I turn to him, blinking back the tears threatening my eyes.

Dinner is ruined, the kids are eating lollipops, there's glass all over my bedroom floor and the entire house stinks of smoke. 'Welcome to the mad house.'

The urge to kiss him consumes me. Nevermind the heat radiating from the cooker, the one burning me up from the inside out is far more lethal.

Our eyes fuse.

'If you keep looking at me like that, Savannah, I'm going to lift you onto your kitchen counter and devour you.' His gaze falls to my lips, and he brushes a thumb over my cupid's bow.

'After the day I've had, I might just let you.' I slump forwards an inch. Strong arms reach for me, tugging me into his chest. He presses a tender kiss to my forehead. I inhale his familiar masculine scent, the base notes of his cologne mostly faded from the day.

'I have a hundred emails I need to reply to, a synopsis to write, a fashion collection to sign off on, and I owe my subscribers a newsletter tonight too.'

'Would it be a good time to tell you I brought dinner?' His hands slide up my spine and across the backs of my shoulders, his fingers gently kneading the knots.

'Are you serious?' Is it possible my fairy godmother isn't

actually a godmother but this gorgeous god-like creature in front of me?

'It's just lasagne, but I made it myself. Stopped at the bakery on the way over and picked up a fresh loaf of sourdough smothered in garlic. There may or may not be a bottle of red wine in the hamper too.'

'Are you hoping for a repeat from the other night? Because if you keep talking that way, you might just get it.' I press my hips into his and slide my arms around his waist.

'There's a reason I didn't bring dessert.' His chuckle muffles across the top of my head. 'It'll need fifteen minutes in the oven to reheat it. Switch it on and I'll go out to the car and fetch everything.' His arms drop from my shoulders and he steps back without breaking our stare.

Something stirs in my chest. Gratitude. Relief. The rare sensation someone cares.

'Why?' I ask.

'Because I heard you on the radio this morning.' He extends his thumb like he's about to make a list. 'I wanted to do something to help take the pressure off.' He extends his pointer finger.

His middle finger stretches outward. 'Because it provided the perfect excuse to call to your house.' His fourth finger extends. 'Because I'm hoping after you've devoured dinner, you'll let me devour you. And because after this weekend, I couldn't stay away from you.' His smallest finger supports his most significant admission.

'I don't want you to stay away from me.' It's barely more than a whisper.

'You haven't tasted my cooking yet.' His lips curl in a teasing smile.

'I did taste you, though.' My stomach flips at the memory. 'And that's something I definitely want more of.'

His head twists towards the door, checking for any young

witnesses, then his lips graze over mine in a teasing, fleeting kiss that sets my skin alight. 'The feeling is mutual.'

I swallow the emotion forming in my throat. His sincerity is my undoing. 'What are we going to do?' I whisper. I don't mean this evening, I mean in general. We both know being a couple will end my career.

'We're not going to panic. That's the main thing.' He sweeps his thumb across my cheekbone. 'One day at a time.' Our eyes meet and a silent agreement passes between us.

'I can live with that.' Can't I?

No labels.

No big drama.

No rush to find the right answers for what we are or what we're doing or what any of this means for my business or my new book.

I want him more than I've ever wanted anything.

I want him here in my kitchen, and in my home, because he's already worked his way into my heart.

God help me. I don't know how this is going to end, but I do know I'm nowhere near ready to find out.

Chapter Thirty
RONAN

When I rushed home to make the lasagne after swimming lessons, I envisaged dropping it at the door. Maybe, if I was lucky, I thought Savannah might text or call when she'd put the twins to bed.

What I didn't envision was sitting around the table with Savannah and the girls for an impromptu dinner and a bottle of wine.

I didn't envision I'd get the chance to see Savannah's shoulders sag with relief or witness a small spark replacing the initial weariness lingering in her eyes when I arrived.

And I didn't envision how good any single one of those things would feel, let alone all of them.

'I can't believe you're here!' Isla exclaims, brandishing a forkful of tomato-soaked mince and pointing it at me.

'Neither can I.' I chance a look at Savannah, who's surveying the scenario with a small smile.

'We never had a boy over for dinner before,' Eden says, glancing suspiciously between Savannah and me.

'It's brilliant, isn't it?' Isla nudges her sister. 'Can you come over more often?'

Savannah clears her throat noisily and takes a huge swig of wine.

'I'll come any time your mam lets me.' I throw a wink in Savannah's direction, and she splutters. For a second, I think she might spit her wine across the table.

I put my cutlery down and push my plate away. 'Do you know what would be truly brilliant, girls? If you could help me clean up and then we could do another one of those dance routines while your mammy finishes her work, then maybe she can relax then too?' My eyes stray to Savannah again, hoping I'm not pushing my luck.

She mouths a silent thank you as her foot finds mine beneath the table.

I thought she was amazing before, but I'm just beginning to see how magnificent she is, how much she contends with on her own.

'Will you stay and put us to bed tonight?' Isla begs, giving me her best puppy dog eyes.

'That's up to your mam.' I swirl my glass, staring at the wine while Savannah thinks about it. If I drink much more of this, someone will have to put *me* to bed.

'I don't want to put you out.' Savannah's foot scales my calf, caressing the back of it. 'You've already done so much.'

I'll do so much more, if only she'd let me.

'It would be a pleasure.' As will the alone time we might get afterwards, if Savannah gets her work finished.

Her tongue slides over her lower lip and she readjusts herself. Bingo. It appears we're on the same page.

'Right. Let's do this.' I nod to the twins and start stacking plates.

Two hours later, the kitchen is gleaming, the laundry is in the drier and I'm all danced out - again. Thankfully, no one videoed this one. The twins coerced me into reading not one, but two bedtime stories before eventually crashing out in their respective bedrooms.

I'm sitting on Savannah's couch with another glass of red, admiring the view from the huge corner window in the sitting area. The sun dips low over the sea, radiating orange and fiery red streaks through the window like liquid warmth. Though the warmth of the evening has nothing on the heat flooding my veins knowing that Savannah is mere feet away in her study, and that any minute now I'll get to touch her, to taste her, to take her as mine.

When she finally emerges, she strides across the open-plan living area with another glass of red in her hand. In a simple, summery blouse and matching skirt combo, she looks effortlessly chic. Her feet are bare and her toenails painted a shade of hot pink. The sinking sunlight brandishes her hair a burnished gold.

'Did you get everything done?' I pat the plush couch next to me, beckoning her over.

'Not all of it, but the urgent stuff. I can't get my head into this synopsis I'm supposed to write.' She shakes her head. 'Seriously, I don't know how I can thank you.' Her voice is thick with gratitude as she sinks into the leather beside me.

'I have a few ideas.' I take her wine glass and place it with mine onto the coffee table beside me.

Slipping a hand beneath the curve of her ass, I lift her onto my quads, facing me. Her thighs part until they're either side of mine. I tug her into my lap until her pelvis rests on top of mine.

She exhales a breathy rasp when she feels my arousal beneath her. 'Ronan,' she moans.

Her face dips and her mouth crashes onto mine, her probing tongue demanding entry. My fingers thread through her soft, silky hair, as her hips roll on top of me, seeking friction.

I pull back, breaking our kiss because the urge to watch her writhing and rocking on my cock is eating me from the inside out.

My hands slide beneath her top, chasing goosebumps across the flat planes of her stomach and up to the underside of her breasts. Her hips pause and she glances at the stairs.

'They're conked. Trust me.' Our eyes meet and she offers a nod of thanks before pulling her blouse off.

Her beautiful breasts are supported by an ivory, silk bra, her pert nipples visible beneath the fine material. She slides the straps down, one by one.

'You're killing me, woman.' I bite out, watching as she traces her collar bone with her finger before lowering it between her breasts. 'Take it off. I want to see you.'

Her hands reach round to her back and three seconds later, the bra falls between us. I rake over every inch of glorious, tanned skin, memorising each and every millimetre.

'You're fucking perfect, Savannah.' I skim her nipples with my fingers, pinching and rolling as her hips buck against me. 'Look what you do to me.' I thrust upwards, and her head falls backwards, her back arching.

'You're going to get me in so much trouble,' she moans, 'but right now, I'm beyond caring. I need to feel you inside me.'

'And you will,' I promise, sliding my hand between us, beneath her skirt. My fingers dart across her inner thigh until I find a triangular scrap of silk. It's saturated already. Tugging it to the side, I swipe a finger through her centre. 'You're so fucking wet for me, baby.'

'I've been wet for you for months,' she admits, parting her legs wider to give me better access.

'I know, Savannah. We've wasted so much time. But I'm

going to make it up to you.' I slide two fingers inside her slippery core, circling her needy swollen clit with my thumb.

'You're so fucking good at that, Ro.' Her hooded eyes stoke the fire in my core and in my veins.

I work her as she watches dazedly, moaning and panting and muttering my name over and over again. When her thighs tremble and tighten, I catch her nipple in my mouth and suck. She whispers my name as she shatters and shudders and comes undone on my hands.

When the trembling finally subsides, I stand, keeping her legs wrapped around my waist as I carry her upstairs to her bedroom. I place her gently on her back and pull her skirt down over her thighs, past her knees and ankles, and toss it on the floor.

The silk panties are destroyed.

Good.

She's not going to be needing them, anyway. I slip them off and kiss my way up her inner thigh.

'Ronan, I can't go again. Not yet. I'm too sensitive.' Her hand reaches out to halt my head as my lips brush over her centre.

'You can go again. And you will go again. Because I'm going to lick your pussy so fucking good, you're going to beg me to never stop.' Her eyes widen. My dirty mouth is her weakness and I'm not afraid to use it.

I want to ruin Savannah Kingsley forever more. Because I can't have her freaking out on me after this. There can't be a day where she turns around and says we can't do this anymore. Because the day will come where she has to choose between what we have, and the single life she's carved out for herself.

And I need her to choose me.

The other option doesn't bear contemplating.

My tongue circles her sweet, dripping sex, and she jerks and exhales a low guttural moan. 'You're going to kill me.'

I halt my tongue just long enough to answer her. 'No, baby, I'm bringing you back to life.'

Her fingernails rake over my scalp. 'No man has ever treated me this way before. Worshipped my body like you do.'

'More fool them, Savannah.' My tongue swirls around her clit as the blood rushes there again. I slip a finger inside her core. 'If you were mine, I'd worship this body every fucking day for the rest of my life.'

I'm testing her. I know I am. Willing her to say the words I've willed from her lips so many times over so many months.

She doesn't disappoint me. 'I'm yours, Ronan. Whether I want to be or not. I'm yours. You have me.'

I tilt my head upwards to meet her eyes, my tongue still swirling circles around that beautiful, sensitive bud. 'Good girl,' I murmur, before sucking her until she screams into her fist.

When I finally slide my throbbing cock into Savannah's slick centre, it takes everything I have not to blow there and then. It's not just the sensation of her body sliding beneath mine, or the tight walls of her taut perfect core, it's the knowledge that she is finally mine.

Mine.

The woman I've wanted for years.

And it sends me spiralling into my own decadent oblivion.

Chapter Thirty-One
SAVANNAH

Ronan's been sneaking into my bed every evening for over two weeks now and sneaking out again before the girls wake up. He's cooked dinner almost every night and ordered in pizza the past two Fridays. I'm almost on top of my work, for once, thanks to his help entertaining the girls.

But there's still one thing I haven't been able to manage - the synopsis for the new parenting book, much to Cassandra's dismay.

How can I write another book on parenting alone while I have a man taking care of my kids every evening, and taking care of me too? It's utterly hypocritical. The words just won't come.

How can I parade around the country with my glossy new hardback preaching about balancing work and life as a single mother, when truthfully, I'm not one anymore?

Granted, Ronan and I aren't married, so on paper, I am still technically single. But the idea of marriage doesn't seem as ridiculous as it did this time last year.

That childhood dream of me in a white dress might not be over yet.

My career would be though.

Half of me worries I'm rushing into this relationship, but the other half is so high on the hit of endorphins that I don't care.

Getting involved with a man was never on my agenda. Getting involved with a former manwhore was never on my agenda.

Yet, we're together.

That night I told him I was his. It seemed like role play at the time, but the truth is, I was his from the moment I met him. I felt the attraction the second I laid eyes on him, which is probably why I was so hard on him. Offence is the best form of defence, right? And I've been defending my heart since Finn fucking Reilly shattered it seven years ago.

The girls are at school and I'm supposed to be preparing a speech for a ladies' charity lunch in aid of the Irish Single Parents' Society in a few weeks. Instead, I'm lounging on the luxurious day bed in my back garden in the skimpiest bikini I own, with Ronan between my legs for the second time today.

Considering I spent almost two years wishing he'd stop moving his mouth in my direction, now I'm grinding against said mouth, unable to get enough of it.

Days like these, I'm eternally grateful for the privacy of the sixteen-foot surrounding fir trees and the half acre between each house on this road.

I scrape my fingers across his scalp and encourage him to slide up my body. 'I want to come on your cock.'

'Demanding little thing, aren't you?' He licks his lips and crawls up the thick luxurious mattress, eyeing me like I'm a goddess. It doesn't matter if I'm in a full face of make-up, or if my hair is matted and standing up on end, the same inexplicable wonder twinkles in his eyes.

'I've been deprived for years,' I remind him. 'Actually, forever. No one ever fucked me like you do.'

'And no one ever will.' His pupils gleam, not with arrogance, but with a defiant confidence.

'Is that right?' I part my legs wider in invitation. There's something so carnal about having sex outside, with the sun beating down on us, and the knowledge one of the neighbours might see us.

'You're mine, Savannah. And I don't share.'

'Neither do I.' For a split-second, my ex's smug face forces itself to the forefront of my mind.

I shared him. Though I hadn't realised it at the time. His wife is petite, with dark hair and porcelain skin and bone structure most women would sell their soul for. I still have no idea why he would cheat on her in the first place.

Or why anyone would cheat on anyone.

If you're unhappy, why not just leave?

Or perhaps he wasn't unhappy. Perhaps he wanted his cake and to eat it.

Argh. Why am I thinking about this now when I've been doing so well?

I close my eyes, count to five and mentally chant Ronan isn't him.

'Look at me.' Ronan hovers over me, his finger traces my jawline before tilting my chin up and forcing my eyes onto his. 'You're beautiful. I'm obsessed with you. And I've got you, okay?'

I've got you.

It's his mantra for me. He says it every time I doubt him, or myself.

Trust is hard to earn, and even harder to give.

'I know I'm supposed to be an independent woman and all that, but I like being "got".' Admitting this somehow feels more intimate than the fact my bikini bottoms are round my ankles and his thick cock is nudging at my centre, weeping with want.

'Having mutually consensual filthy sex doesn't make you any less independent. If anything, you're excelling in championing the women of this world by going after what you want and grabbing it by the balls.' Ronan cups my breasts, tugging my bikini top lower until my breasts spill over the top.

My hand slides over his granite glutes before reaching between us and grabbing him by the balls. 'Like this, you mean?'

Way to get back in the moment. Our lips collide with a fire and lust and longing. Our hands clash as we both fight to tug his shorts down. I scratch and claw at his sculpted ass cheeks, dragging him into my centre.

'Savannah.' His voice is low and guttural, but there's a warning in it.

'What?' I buck impatiently against him.

'I'm not wrapped.' He inches backwards on his knees, but I dig my nails into his ass. 'Did you get tested?'

'Of course. And I've always used protection.' He swallows thickly, those liquid molten eyes melting my soul.

'I'm on the pill. For hormonal reasons.' I nip at my lower lip, wanting nothing more than to feel him inside me, really feel him, not some latex sheath.

'Oh baby, are you saying what I think you're saying?' He drags his huge cock through my slick folds.

'Yes.'

'I think I love you,' he says with a wolfish grin.

Before I can even contemplate a reply, he inches himself inside me, our skin slipping and sliding as he relentlessly thrusts. Those rolling hips hit every sensitive spot I own.

'You feel so fucking good,' he murmurs into my mouth. Deft fingers find my wrists and pin them above my head. Wild wide eyes devour me like he's committing this moment to memory. 'I could do this all day, every day. I could happily live inside you for the rest of my life.'

He's not alone in that sentiment. The more time I spend with Ronan Rivers, the more time I want to spend with him.

My fantasies aren't just sexual either. I fantasise about making breakfast for him. Coming home to him.

This was supposed to be one night, and it's turned into every night and, worryingly, it's still nowhere near enough.

His face dips to my breast, his tongue flicking over my nipples. My orgasm builds higher and higher with each thrust.

'Come for me, baby.'

Every inch of my skin tingles and hums with the promise of hot, white pleasure. Lust lances through every single cell in my body until I can't hold on a second longer and I explode, my core clenching Ronan's cock, coaxing him to his own climax. I'm still spiralling as he spills himself inside of me.

Feeling more satisfied and sated than I've ever felt in my life, I rest my head on his chest and doze in his arms beneath the summer sun.

'Savannah, are you home?' My father's voice cuts into the delicious dream I was knee-deep in. 'I've come to trim the bushes.'

'Fuck.' I bolt upright and turn to Ronan. 'Your shorts! Where are your shorts?' Sometime in the throes of passion, I'd flung them across the lawn.

'Who's that?' Ronan whispers, rocking up to his feet. He's stark bollock naked and never looked more glorious with the sunlight illuminating his sweat-glistening torso, but, if my dad catches him here, I will have more explaining to do than it's worth.

'It's my dad.' I grab my bikini bottoms and drag them up my legs. 'He maintains the garden.'

'Shit.' He cups his privates in both hands, but it's so large it's still exposed.

The two of us scan the vicinity for his shorts, but we're nowhere near quick enough.

Stuart appears from around the side of the house. He's wearing khaki-coloured cargo shorts and a camel-coloured t-shirt. Raybans do absolutely nothing to mask the neatly trimmed eyebrows that shoot skywards when he sees us.

His feet root to the spot as his jaw hits the floor. His mouth opens, closes, then opens again as he looks anywhere but at me. 'Well, I can honestly say there's a first for everything.'

Ronan squats, and finally locating his shorts, holds them over his groin.

'Dad, I err...' My cheeks flame and mortification melts me from the inside out. 'I wasn't expecting you today.'

'So I see.' He shoves the Raybans on his head, pupils daring to dart between Ronan and me. Ronan's shorts are finally in position, but I swear Stuart's beady eyes hover over my man's torso with an awestruck appreciation.

I clear my throat. 'This is er...'

My boyfriend?

My fuck buddy?

The man who has my heart?

The man who calls me his?

'Ronan Rivers, pleased to meet you, sir.' Ronan steps forward. His hand rises an inch like he's thinking about extending it for a handshake, but then he seems to think better of it.

'I know who you are.' Stuart's voice is mockingly stern, but his body language is positively relaxed. 'What I didn't know is that you're sleeping with my daughter.'

'I'm not just sleeping with her…I'm obsessed with her, sir. And I have been for a very long time,' Ronan admits boldly.

Stuart bites back a surprised smile and despite the awkwardness of the situation, my stomach somersaults.

I cough to mask my shock. 'He's teasing you, Ro. Don't mind him.' I swat his arm. 'Dad, stop staring at my –' My what? 'At Ronan, or I'll tell Steve you were perving on another guy.'

Stuart straightens himself and turns away. 'Now now, Savannah, we all know how jealous he can get. No need to upset him. Though he will be delighted at this unexpected turn of events. We might just get a wedding out of you yet, young lady.'

I pick up the flip-flop discarded by the day bed and fling it at him. 'From the day you adopted me, you've done nothing but try to palm me off on someone else.'

'Imagine how good I'd look in a white suit as I give you away,' Stuart muses, stroking a thoughtful finger over the neatly trimmed beard dusting his jaw. His eyes are glowing with devilment.

'I'm so sorry about this.' I turn to Ronan. I'd be so grateful if a natural disaster could strike right now. A tornado that could sweep me away, an earthquake that could split the ground open and drag me into the cracks below.

'Dad, if you wouldn't mind going into the house and sticking the kettle on, Ronan was just about to leave, anyway.'

'Oh, don't go on my behalf,' Stuart says gleefully, clearly now recovered from his initial shock. 'You won't even know I'm here.'

'You will,' I tell Ronan. 'And what's more, he'll ring Steve and tell him to come over, then the two of them will be here gawking at you.'

'Fine, fine.' Stuart struts towards the house, chuckling.

'Great to meet you, Ro.' He emphasises the Ro like they're best buds.

'I'm due at the pool in an hour anyway,' Ronan says, as he pulls on his shorts. 'Can I see you tonight?'

'Absolutely.' I almost took it as a given that he'll come back later.

'It's a date.' He drops a lingering kiss on my lips.

'I distinctly remember you saying you didn't want to date me, that you only wanted to fuck me.' I roll back on the bed, readjusting my bikini top.

'I changed my mind. I want to both.' Ronan's gaze follows my fingers and his Adam's apple bobs. 'Even if it means being your dirty little secret.'

I throw a pillow at him. 'You're not my dirty little secret.' Even as the words escape my mouth, I have to question them.

He's dirty, and this thing between us is a secret, but it doesn't have the sordid connotations that the line implies.

Plus, we've already established there's nothing little about him.

'It's okay. I'm okay with it.' He backs away from the day bed reluctantly. 'For now. But if I get my way, your parents will get a wedding out of you yet.' He fires a wink over his shoulder as he strides across the grass.

Chapter Thirty-Two
RONAN

Starting my day at five a.m. is worth it when I get to wake up with Savannah. These past few weeks I've taken to leaving her house and going for a run along the beach before heading home for a shower.

I've never slept as well, and I've never felt as good.

That's what falling in love does for you, and I am falling hard and fast.

I stride through the lobby of my apartment block, humming a low catchy tune that's all over the radio at the moment.

'Someone got laid last night.' My brother's eyes glint, waiting for the lift and any dirt I might dish. His shirt is creased and his dark hair is dishevelled. He's still drunk, if his slurred drawl is anything to go by.

'Did they?' I flip it back on him. 'Who's the lucky lady?' I send up a silent thanks I've taken to running after working out with Savannah.

'Oh, come on. Don't be like that. We all know you're shagging Single Sav. Or is it No Longer Single Sav, now?' He leans against the magnolia wall and eyeballs me with glee.

Even the mere mention of her name sets a smile stretching over my face. I'd love to tell him, to tell the entire world. I'd shout it from the roof tops if I could, but I can't. Not until Savannah's ready.

Being the man who gets to hold her, to kiss her, to lie with her every night is worth the sneaking around, but I can't help wishing she'd go public with our relationship.

Time. I just need to give her time, but it's hard.

I know she feels the same way about me. I feel it every time I'm with her. Each time I'm inside of her. I see it in the way her eyes lock onto mine.

'I've been for a run.' I smooth a hand over my vest and hold up the bottle of water in my right hand.

'And is running working off all your sexual energy too?' The lift pings and the doors open.

'You're awfully concerned about my sexual welfare, brother.' I dart into the lift beside him.

'I miss my drinking buddy,' my brother admits, rolling back on his heels and shoving his fists into his pockets.

'I'll have a drink with you later, I promise.' It's Sunday, we're due at Mam's for dinner, anyway.

'Wine at Sunday lunch doesn't count.' Richard rolls his eyes, but his voice is teasing. 'Will Savannah be joining us again?'

'I wish.' It's out of my mouth before I can stop it.

Richard's hand darts out from his pocket and he clicks his fingers. 'I knew it! I'm happy for you, man. Really, I am.'

And despite the banter, despite his teasing and the fact he's often a pain in my ass, I know he means it.

'Look, it's very new. Nothing's official, but we've been spending time together.' God, it feels so fucking good to admit it out loud. And if her coming on my hand, my mouth, and my cock every day for the past few weeks isn't making it official, then I don't know what is.

'Spending time together,' Richard scoffs, using his fingers to air quote his words. 'You've been balls deep in her for weeks. That's why you don't come out anymore.'

I could deny it, but my facial expressions give me away every time. 'Unlike some of my previous conquests, I don't kiss and tell. I'm trusting your discretion here. No one knows we've been "spending time together" and that's the way it has to stay. For now, at least.'

'Your secret is safe with me.' Richard draws a cross over his heart as the lift launches upwards. That wicked glint flickers in his irises again. 'Tell me this, though. Is it good?'

My muscle memory kicks in and my dick twitches in my shorts. 'Fucking unbelievable.'

The lift doors open on his floor, and he lingers in the doorway for a second. 'Fair fucks to you. You've been like a lost sheep since you retired. I've never seen you smile as wide since, well, ever really.'

'Thanks. That means a lot.'

'One more thing. Does she have a sister by any chance?' He backs out of the lift, raising his arms as he shrugs.

'Discretion, remember,' I call after his retreating back as he swaggers down the wide corridor to his apartment.

'My lips are sealed as tight as the zip on my trousers.' He pretends to zip his lips close.

'If that's the case, we're all fucked.' I shake my head as the lift doors automatically close.

My apartment looks bare and cold compared to the organised chaos of Savannah's house. I stride through the spacious hallway and into the chrome and black kitchen to make a protein shake, already counting the hours until I get to see Savannah again.

We're meeting at the pool for a final lesson before the shoot next week. She's not about to win any swimming competitions, but she's confident enough to be able to move through the water using breaststroke and front crawl. It's enough for the purpose.

Savannah getting offered the Coral Chic contract was the best thing that ever happened to both of us. If she hadn't needed to learn how to swim, she'd still be shooting me filthy looks from the side of the pool each Saturday. The thought doesn't bear thinking about.

When Savannah arrives at the pool, her long blonde hair is piled up on top of her head and she's wearing that yellow bikini again.

The one I fucked her in on the day bed.

The one I pulled down to her ankles while I devoured her.

The one I fucking dream about every time I close my eyes.

On closer inspection, my girl looks harassed.

'What's up, baby?' Do I normally hate baby as a term of endearment? Yes. Have I done a full one eighty on it, now I have Savannah? Also, yes.

'Nothing. It's fine. This morning ended up being a bit stressful, that's all.' She lowers herself into the shallow end.

'What happened?' I swim towards her, my hands automatically reaching for her waist. No matter how many times I touch her, it's never enough.

'I dropped the girls with my dads as planned, but they forgot to mention they have tickets to a matinee performance at the theatre later and I'm booked to make a guest appearance at a new wine bar on Grafton Street. The woman who's opening it is a single mother. She specifically requested me because I'm Single Sav. It's not like I can send anyone else in my place. I left a message for the next door neighbour to see if Shona can come over, but she didn't get back to me yet.' She sighs, sinking her shoulders beneath the water.

'I'll take the girls for the afternoon.' I lower my chest to bob beside her.

Her head whips up. 'I wasn't saying it for that reason. It wasn't a hint. I know you go to your mam's for dinner on Sundays.'

'I'll bring them to Mam's, if that's okay with you?' I reach out and stroke her spine. 'They'll have a blast playing with Joseph and John. And I'm sure Rachel will let them give Mark his bottle. Mam will be only too delighted to have more females in the house.'

'Are you sure? I hate putting you out.' She glances up from under thick lustrous lashes.

'You're not putting me out. I love the girls.' It's the truth, but judging by the shock on Savannah's face, she had no idea. 'I'd do anything for the three of you.'

She wets her lips, her eyes homing in on mine. I pull her towards me, inching down to kiss the shock straight from her lips, but she pushes me back, a firm hand on my chest.

'Thank you, Ronan. You're a good man.' She swallows thickly.

'Let me help you, Savannah. Let me shoulder some of the responsibilities.'

'You've already done so much, but we need to tread carefully. I don't want to confuse them.' Her eyes dart down to the water. 'They're not used to having a man around. I've never introduced them to a boyfriend before. Hell, I've never had a boyfriend since I had them. I'd hate for them to get used to the idea of you being around and then for you to disappear.'

'Savannah, I'm not going anywhere.' I stand up, the water rolling across my torso in thick, ticklish drips. Taking her hands in mine, I press them against my chest. She springs up, her hips pushing forwards to rest against mine.

'I know nothing about the twins' father or the circumstances, but I know you've been let down in the worst possible way. Look at me when I tell you this.' I cup her chin and force her eyes up to mine. 'I'm not him. I won't let you down. You have no idea how long I've wanted you. I'm not going to mess it up now, trust me.'

'I think I might actually love you.' Her tone is teasing as her palms roam over my torso.

'I don't think I love you.' My voice is thick with emotion as I wrap my arms around her waist. 'I know I do.'

My lips crash against hers.

I've said it now. There's no going back.

Chapter Thirty-Three
SAVANNAH

He loves me.

He loves me.

He said he fucking loves me.

Those three tiny words that have enormous consequences. No man has ever said them to me before. Well, apart from my dads, but that doesn't count.

Then he kissed me and continued our lesson, like it was the most natural thing in the world. I'm trying not to freak out, but it's nearly impossible. Butterflies swirl and soar in my stomach at a dizzying rate. My heart is in my mouth and I'm not sure if it's elation, excitement, or down right panic.

Ronan Rivers loves me.

I barely remember getting ready for the event, let alone arriving at the wine bar and cutting the ribbon. I have no idea what I said in my speech.

All I can think about is getting to Ronan's mother's house. Getting to him and to my girls.

I didn't tell him I loved him back. I couldn't say it out loud, but I do love him. I love him so much my heart might burst.

But what I'm going to do about it is another matter entirely.

I hate sneaking around. I hate that we can't just date like a normal couple, but I have the girls to think about, and my brand, of course.

If I'm not Single Sav anymore, then who the hell am I?

Where do I go from here?

I inhale deep, slow breaths and exhale loudly.

You don't have to decide today.

Just enjoy it.

Enjoy being with Ronan. Enjoy the dizzying endorphins soaring through your soul. Enjoy having someone of your own.

By the time I reach Mrs Rivers' house, my erratic heart rate has calmed.

The garden is a flurry of activity. Ronan is in goal. Isla, Eden, John and Joseph stand in a line ten metres back. They seem to be taking it in turns to take penalty shots. Isla's foot is hovering over the ball as if she's biding her time while she bites her lower lip in concentration.

At the sound of the engine stilling, Ronan's head twists and his big blue eyes seek me out. My stomach flips and my soul sings. I raise a hand in greeting, unable to wipe the grin off my face at the mere sight of him.

Isla sees an opportunity and kicks the ball as hard as she can into the corner of the goal. All four kids scream with glee and Ronan darts out from between the goal posts to chase Isla and sweep her into the air while she howls with laughter. Eden, John and Joseph join in, circling Ronan and Isla, and cheering. Sunlight dances over them, framing them like a picture. And what a pretty picture they make.

This is what Sundays are made for. Ronan's family has it right. Sundays are for families. I silently vow not to take on any Sunday commitments from now on.

I open the car door and the twins come running over to greet me.

'Mammy, did you see that?' Isla's eyes shine brightly with pride.

'I did, honey. You're amazing.' I kneel at my daughters' eye level and hug them both, mouthing a silent 'thank you' at Ronan over their shoulders.

'A pleasure,' he mouths back.

'Who's hungry?' Ronan's mother calls from the doorway.

'Me,' my daughters shout together, leaping into the air and running towards the open front door. John and Joseph run after them, leaving Ronan and me alone in the garden.

'Glad to see they've made themselves at home,' I muse as Ronan brushes his lips over my cheek. It's nowhere near enough, given watching him play dad with my kids does things to my lady parts, but it will have to do for now.

'Why wouldn't they?' His hot breath grazes my ear and goosebumps ripple across my skin despite the summer sun. 'If I get my way, they'll be up here every Sunday soon enough.'

'Hmm, Stu and Steve might have something to say about that.' I glance towards the house to check no one is watching before tilting my face up towards his lips.

'They won't if they get the wedding they've been waiting for.' Mischief crinkles the corners of his eyes, but his tone is serious.

I don't know how to answer, so instead I reach up on my tiptoes and close the distance between us. I part my mouth with his, sinking into the sensations that spin through my body.

'Kids!' Mrs Rivers calls from the front door. I jump back, guiltily, but Ronan just grins at his mother, who looks to be suppressing her own smile, if her twitching lips are anything to go by.

'Coming,' he yells, and takes me by the hand. 'Could be

worse,' he murmurs into my ear. 'She could have caught us on a day bed with our trousers round our ankles.'

'Or no trousers on at all,' I agree. When Ronan leads me into the house, I don't take my palm from his.

His brother, Richard, waggles his eyebrows less than discreetly, his dark eyes darting from our hands to our faces and back to our hands.

Rachel is sitting at the table with sleeping baby Mark cradled in her right arm and a glass of white wine in her left hand. She also takes in Ronan and me, and beams. 'Savannah, welcome back,' she whisper-shouts over her baby's head. 'Your girls are adorable.'

'Thank you.' I turn to Mrs Rivers, who is busy handing out plates of thinly sliced beef and steamed veg. 'Thank you for having us.'

'You have no idea how much I enjoy it.' Mrs River's pauses, her blue eyes water as she places Isla and Eden's dinner in front of them.

Isla's head twists up from her plate and I pray to God she's not about to complain about the vegetables. Instead, she blurts out, 'Is Ronan your boyfriend?'

Eden elbows her sister, but Isla doesn't get the hint.

'What?' Isla gazes between Ronan and me. 'Is he?'

I should have been prepared. I should have dropped his hand. I should have had this talk with them in private, instead of having it in front of Ronan's entire family. My face flames and my mouth opens, but words refuse to form.

Ronan saves me yet again. 'Would it be okay if I was?'

'No,' Isla shouts, pushing her chair back from the table and jumping to her feet. 'It wouldn't be okay. It would be awesome!' Little feet patter across the kitchen towards Ronan and me.

'Please, Mammy, please, let him be your boyfriend.' Her small hands grab my thighs. 'He's so much fun. He splashes us in the pool when you're not looking. He gives us lollipops when you burn dinner. And he has the best dance moves I've ever seen.'

Laughter erupts around the room, but I feel the weight of every eye in the room on me. Especially from the man to my right.

'Well, I guess he kind of is...' Heat flushes from my neck to my cheeks.

'Yeah!' Isla squeals and beckons Eden over to join us. Ronan sweeps both girls up into his arms, positioning one on either hip as if they're weightless. His face leans forwards and he presses a kiss against my forehead.

'Welcome to the family.' Mrs Rivers appears at my side, and I melt into her motherly hug.

I've been alone for so long.

The magnitude of this moment makes me want to cry a river of happy tears.

I have no idea how this is going to work out.

But what I do know is that I want it to.

The question is, do I want it more than I want to be Single Sav?

Because I'm going to have to choose, sooner rather than later.

Even though the twins know Ronan and I are together, he continues to sneak out of my bed each morning before the girls wake up. It's one thing knowing he's my boyfriend, but seeing the implications of that title first-hand is another thing entirely.

The kids are delighted Ronan and I are together.

My dads are delighted Ronan and I are together.

Ronan's family are delighted.

I'm fucking delighted.

But what will the Single Sav fans say?

As happy as I am with Ronan, I feel like there's a shadow lingering over me. A giant question mark-shaped cloud.

What will my business model be?

What about my book deal?

My blog subscribers?

The thought whirs through my head in the early hours of every morning. Ronan stirs beside me, the early morning sunlight filtering over his face. His strong jaw and chiselled cheekbones are a work of art. Is it any wonder I'm considering giving up everything I've ever worked for to be his?

But what if I do give up my single brand and he leaves me? The twins' dad did. Hell, my own mother left me. Why would Ronan stay?

'Morning, beautiful.' Ronan's thick, fair lashes flutter open and he tugs me flush against his bare, taut torso. His muscular chest has become my favourite pillow, the soft thudding of his heartbeat my new sleep soundtrack.

'Good morning.' I nuzzle into his neck, inhaling his deep masculine scent. 'Did you sleep well?'

'I always sleep well next to you.' His lips brush over the top of my head in a tender gesture. 'Probably because you wear me out so thoroughly beforehand.' His palm slides over my skin to cup my ass.

'How is it Friday again?' The time is flying. The shoot is next week. I'm half excited, half terrified.

'I've been meaning to ask, do you want me to come to the shoot?' Ronan rubs the sleep from his eyes and blinks.

I don't even have to think about it. 'Yes.'

'Consider it done.' He presses a kiss against my temple. 'What's on the agenda today?'

'I really need to write my speech for the ladies' lunch at Huxley Castle. It's only two weeks away and I have a half-hour slot on stage as their guest speaker. It's a charity function for the Irish Single Parents' Society.' I shrug and that one simple motion conveys the guilt I feel, the hypocrisy.

'You've been a single mother for seven years.' Ronan traces small circles over my skin. 'You're still a single mother, technically. We're not married – yet.'

'Would you really want to get married one day?' I blurt out, feeling my eyes widen. 'To be a father to the girls?'

'Is that a proposal?' he teases, tickling my ribs. 'Of course, I would. I'm dating their mama. Even if those dates are mostly comprised of stolen hours behind closed doors.' He forces a smile, but it doesn't quite reach his eyes.

I pinch his bum to lighten the mood. He jolts up and flips me on my back in one quick movement, so he's on top of me. I hiss, but I love it really. I love his sheer size and his powerful physique. Love the abs that are so perfectly carved. Love the smooth, full contours of his ass.

I love everything about him. But I still haven't told him. Haven't said the words. Because when I do, there's no going back.

I glance over his shoulder towards the window. The sun is creeping higher in the sky. The girls will wake before six. They're like clockwork, no matter what time they go to bed. Like he can read my mind, he releases me with a small sigh and rolls out of bed.

'What are your plans for tonight?' I prop myself up on my elbows and watch as he pulls on the shorts I tore down last night.

'Is that a joke?' He stills, his blue eyes smouldering.

'No. It's Friday night. Maybe you want to go out with Richard or something...' I can't presume he wants to spend every night with me, just because I want to spend every night with him. I've got to be at home with the kids, but that doesn't mean has to.

'Or something,' he answers with a grin. 'There is nowhere

else I'd rather be than between your long, toned legs, lady. Though, seriously, I wouldn't mind being able to take you on an actual date sometime soon.' He raises his palms like a white flag. 'No pressure or anything, but our families know. The kids know. While I'm ecstatic being here with you, we can't go on sneaking around forever.'

I sigh, rocking up to a sitting position.

'I'm not trying to rush you.' Ronan hovers by the bed, his blue eyes boring into mine. 'But I can't wait to spoil you.'

'You spoil me every day,' I tell him earnestly.

He gives me a pointed look. 'I want to take you to the best restaurants. To the movies. Whisk you to fancy hotels for dirty weekends away.'

It can't be easy on Ronan, living in the shadows. Creeping out at the crack of dawn every morning. Cooking for us. Cleaning up after the girls. It's completely unfair on him. If the roles were reversed, how would I feel?

Like shit, that's how.

He deserves recognition.

He deserves better.

He said he loves me. He's proved it over and over again by showing up for me and the girls every damn day since we went to Ballybowen.

I inhale deeply through my nose.

It's time. Whether I want to be or not, I'm no longer Single Sav.

'You're right. It's time we came out.'

Ronan drops back to the bed, perching on the edge of it, clasping my two hands in his. 'I won't let you down, Savannah. What we have is the real deal.'

'I know you won't.'

'There might be a bit of backlash, but I'm sure a lot of your followers will be ecstatic to see you happy and settled.'

He squeezes my fingers encouragingly. 'Did your contract with Coral Chic stipulate you have to remain single?'

'No.' My fingertips turn white where they're gripping his so tightly.

'Do any of your commitments? What about your clothing range? Did you take an oath I'm unaware of?'

'No.' I shake my head gently. Maybe it's time to focus on the clothes. I did always want to open a store.

'Look, I know this is a huge change for you, Savannah. I get it. But you can still offer sublime parenting advice, whether you have a boyfriend or not. You can design children's clothing whether you have a boyfriend or not. Life changes. Nothing stays the same. We grow and evolve. You, my love, are evolving. And your fans can either like it or lump it.'

'Tell that to my agent,' I snort. 'I still haven't started that damn book.'

'So, write a different book. Write a different synopsis. Write for a different imprint. This is your life, my love. It's time to start living it. We have each other. We'll get through a little backlash.'

'We'll have to. Because life without you by my side isn't an option.'

'That we can agree on.' He presses a kiss to my cheek.

I roll my lips together as a wave of nerves washes over me. 'I'll draft an email to go out this weekend to my blog subscribers. It's only fair they hear it from me first, after all the support they've given me over the years.'

'That's probably wise.'

'I'll tell them the truth. I wasn't looking for love, but I found it anyway.'

'You did?' Disbelief hitches in his throat.

'Yes. I love you.' Those three words are out of my mouth. There's no going back.

Chapter Thirty-Four
RONAN

Since Savannah said those three little words on Friday, I haven't been able to wipe the grin from my face.

Every stupid love song on the radio sets me smiling like a goofy schoolboy.

Every time I look at her, I vow to never make her regret choosing me over her brand.

Speaking of branding, I scoured her Coral Chic contract. It doesn't mention her relationship status, but I wouldn't put it past Lucas Beechwood to pull her from it just because he wanted her for himself. But in case the shoot is going ahead, Savannah needs another trip to the open water. Her confidence and abilities in the pool have improved immeasurably, but wild swimming is a different beast altogether. It's imperative she's prepared.

Jake and I always maintained the only way to overcome your fear is to face it head-on. And while Savannah has faced her fear of the water, she's never returned to the lake where her fear originated.

Taking her there is either the best idea I've ever had, or the worst.

It's Sunday morning, so we're due a lesson, anyway. It's just a simple change of location.

Having crept out of Savannah's bed only a couple of hours earlier, I've already been for my morning run, home for a shower, and swung by the twins' favourite bakery to pick up donuts, gingerbread men, and a selection of fresh pastries.

When I'm five minutes from Savannah's house, I call her. She answers on the second ring. The sound of the twins squealing in the background resounds through my in-car speaker system.

'Miss me already?' There's a taunting to her tone.

'I missed you the second I left you.' When will she ever accept the magnitude of my feelings for her? Sometimes I feel like she's waiting for me to turn around and say, 'I'm only joking.' Sometimes I feel like she's waiting for me to leave her.

She'll be waiting a long time for that to happen.

'That was only three hours ago.' She tuts, but I hear the pleasure in her voice.

'Three long, cold hours away from your bed,' I groan. When will it be acceptable for the twins to know I stay?

'Hmm. I miss you too.' The background noise subsides, like she's moved rooms. 'What time is our swimming lesson today? You know it'll be the last one before the shoot.' As if I could forget.

'I was thinking we could go wild swimming. Think of it as an end of term excursion.' My fingers thrum the steering wheel as she contemplates the idea. 'Are your dads taking the girls?' I wince thinking about her fathers.

Meeting Stuart Kingsley with my pants round my ankles wasn't my finest moment. I hope it's months before I have to face him again.

'Yeah. They've got tickets for the zoo. They're picking the girls up any minute.'

'Oh, fuck.' I shake my head vehemently.

'That's a problem?' Savannah's voice peaks.

'I'm three minutes away from your place.'

'And?'

'I'm still recovering from meeting Stuart naked,' I confess.

'So is he.' Savannah's laughter splutters around my car. 'You made quite the impression.'

'It wasn't exactly the impression I was aiming for.'

'He was impressed, nonetheless.' She snorts and chuckles again.

'See you in a minute.'

Five minutes later, I'm helping myself to a Nespresso in Savannah's kitchen while she slices up the pastries and places them in the centre of the dining table. In a tiny vest top and sleep shorts, she'll be lucky if she makes it out of the house at all today.

I inhale a deep breath and revel in the fact that she's mine. That the woman I've wanted for two years is finally mine. Mine. And I get to bring her breakfast.

She hovers beside me, looking up at me from under fluttering eyelashes. 'I'd rather have you for breakfast.' She bites her lower lip as my hands land on the perfect curve of her ass cheeks and tug her against me.

'Greedy girl. Didn't you get your fill last night?'

'Nowhere near.' Her hips grind against mine.

The sound of pattering feet approach on the stairs and we jump apart.

The girls race towards us, greeting me with squeals, hugs and excited exclamations of, 'Is that a gingerbread man?'

'You're spoiling them.' Savannah gives me the side eye, but she doesn't sound cross.

I help the girls up to the table before returning to Savannah's side by the coffee machine, and murmur, 'I figured

Mammy's boyfriend might not be allowed to stay over, but turning up with breakfast from the bakery is acceptable.'

'Boyfriend.' She churns the word out like she's still adjusting to it. 'Am I not too old for a boyfriend? Should we call each other partners or something?' she whispers into my ear.

'You don't turn thirty for another four months.' I arch my eyebrows and waggle them. 'Maybe after then we can agree on a different label for what we are.'

Her throat bobs as she swallows hard.

My meaning isn't lost on her.

Good.

I'm in it for the long haul. I want to spend the rest of my life with her and her daughters. I want them to become *our* daughters.

The front door opens and Stuart appears, dramatically holding his hand across his eyes, though his fingers are splayed so wide he wouldn't miss a mouse. 'Hello, is everybody decent?'

'Funny, Dad.' Savannah shakes her head and shoots me an apologetic glance. 'Come on in.' She beckons him towards the kitchen.

'What does decent mean?' Isla asks, her lips dusted with pink frosting from one of the donuts.

'It means a nice human,' Eden explains, matter-of-factly.

Another man appears in the doorway. Like Stuart, he is athletically built, and impeccably dressed in chino shorts and a short-sleeved shirt. His facial hair is trimmed into a neat stylish beard and his eyes are wider than saucers as he takes in the scene in Savannah's kitchen.

'Good morning.' He strides over to me and extends a hand. 'I'm Steve, pleased to meet you.' His grip is firm and full of unspoken warnings regarding his daughter.

I nod and squeeze his hand. Message received. 'I'm Ronan, pleased to meet you, sir.'

'No need for those type of formalities.' His voice lowers lewdly. 'The only formality required in my presence is keeping your pants on.' His eyebrows rise but the twinkling in his coffee-coloured eyes implies he's teasing.

'Dad,' Savannah hisses, swatting his arm.

'How are my two princesses today?' Stuart heads towards the table and coos over the twins, while Steve continues to stare between Savannah and me, assessing the situation.

'Ronan brought us donuts,' Isla exclaims and I could kiss her for leading her grandfathers to believe that I just arrived. That I didn't spend the night buried between their daughter's legs.

'That was kind of him.' Stuart nods approvingly.

'Yeah, he sneaks out every morning, but he doesn't always bring donuts back,' Isla announces with a toothy grin.

A wince crinkles at the corner of my eyes. Stuart snorts and Steve harrumphs.

Savannah's chuckle echoes around the kitchen. 'I guess that's the end of your five a.m. starts.'

'Come on, girls, let's go brush your teeth and find your shoes. Grandad Stu and Steve are taking you for a special day out.' Savannah presses a kiss to Eden's head and ruffles Isla's hair. The girls leap up from the table and Savannah follows them up the stairs leaving me alone with the two men who raised her.

Stuart and Steve corner me against the kitchen counter.

'So, it's serious.' Steve folds his arms across his chest.

'I told you it was, didn't I?' Stuart insists. 'Savannah doesn't mess around.'

'Neither do I,' I assure them.

Steve eyes me warily. 'That's not what the gossip blogs say.'

I flinch and close my eyes for a second trying to articulate the right words. 'When I retired from competitive swimming, there was a giant void in my life. A void which I filled anyway I could; drinking, partying, playing the field.' I swallow hard. 'Believe it or not, I've been obsessed with Savannah since she totalled my Aston Martin two years ago. And the void I was trying to plug morphed from being a sport, to being a person. I never dreamed I'd be lucky enough to be the man that Savannah chose when she started dating again.'

'I actually thought she hated you.' Stuart shrugs. 'But then, love and hate are so finely entwined, isn't that right, Steve?' He nudges his partner.

'Just don't hurt her, okay?' Steve warns.

'Never,' I promise, holding out my hand to Steve again.

He nods and shakes it with a little less aggression this time. 'She seems... happier. Take care of her.'

Savannah's fathers finally load the twins into their Audi, and crunch down the driveway, Stuart waving a little more enthusiastically than Steve. I breathe a sigh of relief.

'That wasn't so bad, was it?' Savannah's hands snake around my waist as her chin rests on my shoulder.

'At least I had my shorts on this time.'

'Not for long.' Savannah reaches for my waistband, but I catch her hand in mine and still it.

'Patience. We're going on a road trip.' As tempting as it is to lay her out across the kitchen counter, I'll feel so much better knowing Savannah is ready for next week. Once we get the shoot wrapped up, we get to come out as a couple to the world, and I, for one, cannot wait.

'We are?'

'Yep. Pack a bag.'

Twenty minutes later, she's strapped into the passenger

seat of my Tesla. 'Where are we going? And why can't I drive?'

'Because I don't want you ploughing into any unsuspecting Aston Martins.' I fire her a wink as she tuts.

We spend the next half an hour in relative quiet. My hand homes in on Savannah's thigh while she taps the keyboard on her phone, pausing intermittently and biting her lower lip.

No matter how much I touch her, I still can't get enough.

'Everything okay?' I nod to her mobile.

'Yep. Just trying to find the words to articulate my new status.' She exhales heavily.

'You're sending the email today?'

'Yep. I'm sick of lingering in no-man's land.'

'Honey, you've never been in no-man's land.'

Her fingers hover over the send button. 'Are you one hundred per cent about us?' she checks.

'I am. Are you?'

In answer, she inhales deeply through her nose and hits the send button. Within thirty seconds, her phone is buzzing like a million bees in a meadow.

'Holy shit.'

'Yep.' Her fingers thrum the dashboard as she stares defiantly ahead. 'I'm going to ignore that until later. Cassandra, my agent, is going to kill me. Please distract me. Where are we going?'

'Meath.'

I indicate to take the next exit towards the same lake her mother took as a child. The same place she incurred the trauma that rendered her afraid of the water in the first place.

'Is this okay?' I nod towards the sign for the waterfall.

She offers one curt nod but doesn't say a word.

My thumb caresses the silky flesh of her thigh. 'I've got

you. I won't let anything happen to you. In the water, and in life.'

She nods again but doesn't say a word. As I pull up at a secluded spot by the lake, the sun chooses this precise moment to break through the clouds and illuminate the water. Savannah exhales slowly, surveying our surroundings.

'I forgot how beautiful it was.' Her neck cranes as she arches forwards to soak it all in. 'I always remember it being so dark, so full of despair, but it's so beautiful and bright.' Her hand reaches for the door.

I set up a blanket by the water's edge and we inch into the lake together, holding hands. Savannah's face is pale as she slips her summer dress over her head. I don't know if it's the water, or the fact she's basically just renounced everything she's worked for. Either way, I've got her.

She's wearing a new bikini, one I've never seen before. It lifts her pert, perky breasts even higher than usual and sculpts her ass to perfection. My cock stirs at the mere sight of her. I will him down. Now is not the time.

'You okay?' I check for what feels like the fiftieth time.

She slips her palm into mine and squeezes, tugging me towards the water's edge. 'I will be. Let's do this.'

We inch into the cool blue water together, our fingers entwined. I walk a step ahead of her, to assess the depth, hissing as my balls hit the chill factor.

A snigger sounds from behind me.

'We'll see how funny you think it is when your perfect tits are so cold you're begging me to suck them back to life.'

'Oh, Ro,' Savannah follows me in with a yelp of her own. 'You've already sucked the rest of me back to life. There's no point stopping now.'

We stand, hip-to-hip, toe-to-toe, chest-to-chest. Her gaze roams over the lake, lingering on the waterfall at the far side. Her expression is so solemn, so serious, but it's not scared.

Her head tilts back towards me, her pupils bore into mine, fire flickering in her irises despite the chilly water. 'You know, when I'm with you, I feel like I can do anything. Be anything, without the pressure of being this independent woman I've built up on social media.'

'You're still independent, no matter what your relationship status is. You're the smartest, sassiest, sexiest woman I know. I'll never hinder your growth. I'll support you in everything you do.'

'I know.' Her tongue darts out to wet her bottom lip as her fingers disentangle from mine to drift over the planes of my chest, settling over my heart. 'And that's why I love you.'

My triumphant smile moulds against Savannah's mouth as her legs wrap around my waist.

Chapter Thirty-Five
SAVANNAH

I've thought about this place more times than I can remember, but in my hazy traumatised memories, the water was always darker, the isolation sinister instead of serene. It's nothing like the child-sized me remembered. I'm ecstatic Ronan thought to bring me back.

Whenever I summon a picture of this lake, it'll be an image from today. One of happiness, joy, and fun in the sun.

This is the day I faced my fears. The fear of the lake, and the fear of shedding my old identity.

The fallout from my email could be colossal.

But losing Ronan would be worse.

We splash around for a while. Ronan adopts his bossy teacher persona and insists we swim a couple of lengths.

'Here,' I beckon him towards the lakeside, where my phone is lying on the dewy grass.

Ronan glances at the phone, then at me. 'You want me to pose with you?'

'Yep.' I wade through the shallows and snatch it up, careful not to drop it into the water.

'I absolutely hate the camera. I never willingly get in front of one. Worst invention ever.' A sly smile crooks his lips.

'You would say that, given how many times you've been papped in compromising positions.' I poke my tongue out at him.

'I was only passing the time until I could convince you to take me up on one of my filthy offers.' He slips an arm around me. 'I'm sorry.'

'Don't apologise. We all have a past. I'm not exactly proud of mine either.' An image of Finn's wife forces itself to the forefront of my mind. I had no idea she existed, but that doesn't stop me feeling bad for sleeping with her husband.

'Come on then.' Ronan tilts his head towards mine. 'One for the wank bank?'

'No. It's for Instagram. Let's do this.'

'Seriously?'

'No point ripping off half the plaster.' I shrug. 'Besides, the brand ambassador for Coral Chic is supposed to endorse their products.' I run a hand over the gorgeous new bikini I'm wearing and shimmy closer to Ronan.

'Damn you look hot in that Lycra, but it would look better on the floor.' Ronan's hand grabs my ass beneath the water, and I squeal.

'Smile and try not to look like you're groping your student.' I snap images from several angles before scrolling back through them.

To the naked eye, we aren't touching, but the chemistry between us is palpable. Probably because Ronan's fingers are inching over my bikini bottoms in a way that has heating pooling between my legs.

Despite the uncertainty around my career and my brand, my smile is brighter than it's been in years. My eyes are glowing with happiness. My skin is radiant, a fact that can only be attributed to multiple daily orgasms.

Ronan towers over me like the cat who got the cream, and even though his hand can't be seen, his face says he's up to the best type of badness.

'Are you really going to post that?' His fingers slip inside my bikini bottoms, tracing the curve of my ass.

'Do you mind if I do?' I open the Instagram app, hovering over the upload button.

'Do I mind?' His tone is incredulous. 'Baby, I've wanted to claim you as mine from the second you smashed up my car.'

'You mean the second *you* smashed up *my* car?' He slaps my ass, and the sensation sets tingles down my spine. 'Post the picture.' He gestures to the phone.

I type the caption, 'Sunday Funday with my swimming instructor,' and tag both Ronan and Coral Chic into the post with the hashtags #secretsout #datingintthedeepend #brandambassador #paidpartnership and #whataview. I don't mean the sun glittering off the turquoise lake. I mean the ripped Adonis beside me.

'If we're coming out, we may as well do it in a baptism of fire.'

Ronan picked up more than just the donuts and pastries this morning. He picked up an entire picnic basket's worth of freshly made sandwiches, cold meat salads, a punnet of fresh, juicy strawberries, and a half-sized bottle of Tattinger.

I'm under no illusion this is the calm before the media shitstorm, but at least we'll weather the shitstorm together. And maybe it won't be that bad. Two people in love should be celebrated, not condemned.

We sprawl across a fleecy blanket, side by side, faces tilted up towards the hazy sunshine. Ronan took pity on my chattering teeth and lent me his Dryrobe. He's wearing a hoody and his wet shorts, the same fire engine red ones I stared at for months before uncovering what's inside them.

Our fingers are interlaced, both of us propped up on our elbows, each clutching a plastic flute filled with bubbles.

'Thank you.' I tear my eyes away from the glistening water.

'What for?' He shoves his sunglasses onto his head to squint at me.

'For bringing me here. For teaching me to swim. For loving me.' I offer a small shrug. He's changed my life. I'm not sure what the future looks like, but with Ronan by my side, I'm excited about the next chapter.

'Thank you for letting me.' He rocks forwards, his lips locking with mine in a slow sensual kiss. I peep over his shoulder without pulling away, checking for prying eyes, but this place is just as remote as it ever was.

It's one thing to post an image of us together and announcing our relationship, but if someone were to snap pictures of this sensual scene, they would be worth a fortune.

The low rumbling of a large vehicle approaching in the distance is the only reason I tear my mouth from my man's.

My man.

I love it.

And I love him.

'Looks like we've got company.' I rock back onto my elbows, grateful for my oversized sunglasses as a minibus pulls up and fourteen babbling women pile out with various coloured yoga mats tucked beneath their arms.

Several of them glance our way. Ronan drops his sunglasses back down from his head to cover his eyes.

'Ah, young love.' A curvy woman in a polka dot swimsuit and shorts approaches us, eyeing the champagne flutes and our entwined fingers. 'This is how it starts,' she says, pointing her index finger between us. 'Isn't it, Rose?' Her head cranes as she searches for her cronies, beckoning them over.

'Enjoy it, while it lasts.' Another yoga pant wearing woman strides over, flanking the first. 'Once you have kids, it'll be the end of these lazy days.'

The rest of the women migrate towards us and my sweaty fingers grip Ronan's like my life depends on it.

'Are you on your holidays?' Another kind-faced lady asks, peering into the picnic basket and sniffing.

'No, we're just on a day trip from the city.' Ronan flashes a winning smile. Considering he doesn't elaborate, you'd think they'd get the hint and move on, but no.

Mind you, if I were them, I'd probably stand and gawp at the man beside me too. Hell, I gawped from the poolside for long enough, didn't I?

'Ladies, come on.' A woman in her forties booms from beside the bus in an authoritative tone. 'This is supposed to be a wellness excursion, not a gossiping session.'

I exhale a sigh of relief as, one by one, the women bid us goodbye. All but one. The first.

'I recognise you.' I flinch at the accusation in her tone, but when I dare to glance up, it's Ronan she's pointing at, not me.

'Yeah?' He cocks his head and forces another dazzling smile.

'I can't place you, but I've definitely seen you before.' Her head angles to the side, her beady eyes narrowing. She hesitates, hopping from foot to foot, staring at Ronan like he's a jigsaw puzzle, one piece short.

When her eyes fall to his swimming shorts, I know she has it. She clicks her fingers and squeals, 'You're Ronan Rivers. The Olympic swimmer! I watched your last race ten times over.'

I bet you did, you saucy minx. Her eyes continue to flit

between Ronan's face and his swimming shorts. She's probably wondering where the budgie smugglers are.

'You have me.' He raises the hand that's holding his champagne flute and offers a silent cheers.

'And who's this you're with?' Beady black eyes glint with glee as they land on me again. Thank God she's not one of my subscribers.

He hesitates for a second, glancing towards me. 'This is my girlfriend.'

'You'll make beautiful babies one day,' she coos.

'Here's hoping,' Ronan mutters. She backs away reluctantly as her friends impatiently beckon her back to where they're laying out their mats in a semi-circle facing the lake.

'Beautiful babies, hey?' Ronan murmurs in my ear.

'Do you want children?' I can't even attempt to sound nonchalant.

If he's serious about a future with me, he's going to inherit two, anyway. What difference would one more make?

He inhales and blows out a slow, thoughtful breath. 'Yes, I do. I want to put a baby in you.' His fingers roam inside the Dry robe, tracing the flat of my stomach. Fireworks burst beneath my skin. 'Do you want more kids?

I swallow thickly. 'I'd love another baby.'

'Home?' we say in the same breath.

We spend the rest of the afternoon in my bed, ignoring both of our buzzing phones.

Monday will be here all too soon.

At five o'clock my dads swing into the driveway wearing matching expressions of excitement. 'We're so happy for you, darling,' Stuart whispers in my ear as he pecks my cheek.

'You saw my Instagram then?' I pinch the bridge of my nose.

'Honey, the world and his wife saw your Instagram. It's the biggest scandal since Holly's boobs went viral,' Stuart says. Poor Holly. But it turned out well for her in the end. Hopefully, it'll turn out well for me too.

Ronan scoops up Isla with one arm and Eden with the other as they pull at the strings of the apron he's put on to cook dinner.

'Oh, what are you cooking, Ronan?' Steve's hint is as subtle as a brick.

'Just fajitas. There's plenty, if you want to stay?'

'Oh, we'd hate to impose.' Steve's voice implies the total opposite. Then he runs up the steps and into the house without a backwards glance.

Ronan whips up a huge platter of chicken fajitas complete with salsa, guacamole and sour cream, whizzing around the kitchen like a younger, more attractive Gordon Ramsay.

'Show off.' I nod at the silent smoke alarm.

'You're just too hot to handle.' He brushes his lips over mine and Stuart wolf-whistles.

'Told you we'd get a wedding out of her yet, didn't I, Steve?' Stuart downs his second glass of wine and reaches for the bottle. Even Steve's expression softens.

I set the table while the girls chatter incessantly, regaling us with a blow-by-blow account of every animal they saw at the zoo.

My kitchen is full, but not nearly as full as my heart.

I have no idea what tomorrow will bring, but with Ronan by my side, we'll deal with it together.

Chapter Thirty-Six
RONAN

My alarm buzzes on the floor beside Savannah's huge, comfy bed. I disentangle my legs from hers and roll across the mattress to snatch the phone up, silencing it with a single swipe. I don't begrudge these early mornings. Not when they enable me to spend every night in Savannah's bed. Under her. Over her. Inside her. But I'd be lying if I said I wasn't tired.

What I wouldn't do for a lie-in.

I brush a tender kiss across Savannah's glossy head and toss back the covers.

'Stay,' she mumbles, her arm reaching for my waist.

I hesitate, torn between what I want to do and the right thing to do. 'But what about the girls?'

Savannah's eyes prise open. 'They've been watching you sneak out for weeks. It's not like they don't know you're here, anyway.'

'And you're okay with that?' Hope rises in my chest. First the Instagram picture, then dinner with her dads, now staying past the girls' wake up time. It's everything I ever dared to dream of and more.

'I'm okay with that.' She throws the cover over me and

snuggles against my chest, pushing me back against the plump, plush pillows. 'When we get up, we'll have to face the music. I want to hide here for a bit longer. I'm not ready yet.'

'You were born ready, Sassy Sav.' I snuggle closer, wrapping my arms around her. 'It won't be as bad as you think, I promise.'

Within seconds, I drift back to sleep again.

I'm woken an hour later by Isla giggling. 'Do you think he's got clothes on under there?' A tiny finger prods my back over the duvet. 'I never saw a naked boy before.'

'Gross.' Eden's voice overflows with disgust at the mere prospect. 'Well, what about Barbie's boyfriend, Ken? Does he count? I took his pants off, but you can't really see anything.'

Savannah's slim frame shakes slightly like she's suppressing a laugh.

'Weird, right?' Isla mutters, her breath brushing over my skin as if she's poring over me like a science experiment while I sleep.

Thank God I'd had the foresight to pull my boxers back on last night.

I blink the sleep out of my eyes and roll onto my side to face the girls. 'I do have clothes on. And nakedness isn't gross, it's natural.'

'You're awake!' The twins yelp, bouncing up and down next to the bed, their matching pink pyjamas crinkled from sleep.

'Hard not to wake when you're being poked and prodded.' I smile to show I'm teasing, while Savannah harrumphs beside me. I pinch her ass beneath the covers, and she muffles a squeal. She doesn't mind being poked or prodded. Not by me, at least.

'Let's go get some breakfast before school, girls. Let

Mammy sleep in for a little while longer.' I pull the covers back and grab my t-shirt from the leather tub chair in the corner of the bedroom.

Savannah hauls herself up into a sitting position, her fingers raking through her golden mussed hair. 'I'll sort them out, Ro, don't worry.'

'Let me, please.' I pull the t-shirt over my head. 'I'll bring you up a coffee.'

A pink tinge flushes Savannah's neck. 'You don't have to do any of this.'

'I want to.' I've wanted to for a long time. 'Besides, you should probably check that.' I nod towards her phone and she groans.

I leave her to it, padding down the stairs after the girls as they bombard me with a million questions.

Isla heads for the cereal cupboard. 'Do you live here now?'

'Are you taking us to school today?' Eden asks as she takes a seat at the kitchen table.

'Can I have Coco Pops for breakfast?' Isla pulls out the yellow cereal box and shakes it hopefully.

'Are you our dad now?' Eden peeps up shyly from under her thick, dark lashes.

'Wow.' I laugh. 'One thing at a time.'

'Phoebe's mammy left, and her dad found her a new mammy. We're going for a sleepover there on Friday night. It's Phoebe's birthday,' Isla states, taking the seat beside her sister and plonking the Coco Pops on the table.

'Is that right?' I grab a couple of bowls, spoons, and the milk from the fridge and place them in the middle for the twins to help themselves.

'How old's Phoebe going to be?' Anything to distract them from the other questions. The ones I don't know how to answer, even if I know how I want to answer them – yes, yes, yes and yes would be my preference.

'She's going to be seven. She's allowed three friends to sleep over, so she asked us and Sarah Snowden.' Isla thumbs her chest proudly.

I head to the coffee machine, load a capsule, hit the espresso button, and add two sweeteners. I know exactly how Savannah likes it.

'I'm just going to take Mammy this coffee, okay?'

'Sure,' Isla says, pouring a mountain-sized portion of Coco Pops into her bowl.

Eden's voice wafts up the stairs as I carry the coffee up. 'I like having him here,' she says. 'And not just because he gives us treats.'

'Me too,' Isla agrees.

'I hope he stays.' Eden's voice is wistful. She sounds way older than her years. These girls, my heart breaks for them. Where is their father? Who is their father? And why wouldn't he play a role in their lives?

His loss is my gain.

Given half the chance, I'm going to be everything they ever needed and more.

I nudge open Savannah's bedroom door with my knee. She's propped up against the headboard, her face is stricken as she stares blankly out of the window. Quick hands swipe across her cheeks, wiping away her tears, but not quickly enough.

'Are you okay?' Placing the coffee cup in her hands, I perch on the edge of the bed.

'Oh God, Ro, I knew it would be bad, but you should see what they're saying about me. It's absolutely hateful. The damage is colossal.' Tears stream from her eyes. This time she doesn't even try to wipe them away.

'It'll pass, sweetheart.' I brush her hair from her face and tuck it behind her ears.

'The things they're calling me are beyond cruel.

Hypocrite. Whore. It's unreal. I don't know if I'll ever recover from this.' Her stunning azure eyes well again.

My jaw locks hard enough to hurt. How dare they judge her? Judge us.

'You will. We'll get through it together. Next week, they'll be talking about someone else.' My fingers blaze a trail across her shoulder, sweeping soothing strokes across her skin.

'Did you check Instagram?' She places the coffee cup on the locker beside the bed.

'No.' The only thing I ever used Instagram for is to check on the woman beside me, and given I haven't left her side in almost twenty-four hours, I didn't feel the need.

'It's fucking mental...the abuse...' She trails off.

I flick open the app on my phone.

She's lost almost half of her following, and the other half aren't holding back on their opinions. I scroll through the comments under the picture she posted yesterday.

Slutty Sav.

Oh, er...Sexy Sav

Sneaky Sav. I want my money back! I can't take advice on how to parent single from a woman who isn't single.

Go on, my son!

Single Sav's a hypocrite, preaching about being an independent woman, then banging the biggest playboy around.

At least she got a nice photo - let's be honest - we all know she'll never get another one with him.

Rage roils inside of me as her head falls into her hands, and she sobs. 'Cassandra emailed. Inkwell Imprint has withdrawn their offer for a second book. Bella Baby is renouncing me as their ambassador, and I've had three missed calls from Lucas Beechwood, so you can guess how that will probably go.'

The enormity of what she's potentially given up for me hits me like a punch to the gut.

Chapter Thirty-Seven

SAVANNAH

I had almost two-hundred-thousand women unsubscribe from my blog.

I've been bombarded with links to gossip blog sites showcasing photos of Ronan's playboy days. Eugh, even the image of him leaving a nightclub with the weathergirl.

Hundreds, if not thousands, of the comments speculate the same stupid opinion. 'It won't last.'

'Want me to take the girls to school?' Ronan offers.

'Is it too much to ask? I know you're due back there this afternoon as it is.' The prospect of facing the mothers at the school gate is one I can't bear.

'Nothing is too much to ask.' Ronan stands, shoves his phone in his pocket and drops a kiss on my mouth. 'I'll be back as soon as I can. We're in this together, Sav. Don't worry, I've got you. I promise.'

He also promised it wouldn't be as bad as I thought and look how that turned out.

'The girls' uniforms are hanging in their wardrobes. Their lunches are in the fridge.' My gaze lifts to his. 'Thank you.'

He lingers in the doorway gripping the architrave tightly

enough to turn his knuckles white. 'No, Savannah, thank you for picking me.'

'I'd do it again.' I force a small smile his way. 'But whatever you do, please don't make me regret it.'

'Never, baby. I love you.' He blows me a kiss.

'I love you too.'

When I hear the front door slam, and I'm certain the house is empty, I pick up my phone to call Lucas Beechwood. The shoot is this Friday, if it's still going ahead. Either way, I need to find out. Time to face the music.

'Savannah,' he snaps by way of greeting. 'Quite the scandal you're starring in. And you told me you don't date.'

I wince, screwing my fist into a tight ball.

'I don't,' I stammer. 'Well, I didn't. Ronan agreed to teach me how to swim for the shoot and, well... it went from there.'

He blows out a long, slow breath like he's in pain. 'I made it clear from the beginning that I was looking for a certain type of person to represent our range. Someone wholesome. Someone respectable.'

'I know, Lucas.' My head hangs. 'This thing with Ronan isn't just a flash in the pan. I know he has a past. Don't we all? But this thing between us is serious.'

'The man doesn't know the meaning of the word.' Lucas tuts. 'I should have guessed when I saw you that night at the gallery.'

'Like I said, we only got to know each other properly when I asked him to teach me how to swim. I was terrified of the water until recently.'

'You were?' Lucas's tone peaks. 'Then why did you agree to a swimming shoot in the sea?'

'Because I'm a huge fan of your brand. And I loved the fact that you approached me, a real woman whose body bears the scars of motherhood.'

Lucas exhales warily. 'You have to understand why I'm

upset, Savannah, given Ronan's reputation. If he makes you look bad, we all look bad.'

'Look, it's your choice. Your brand. If you still want me to do it, I'll do it. Just let me know asap.'

I'm tempted to cancel all bookings in Ballybowen and hibernate there until this all blows over.

'Let me think about it, Savannah. I need to talk to the PR team,' Lucas says resignedly. 'I'll call you back.'

'Sure.'

'Oh, and Savannah,' Lucas adds wistfully. 'Ronan is one hell of a lucky bastard.'

I can't even bring myself to feel flattered, let alone say thank you.

While I wait, I pad through the house, roaming from room to room wearing one of Ronan's t-shirts and a pair of shorts. The familiar scent of his cologne lingers round the neckline, offering a tiny modicum of comfort.

It's eerily silent with the girls gone. It occurs to me that this is what my life would have amounted to if I'd chosen to be Single Sav forever. Wandering around the quiet house alone. One day, the girls will grow up and leave to live their own lives. One day they won't need me in the same capacity. And I don't want to be left here alone. I want to have someone to share my life with.

I made the right decision.

And I'm going to stand by it.

I open my Instagram app, ignoring the fresh influx of notifications, and change my username to Sassy Sav. Ronan will approve if no one else does.

I change my profile picture to the one of Ronan and me at the lake.

And then I head into my office to start updating my website.

When the phone finally rings, I almost jump out of my skin.

'Savannah,' Lucas's tone sounds slightly more upbeat, 'I've had a chat with the PR people. They've come up with a solution.'

I bite my lip dubiously, not daring to hope the solution might be a viable one. 'Go on.'

'We're going to have an entire film crew at our disposal tomorrow for the shoot. It's been suggested that we use this scandal to our advantage. We're about to test the age old saying, "No publicity is bad publicity"'

I hate that the love I feel for Ronan is referred to as a scandal, but I'll suck it up for the sake of his potential solution. At the end of the day, I have a business to run and with a massive loss of paying blog subscribers, the money from the Coral Chic contract will come in handy. 'What do you mean?'

'You said you and Ronan got together while he was teaching you to swim.' Lucas annunciates every syllable painfully slowly.

'Yes.'

'How would you and Ronan feel about doing an Instagram live after the shoot? We have over six million followers on there, Savannah. If you and Ronan are as serious as you say you are, it would be a chance to redeem yourselves.'

'What kind of an Instagram live?' Doubt inflects my voice.

'Tell Coral Chic's followers how the company indirectly lead you, one of the most famous single women in the country, to love.'

I pause for a beat to consider it. I'll never get a bigger platform to explain I wasn't preaching one thing and practising another.

Lucas continues pitching his idea. 'We'll film it straight

after the shoot while all the equipment is set up, but both you and Ronan would have to be willing to go on camera.'

Ronan hates the camera. He's made absolutely no secret of that. But this would be different.

'If Ronan were to confirm you guys are in a relationship, explain he's absolutely smitten with you, it would transform this from a scandal to a true love story. Everyone loves a happy ever after, right?'

'I don't know...' It would mean putting myself out there for another absolute slating, but if we pulled it off, it would spin the entire scandal on its head.

'Savannah, your reputation is in tatters. You don't have many other options.'

I inhale deeply. He's right. 'We'll do it. I'll have to run it by Ronan, but I'm sure it won't be a problem.' I'm not sure truthfully, but hopefully he'll do it for my sake.

It's the best chance we'll get to show we're serious. And for my Sassy Sav business to have any chance.

'He's not there with you? I thought given the morning you must be having he'd be there to support you.' Pity inches into Lucas's voice.

I don't need his pity. Or anyone else's. 'He's doing the school run.' Stick that in your pipe and smoke it.

'Oh, I see.' Lucas clears his throat again.

You don't, but you're about to.

'I'll call you back once I've spoken to him.'

'Great,' Lucas says before hanging up.

Chapter Thirty-Eight
RONAN

Traffic is heavy on the way back from St. Jude's. It takes me the best part of an hour to get home to Savannah. I consider stopping at the bakery to pick up her favourite breakfast pastries, or stopping at the florists to pick up flowers, but flowers always seem to say, 'I'm sorry,' and I'm not sorry.

I'm not sorry we came out as a couple.

I'm not sorry that we no longer have to sneak around.

And I'm not sorry that I get to take the girls to school.

The public is so wrong about us. It's going to give me enormous pleasure proving every single one of those negative comments wrong. Sooner rather than later. Which is why I'm planning on paying a visit to her fathers, sooner rather than later.

I pull up outside Savannah's house and let myself in. She's barefoot, pacing the kitchen in one of my t-shirts. She clutches a pink sparkly notebook in one hand and a fluffy pink pen in the other.

'You look like you're ready to take on the world.' I nod towards the notebook as I stride across the open-plan space and close the distance between us, encircling her in my arms.

'You have no idea. I spoke to Lucas.' She tilts her head back to look up at me. 'He made a suggestion.'

I bet he did.

I make us both a coffee while she fills me in.

'So, basically they want us to go on camera and explain how our relationship developed?'

'Yes. What do you think? Will you do it?' Earnest eyes, tinged with both hope and vulnerability, bore into mine.

'Of course I'll do it. I'll do anything for you, Savannah.' I've been dying for the world to know she's mine, and now I get to be the one who tells them. It's a win- win.

Her chest sinks with a substantial sigh of relief. 'I know you hate the camera.'

'I do, but I'd do it for you. I was coming to the shoot, anyway. And putting my hands on you and telling the world I'm obsessed with you is no hardship. Trust me.' I slip a hand under her t-shirt. My t-shirt. It's the same thing.

She swats it away. 'Later, Ro! I have a million things I need to do right now and sadly, you aren't one of them.'

'I'm just glad to see you feeling more like yourself. I hate seeing you cry, Sav. Especially over a bunch of strangers' opinions.' I drain my coffee and stick the cup in the dishwasher.

'I've changed my blog handle to Sassy Sav, as chosen by you,' she announces, with a wobbly smile. 'It's all part of the rebrand.' She taps her notebook with the pen. 'I'll still offer parenting advice, but I'm going to start documenting my dating life. Sassy Sav's Guide to Dating After Kids, if that's okay with you...' She trails off.

'I absolutely love it, baby.' I grab her waist and pull her flush against me. 'I'm so fucking proud of you. You've always been Sassy Sav to me.'

'Right, let's call Lucas.' She grabs her phone from the table.

Lucas's polished voice answers on the first ring. 'Savannah.'

'We'll do it,' she says.

'Great news. It's the right decision if you two want to be taken seriously.'

'And you're basically getting two ambassadors for the price of one.' Savannah shrugs.

'Oh no, I signed the male ambassador this morning. He flew in yesterday. You'll meet him at the shoot,' Lucas says with a slight superiority.

The thought of Savannah posing in one of those skimpy bikinis with another guy sets my skin simmering with annoyance, but I keep my mouth shut. I'm not her keeper. I'm her boyfriend. And as soon as the photos are done, I'll get to shout it to the world.

'Who is he? Do we know him?' Savannah bites down on her pen lid.

'Finn Reilly. You've probably seen his fitness videos online. His wife is a nutritional coach. They're opening gyms left, right, and centre,' Lucas says. 'He has a huge fitness following. He's wholesome. Likeable. He's exactly what Coral Chic needs.'

An image of Finn Reilly springs into my mind. I've seen his 'Get Fit With Finn' routine on Instagram. With his dark hair, hazel eyes and athletic physique, I suppose he's a good fit for the role. And at least he's married, so he won't be pawing all over my girlfriend.

The phone slips from Savannah's fingers and hits the kitchen floor, shattering the screen. She looked stricken this morning, but right now she looks like she's about to pass out.

'Jees, are you okay?' Grabbing her elbows, I guide her back to one of the kitchen chairs. She slumps back unsteadily.

Her mouth opens and she stares at the phone on the floor like it's poisonous.

'Baby, you're scaring the shit out of me right now. What is it? Do you feel sick?'

Her entire body trembles beneath my touch. 'I can't do it,' she eventually blurts out.

'Why not?' I'm missing something, but I don't know what. She was all for it earlier. She was the one trying to convince me it was a good idea.

'I haven't seen him since...' Her eyes snap to mine meaningfully.

She knows Finn.

Finn, with his dark hair and hazel eyes.

Realisation churns in my stomach.

'Savannah?' Her name hitches up like a question.

Her eyes fuse with mine and she nods once, but it's enough.

'He's the twins' dad,' she confesses.

The conversation from the car journey back from Ballybowen replays in my mind. *'He's married. I had no idea.'*

I slide into the seat next to her and pull her onto my lap, cradling her like a baby. She nuzzles into my neck as I rock her back and forth.

The only sound is the ticking of the clock.

'You want to tell me what happened?'

Eventually, she speaks. 'I was working in London for a women's fashion magazine when I met him at the local gym where he was a personal trainer. We spent three months together before I found out I was pregnant. Which, coincidentally, was when he admitted he was married.'

Rage rises like a riptide in my thorax. I squeeze her tighter against my chest. 'Bastard.'

'I left my forwarding address at the gym should he ever want to contact me about his child, little did I know I was carrying twins, but he never did. Then he shot to fame as a celebrity fitness trainer and started on Good Morning Britain. I hated seeing his smug face on those daily 'Get Fit with Finn' fifteen-minute work outs.' Savannah's fingers ball into an angry fist on my chest.

'I'm so sorry he did that to you.'

Savannah shakes her head. 'The shame.'

'What shame?'

'He was married. And I slept with him. The thought makes me sick.'

'He's the one who should be ashamed. Not you.' Sick fuck. If I ever lay eyes on him, God fucking help him.

'I can't face him. I just can't.'

'It's fine. I'll call Lucas and tell him you're not doing it.' I stand, lifting Savannah with me in the process. 'We're going back to bed.' It's not even sexual. She needs to be held. To feel safe and secure. And that's what I'm going to give her.

'What time do you need to be back at school for lessons?' she asks.

'Not for another couple of hours.'

We spend those couple of hours spooning in silence.

Chapter Thirty-Nine
SAVANNAH

Ronan offered to bring the girls home after his afternoon swimming lessons, but I need to get out of the house. These four walls are starting to feel like a cage, and I could really do with the comfort of seeing my best friend.

I park outside St Jude's twenty minutes early and swallow down the anxiety swirling in my sternum. It's not just the mention of Finn. It's not just the insults being hurled my way. It's everything combined. I feel like my whole world is spinning on its axis and I can't breathe.

The mothers are gathered at the school's wrought iron gates for their daily chat, but I cut through them without making eye contact.

Several greet me with calls of, 'Savannah,', some with knowing smiles, others with sympathetic stares, and there are even a couple with sneers.

'Is it true?' The wife of the local MP steps forwards. Celeste, I think her name is. 'Are you sleeping with Ronan Rivers?'

'Is it any of your business who I am or am not sleeping with?' I snap, without stopping.

'Keep your hair on.' Her voice is thick with false concern. 'We're simply concerned about you. A man like him is no good for a woman like you.'

'You have no idea what kind of man he is. Or what kind of woman I am, for that matter.' *Keep talking and you might just find out, though. Especially after the day I've had.*

I stalk across the asphalt yard and into the old Victorian building to my best friend's office. I knock twice and let myself in. Ashley's sitting behind her huge mahogany desk with a stack of reports piled up. She looks every bit the private school principal in a tailored navy power suit. Her auburn hair is twisted into a tight classic chignon.

'Come in.' She stands and beckons me in. 'Are you okay? I've been trying to call you all day.'

'I will be.' I stride across Ashley's office, which is like a miniature library. Floor to ceiling bookcases line the walls, stacked with dusty leather-bound books. 'It's been one of those days.' I'm not ready to tell Ashley about Finn yet. I will, but not right now. I'm still processing his presence here in Dublin.

'How are the girls? Did you see them today?'

'The girls are fine. Ronan's with them at the gym. One of the baby infants shit in the pool so the janitors closed it down and are cleaning up. Ronan kindly offered to teach basketball instead of swimming this afternoon. He adores Eden and Isla.' Ashley motions to the seat opposite before sitting down again.

'He's really great with them.' I slump into the leather. And really great with me.

'It seems like he's a man of many talents.' Ashley's lips quiver as she battles a smirk.

'You have no idea.' I shake my head.

'When Ms McNamara asked the girls to share their news from home this morning, Isla told the entire class that Ronan sleeps at their house now and he lets them have Coco Pops on school days.' Ashley sniggers. 'Nothing is sacred when there are little eyes and ears watching.'

'Oh God. I don't know whether to laugh or cry,' I confess, massaging my temples. 'I feel like the world as I know it is caving in on me from every direction.'

'Breathe.' My friend reaches across the table and takes my hand. 'The most famous single mother in the country hooking up with a famous man – ahem, man about town – was always going to cause a scandal. Just hang on in there. Friday marks the start of the summer holidays. Let the dust settle. Spend the summer having red hot sex with Ronan Rivers, and by September everyone will be busy talking about someone else.'

'Maybe.' If it weren't for Finn fucking Reilly, I might have had the chance to spin the 'scandal' on its head.

'There's no "maybe" about it.' Ashley rocks back in her chair. 'Trust me.'

I twist my lips and stare at my friend. With the return of Finn, the same old ugly insecurities are rearing their head.

'What if I've given up everything for him and he leaves?'

Ashley laughs, but not in a cruel way. 'Oh Savannah. You have no idea, do you? He's absolutely smitten with you. He's not going anywhere.'

'You think?'

'I know.'

The panic in my stomach eases slightly.

'Now stop worrying. Everything is going to be okay,' Ashley assures me. Her tone is so confident, I almost believe her.

A knock sounds on the office door.

'Come in.' She straightens her spine, holding her shoulders high.

The door opens and a familiar blond head appears. Ronan.

'I saw your car outside. I thought you might be in here. I can keep hold of the girls for a while if you're still talking.'

'No, it's fine.' I push my chair back.

'Actually, I do need to talk to Savannah about something, while I have her here, so that would be great.' Ashley beams at him.

Ronan focuses his attention on me. 'Why don't I take them for a smoothie and a run around the park? No swimming lessons this afternoon due to an unforeseen… turd.' He sniggers. 'I can meet you at home later, if it suits?'

Home. It sounds so natural.

'That would be amazing,' my friend answers for me.

'I'll pick up dinner, too.' Ronan blows me a kiss before closing the door.

'OMG, hang onto him with two hands.' Ashley slaps the desk with her palm.

'He's special alright.' Which is precisely why I'm terrified of losing him. Nevermind losing my identity, losing him is something I'd never recover from.

Before I can spiral again, Ashley hunches forwards conspicuously. 'So, I've made a decision.'

'Go on.' Her hushed tone is enough to distract me from my own drama.

'I'm going to propose to Matt,' she announces, shuffling the papers on her desk, probably so she doesn't have to meet my eye whilst dropping this bombshell.

'You're what?' Whatever doubts I have about my own future, I have no doubt that Matt is *not* the man for Ashley.

He's not good enough for her. Not by a clear mile. And not because he lives in her house and contributes absolutely nothing, including his love and affection, but because he has absolutely no interest in spending any time with her. They're only ever spotted together once a year, on a Christmas card.

'I know, I know, it's a bold move.' Ashley catches her

lower lip between her teeth and places the papers in a neat pile before finally raising her eyes to meet mine. 'But the pressure is coming from every direction.'

'What pressure?' I cross my legs and pray the horror I'm feeling inside isn't reflected on my face. 'What's the rush?'

'Ha.' Ashley scoffs. 'What's the rush? It's been eleven years. *Eleven* years. I can hardly bear to visit my own parents these days because every time I do, my mother's eyes stray straight to my empty left hand with a disappointed sigh. My biological clock is clicking louder than a ticking time bomb. And this week, the board of governors questioned if I'm qualified to teach sex education at a Catholic school given that I'm unmarried, "cohabiting with a man", and apparently "perhaps not the most suitable role model for the students."'

'Fucking hell.' I thought I had problems. I can't imagine what Ashley's going through. Still, her reasoning isn't solid enough to sign her life over to another person.

I'm no expert at relationships, clearly, but it doesn't seem like a great foundation to build on.

Not once did she mention the most import word in any relationship. The only word I'm certain of when it comes to Ronan Rivers.

Love.

I love Ronan. So much it terrifies me.

That's the crux of it.

That's what it boils down to, if I dig deep.

I'm fucking terrified that I've fallen hard and fast and that he might leave me. Like Finn did. Like my own mother did.

What if I'm not enough?

I squash that thought immediately.

It isn't about me right now. It's about Ashley making what I believe will be the biggest mistake of her life.

Ashley exhales a huge sigh, yanks open the top drawer of

her desk and produces a bottle of scotch. 'One to take the edge off?'

'Sure.'

The amber liquor slides down my throat with a sharp burning sensation. We should probably be drinking something celebratory, like pink champagne. My friend is about to get engaged and here we are, 'taking the edge off.'

It's certainly taken the edge off my problems, for now anyway. I'm worried because I have a boyfriend who loves me, and people don't like it.

Fuck the book deal.

Fuck what everyone else thinks right now.

And fuck Finn Reilly.

Then it clicks. My conversation with Lucas. *'Your male counterpart wants me to invest in his business as he starts up in Dublin.'*

'And you don't want to?'

'Between you and me, I'm not sure about him. On paper, he's squeaky clean, the perfect role model, fit, and fun and relatable.' Lucas sat back, clasping his fingers together on the table in front of him. *'But I just get this vibe off him. Like something's not quite right.'*

Lucas's vibe was spot on. And maybe it's time he knew it.

Perhaps it's time to face my past instead of running from it.

Chapter Forty

RONAN

'Did you get on okay with the twins?' Savannah emerges from her office just after eight. Shadows linger beneath her eyes. The day is taking its toll on her.

'Perfect. There hasn't been a peep out of them.' With Savannah's nerves shred, it seemed kinder to everyone if I did the bedtime routine.

'Great work.' She sashays towards me, her long legs flexing gracefully. 'I hope you don't feel like I'm taking advantage. You're so good with them.'

'Sweetheart, believe me, you're not taking advantage.' I gesture towards my crotch. 'If you want to try, though, you can start here.' Anything to make her laugh. Raise a reaction from her, though I'm not entirely joking.

'You're insatiable.' Her lips lift in a slight smile for the first time all day.

'You have that effect on me. No matter what else is going on in the world, Savannah, no matter what anyone says about us, we know what we have.'

'I just reimbursed my blog subscribers the last three months' subscription fees,' she says, sliding onto my lap and curling against my chest. 'I won't have them calling me a hypocrite.'

'You're not a hypocrite, honey. You're an inspiration. First, you prove you can go it alone. Then you prove you're brave enough to trust again after everything you've been through.' Finn's smarmy face fogs my vision again. I've never wanted to punch someone as much in my life.

'Can I ask you a question?' I rock back slightly so I can see her face.

'Sure.' There's a slight wariness in her tone.

'Why did you hide his identity for all these years? Why protect him?'

'Honestly, I'm beginning to wonder the same thing. Initially, I was ashamed because he was married.' Savannah's fingers thrum over her mouth.

'That wasn't your fault.' I cup her chin and tilt her eyes to me.

'It's taken me almost seven years, but I'm finally beginning to realise that. Did you call Lucas?' Her hand moves to the base of my neck, threading through my hair.

'Not yet. It wasn't a conversation I wanted to have in front of the girls.' I readjust Savannah on my lap to reach for my phone in my pocket.

'You know I've been thinking...' She sucks the inside of her cheek. 'I was wondering if I should do it after all?'

'Seriously?' I flip her around to face me, positioning her legs either side of my hips.

'Yeah, I mean, it was my big break. And I worked so damn hard to be ready for it. I hate the fact that... he,' it's like she can't even bring herself to say his name, 'is the one to take that from me. And with my Single Sav business collapsing around me, the money might come in handy too.'

'Don't worry about the money. I'll take care of everything.' I sweep my hand over her thigh in a reassuring motion. 'You're not Single Sav anymore,' I remind her.

'It's not just about the money, Ro. If I don't do the shoot, it looks as if Coral Chic is condemning me too, when in reality they're the only company that gave us the chance to speak out.'

'I know. I get that. But can you seriously stand next to him and smile for the shoot?'

'No, I can't.' Silver flecks sparkle in her irises. 'But I don't plan to. He's got away with far too much, for far too long. And it stops today.'

Chapter Forty-One

SAVANNAH

The day of the shoot dawns bright and warm. As far as summers go in Ireland, it's the best we've had in a decade. For that, I should be grateful. At least the sea conditions are good. I thought facing the water was going to be the biggest challenge of this job, but facing my ex is so much worse.

Finn must know I'm the female model. It's been all over Instagram.

Is he stupid enough to think we can work together amicably?

Or does he think I'm too meek to protest?

I've run over every possible scenario in my head. What he might say when he sees me. What I might say. What Lucas will say when he realises the connection between us.

I could have called Lucas, explained the situation. I could have told him that Finn is the father of my children, but he said it himself, my reputation is in tatters. If Finn denied it and Lucas believed him over me, I'd have lost the Coral Chic contract and the chance to defend mine and Ronan's romance. Plus, Lucas needs to know what type of a snake he's dealing with, and after all these years of staying silent, it will give me immense satisfaction to tell him.

Even though it's terrifying, deep down, a part of me *wants* to confront him. Wants to ask him why he never once enquired about his children.

I jog down the stairs to where Ronan is giving the girls their breakfast. 'You sure you don't mind taking the girls to school again?' I check for the hundredth time.

'I may as well get used to it.' Ronan is leaning against the kitchen counter in a pair of dressy shorts and a fitted white t-shirt that sculpts his pecs to perfection, scrolling on his phone.

'Mammy, did you pack me a dress to change into at Phoebe's house?' Isla asks over her Coco Pops.

'Yep, sure did.' I ruffle my daughter's dark hair. 'I packed you the pink unicorn one and Eden, I packed the purple unicorn one for you.'

'Thanks, Mammy.' Eden and Isla beam with excitement.

A buzzing sound catches my attention and I pause, listening for the source. It's coming from Ronan's pocket. He pulls his phone from his pocket and stares at the screen, but makes no move to answer it.

'Who is it?'

'Unknown caller.' He tilts the screen towards me.

'Maybe you should answer it?'

'No. If it's important, they'll leave a message.' He shoves it back in his pocket. When the vibrating starts again, he continues to ignore it.

I shake away the niggling insecurity. Today is a big day with the shoot and understandably I'm jittery.

Grabbing my keys and my bag, I kiss the girls goodbye. I haven't had time to get a new phone yet and in truth I haven't missed the million notifications filled with other people's opinions of me. 'Have a great time at Phoebe's, okay? Mammy loves you so much. I'll see you tomorrow.'

Eden wraps her tiny arms around my neck and squeezes while Isla merely waves.

Ronan walks me to the front door and out onto the top step. The sun is blinding. I pull my sunglasses from my head and push them up onto my nose.

Ronan presses a quick kiss to my lips. 'I'll be right behind you.' His strong supple arms pull me flush against his chest in a reassuring embrace.

The buzzing continues in his pocket.

'You promise?' I check. My hands are shaking, my legs feel like jelly, but with Ronan by my side, I can do this. I know I can.

Ronan presses another kiss to my lips and squeezes my shoulders encouragingly. 'I promise I'll be there. I've got you.'

Half an hour later, I pull up at the Velvet Strand, one of Dublin's most scenic beaches. It's been cordoned off from the public with white and red striped tape, like it's a crime scene. It might just turn into one yet, if Ronan can't control his rage. Any time Finn's name has come up this week, a vein pulses furiously in Ronan's temple and his fists clench into tight, angry balls.

The tide is out, leaving plenty of room on the beach for a huge coral-coloured marquee, which I assume is our base for the day. Burly security guys man the vicinity, halting any attempts to infiltrate the area. Several passers-by stop to stare, scanning the space for the source of excitement. I strut across the grass, taking deep controlled breaths.

A grey-haired woman with a clipboard approaches as I duck underneath the tape.

'Savannah.' She positively beams at me. Her voice is familiar from our telephone conversations.

'Susie. It's great to meet you.' And to find a friendly face in a sea of strange ones. I raise my hand to my face to shield the sun from my eyes as I scan the beach. There's no sign of Finn yet. My stomach churns.

'And you, too. We've been so lucky with the weather this year, haven't we?' Susie's small talk is doing nothing to distract me from the situation at hand.

Susie steers me by my elbow towards the marquee. 'This way to hair and make-up.'

'Where's Ronan?' Susie ducks through the opening of the marquee, the makeshift doors flapping in the gentle breeze.

I follow her in. 'Dropping the girls to school. He'll be here soon.'

A niggling inner voice pipes up out of the blue *What if he's not? What if he doesn't show up and I'm left standing here like a fucking fool all on my own?*

I mentally shake myself.

Ronan is not Finn. He's not married. He'd never hurt me. He'd never let me down.

The hair and make-up staff manage to tame my hair into perfectly tousled-looking beach waves. My complexion looks naturally sun-kissed, even if it took over an hour of dabbing and patting to hide the pallor at the prospect of facing the man who put me off men for years.

There's still no sign of Ronan. Panic swells in my stomach with every passing second. I need him. He's like my six-foot-two security blanket. My own personal life raft.

I was worried about the water, but it's not the sea that's threatening to sink me.

Where is he?

Maybe he couldn't get past the security. I reach for my

bag, digging around for my phone before remembering I still don't have one.

I inhale deeply through my nose, trying to quell the anxiety.

Susie returns with her clipboard, her gaze roaming over my bikini-clad body. The first bikini I'm modelling is a strapless number made from uplifting synthetic material, in a vibrant shade of coral, just like its brand name 'Perhaps a slight bit more bronzer across here,' she points to my chest, 'to accentuate the collarbone.'

Two of the make-up artists dart over with brushes in hand while I continue to obsess about where my boyfriend is.

Susie gives me another once over and nods. 'The camera crew is waiting for you. Where is Ronan?'

'He's on the way,' I say, with a lot less certainty than I did an hour earlier.

He wouldn't let me down.

Would he?

I haven't been the best judge of character when it comes to men.

Ronan's different, though.

He loves me.

Finn said the same thing though, didn't he?

Fuck.

I already feel like I'm drowning, and I haven't put a foot in the water yet.

Susie leads the way through the marquee and out of the doors. I follow her into the heat of the sun and look around for my boyfriend, but there's no sign of him.

'Ah, at least your male counterpart is on time.' Susie nods to where the sea slaps the shore.

Two men stand facing each other, engrossed in conversation. From this far away, the context isn't clear, but the boyish backslapping and raucous laughter radiates a playful vibe.

Lucas Beechwood is on the right, wearing sand-coloured shorts and a fitted shirt.

The other, wearing Coral Chic for Him shorts and no shirt, looks sickeningly familiar. A million memories of our time together play like one of those digital photo frames in my mind.

Nausea rushes from my stomach to my sternum. Where is Ronan?

I'm not ready for this. I'm not ready for this. I'm not ready for this.

As if Finn senses my eyes on his back, his head twists, and narrow eyes stare back at me, the exact same shade of hazel as my daughters'.

And for the first time in seven years, I come face to face with Finn fucking Riley.

Chapter Forty-Two
RONAN

As a rule, I never answer withheld numbers. It's usually someone trying to sell me something I don't want, or a sports journalist chancing their arm looking for an interview, or an ex. I don't have time to deal with any of those right now, but by the time I drop the kids at St. Jude's, the phone rings for the thirtieth time.

I have somewhere I need to be. Savannah didn't get the support she deserved this morning because I was distracted, not just by these calls, but by overthinking the logistics of moving in with her.

Should I sell my apartment, or rent it out?

Should I propose to her?

Or is it too soon?

I don't want to terrify her by coming on too strong, but isn't committing to living together and raising kids together an even bigger commitment than marriage?

I've wanted her for so long, I'm terrified I'll fuck it up at the last hurdle. I'm so close to reaching everything I ever wanted, I'm scared it'll slip through my fingers.

Another incoming call resounds through the car speaker

system. I hit the green button flashing on the dash of my in-car speaker system out of sheer irritation, because I can't think straight.

'Someone better be dying,' I bark, rage rippling through my core.

'Thank fuck.' My friend Jake's haggard tone seeps through the air and straight under my skin.

'Jake, what is it? Are you okay?' Panic pools inside.

'I've been trying to get you all morning. It's Jess. They airlifted her to Dublin National Maternity Hospital in the early hours of the morning. She started haemorrhaging.' His voice cracks with emotion. 'There was so much blood, Ro. It was everywhere. The baby. I don't know if they made it...'

'Where are you?' I glance at the clock. I'm forty minutes away from the hospital, give or take, depending on traffic.

'In the car. I'm about two hours away. They wouldn't let me travel with her. I can't get there quickly enough. Can't get through to anyone on the phone. I keep getting the same bulldog of a receptionist who won't tell me anything. You're closer than me, bro, can you please go to the hospital? Find out what's happening. I'll get there as soon as I can, but I can't bear the thought of Jess being alone. If anything happens to her... or the baby.'

Jake's had my back since the day we met. Through training. Through competitions. When I struggled to adjust after retirement. But it's the biggest day of Savannah's life too. Guilt twists my guts. I hate having to choose between the two people I love most in this world.

I glance at the dash. She's doing the solo shoots first. Finn shouldn't be anywhere near her until this afternoon. The thought of that makes my blood boil, but this is life or death. If something happened to Jess or the baby, I'd never forgive myself.

I'll make it for the interview.

I suck in a breath and blow it out slowly. 'I'm on my way.'

'Thank you, thank you, thank you, thank you.' Jake's relief resonates through the car.

'Call me as soon as you find out anything. I'll keep calling from here. I had to switch my number to private because the receptionist must have caller ID and she keeps answering my calls with "I still don't have an update".'

That explains that then.

'I'll call you within the hour, I promise.'

'Thanks, man. I owe you.' Jake sounds like he's on the verge of tears.

'You owe me nothing.' I hang up. I need to call Savannah and explain what's happening.

I scroll through my contacts until I find her details, listed under 'Future Wife.'

It rings and rings until her answerphone kicks in. 'You've reached Savannah. Leave a message and I'll get back to you.'

Fuck it, she's got no phone. I should have insisted we replace it immediately, but after everything, she liked the idea of a few days reprieve from the millions of notifications.

Forty minutes later, I pull up outside the hospital. There's no parking anywhere. Fuck my life, of all the days. I crawl around the car park twice before finally giving up and abandoning the Tesla outside the hospital doors. I'll pay the fine. Whatever.

The sickly scent of disinfectant hits my nostrils as I enter the building. I run towards the reception desk, but there's no one behind it and the phones are ringing off the hook. A small bronze bell sits to the left of a leather-bound clipboard and a medical history form. I press my finger on the bell and leave it there for a good ten seconds.

Two harassed-looking receptionists emerge from a room

behind the desk, each clutching chipped china mugs, each wearing an expression of irritation.

'Can I help you?' One of them who's wearing thick red-rimmed glasses, her grey hair twisted into an elegant bun on top of her head, asks. She radiates a no-nonsense sort of headmistress vibe.

'Yes. Jessica Jones was airlifted here this morning from Ballyshanway. I'm her...' I scratch my head, 'brother.'

'Really.' She arches her eyebrows. 'And there was me thinking you looked awfully like that swimming champion. The one that's supposedly dating the single mam blogger.'

'Okay. I'm Ronan Rivers, and yes, I'm dating Savannah.' I bang the flat of my hand on the wooden desk hard enough to startle them. 'Now please, for the love of God, tell me where Jess is. She and Jake are like family to me. I need an update.'

She pushes her glasses up on her nose, takes a seat behind the glass panel and places her mug on the worn wooden desk. Her fingers glide across the keyboard as she stares at a computer screen.

Finally.

'What room is she in? I need to see her.'

She glances up after a few seconds of scrolling and clicking, sympathy creasing the corner of her eye. 'I'm afraid that won't be possible.'

'What do you mean, it's not possible? What's happening?' I pace back and forth and fling my hands in the air in frustration. No wonder Jake is going out of his mind. If that was Savannah in there, I'd be sick with worry.

She tsks, more to herself than me, I think. 'She's in surgery right now. You can't go in.'

'What kind of surgery? Is she going to be okay? Is the baby okay?'

The other receptionist steps forward with a haughty expression. Her index finger taps the name badge pinned to the front of her navy and green striped blouse. 'See this,' she says. 'Receptionist. We aren't doctors, pal. We understand your frustration, but we can't tell you what we don't know.'

My chest tightens as I rest my head against the glass panel. 'Well, can you point me in the direction of someone who can? *Someone* must know what's going on around here.'

'Family waiting room is at the end of the corridor. Turn right, then left again. Someone will be out to you as soon as they can. If anyone asks, you're her brother.'

I take off down the corridor, tossing a 'thank you' over my shoulder as an afterthought.

The waiting room is overflowing with people. Men, women, children. All of them wearing expressions of worry or fatigue.

There's one free seat available and I take it, deliberately avoiding eye contact with anyone. The last thing I need is the 'are you Ronan Rivers?' shit right now.

Pulling out my phone, I text Jake, explaining I'm here and waiting for an update

Of all the days.

I'm just grateful it's not Savannah in surgery.

An hour and a half later, a white-haired man in his sixties enters the room. The disposable doctor's hat and navy scrubs eliminate the need for an introduction. 'Mr James,' he calls, scanning the room.

I leap to my feet and follow him out of the room into the lime green corridor.

'Your wife is out of surgery.' His neutral expression gives away absolutely nothing.

I open my mouth, ready to correct him, then close it again.

'It was touch and go. She lost a lot of blood, but she's going to be okay.'

'Oh, thank God.' I exhale the breath I'd been holding. 'And the baby?'

His lips crook upwards into a small, weathered smile. 'Congratulations, you have a son.'

I clutch my chest, as if to silence the hammering of my heart. 'Can I see them?'

'Your wife,' he raises a questioning white eyebrow at me, 'is in recovery, sleeping off the anaesthetic. I don't expect her to wake for at least another hour. Your son is in NICU, receiving oxygen. A nurse will be down shortly to take you to him. Given his premature arrival, he could be in there for a few weeks. It could be a long road, but they're both in great hands.'

'Thank you so much, doctor.' I could cry with relief, so I fully expect Jake to.

'You're welcome, Mr Rivers.' Knowing eyes gleam. 'Pity you didn't get the third gold. It really would have been something. How's the shoulder now?'

I should have known better than to pretend to impersonate Jake James.

'It's okay. I won't be winning any medals anytime soon, but thankfully, there are more important things in life.'

'That there is, son.' He offers a curt nod before turning on his heels and striding away.

I whip out my phone. Jake answers on the first ring. 'Any news?'

'Jess is okay. She's in recovery, but she's fine.'

Jake's exhaled breath is thick with relief. 'And the baby?'

'Congratulations, Daddy. You have a son.'

'A son!' His whoop threatens to burst my eardrum.

'Where are you?' I pace the corridor, not wanting to leave until he gets here, but acutely conscious of my other commitments to Savannah today.

'About forty-five minutes away.'

'I'm so sorry man, but I need to go. I have somewhere I need to be, but I promise I'll come back later.'

'You don't need to,' he says. 'You've done enough. Thank you. Just knowing you were there made the waiting that bit easier.'

'It was the least I could do.' It's the truth.

'See you soon, Vito.'

'Vito?' I don't get it.

'Vito Corleone. You know, the Godfather.'

I roll my eyes. 'Drive safe.'

I race out the hospital doors back to my car, and no doubt a hefty fine. Fuck it. It was worth every cent.

Chapter Forty-Three
SAVANNAH

'Are you okay?' Susie stops and turns towards me. 'You look like you've seen a ghost.' Her big brown eyes are wide with concern.

My feet are rooted to the sand.

Finn fuckface Riley stares back at me without so much as a flicker of remorse. The man treated me worse than a dog and he's standing there smiling at me like we're old fucking friends.

Get Fit With Finn is his mantra. It should be get fucked with Finn.

'Do you need something?' Susie steps forward.

'I...' I need my boyfriend.

No, truthfully, I don't need him. I want him, and that is wildly different.

Finn's thin lips press into a smirk, and something flicks like a switch inside of me.

A pint-sized shot of adrenaline shoots from my adrenal glands straight into my bloodstream as I eye the men before me.

I've stood on my own for six hard years.

Put the work in to get where I am today.

Whether I'm Single Sav or Sassy Sav, I am a strong, capable woman, and I can confront this prick, with or without Ronan.

'I've got you.' Ronan's words from the last time we were here whisper into my subconscious.

The reality of the situation is, I've got me.

Ronan might have been the reason I initially gave up my single status, he was the one to pull down the wall I've been hiding behind, but truthfully, I gave it all up for me. For that little girl who used to walk around with a pillow on her head singing *Here Comes the Bride*. For the woman who built up an entire persona to hide behind.

Abby Connolly asked me for advice all those weeks ago and it rolled from my tongue. *'Don't let anyone put you in a box because that's what they're comfortable with.'*

The truth is, I put myself in a box for safekeeping.

I'm sick of playing it safe.

Sick of sleeping my way through this life, frightened to open my mouth, frightened to chase after something I want in case I get hurt, or someone leaves me.

Whatever this life throws at me, I'll deal with it. Like I've always done.

'Do you feel okay, Savannah? Is it the heat?' Susie's pristinely shaped eyebrows draw together. 'I'll go get you some water.' She turns and stalks back to the marquee.

'I feel great,' I mutter, but she's already gone. Straightening my spine, I stride towards the shoreline.

'Finn.' My gaze roams over the man I once thought I loved. I feel nothing for him now. Nothing but disgust. I flick my hair from my shoulders and jut my chin. 'It's been a while.'

'You guys know each other?' Lucas steps towards me, a curious expression etched onto his handsome face.

'Not really,' I bite. 'I thought I knew him a long time ago. Turns out I didn't know him at all.'

Finn's not as tall as I remembered, nor as broad, but there's no denying the man is ripped. He'd have to be, given his job, I guess. He's nowhere near as big as Ronan, in any sense of the word. His gym chain might be called Peak Performance, but he rarely made me peak in any shape or form.

His dark hair is styled into a quiff, which makes him look like he spent more time in the bathroom than any self-respecting man.

Hued hazel eyes, the same shade as Eden and Isla's flicker close. Finn flinches like he's been sliced with a knife, but he recovers quickly, a smarmy smile splitting his face, exposing unnaturally white teeth. 'Savannah used to train at one of the first gyms I worked at.'

'Oh, what a small world.' Lucas frowns like he's one piece short of a jigsaw puzzle. 'I thought Finn would be the perfect role model for what we're trying to capture at Coral Chic. His success, like yours, Savannah, has soared in the past few years.' Lucas's head jerks towards Finn. 'How many gyms do you own now?'

'Twelve across the UK.' Finn's face stretches into a smug expression. 'Lucas and I are discussing a potential flagship branch in Dublin.'

'Over my dead body,' I spit. My lips tremble. Rage roils from the top of my head to the tips of my toes.

Lucas takes a step back, recoiling in horror.

'Oh, don't be like that, Sav. We used to be buddies.' Finn has the audacity to step closer and bump his elbow against mine. The contact makes me want to physically vomit.

Yeah, fuck buddies.

Except I didn't get that memo. I stupidly thought him spending most evenings at my place meant we were together.

God, I was so naïve.

Not anymore.

'From what I've been hearing, you've got a new buddy now.' Finn waggles his eyebrows. The man clearly has a death wish. 'Single Sav has been sneaking around again. Naughty girl.'

Is this fucker for real?

'I wasn't the one sneaking around.' My fingers knit into tight fists. Blood throbs furiously through my temple. I'm shaking with a red-hot uncontrollable rage.

'Neither was I.' Finn puffs out his chest like a pigeon and folds his arms. How did I ever find this man attractive? He physically repulses me. 'Cheryl doesn't care who I fuck, as long as it doesn't damage our reputation or affect our fitness brand.'

Lucas's jaw almost hits the beach. 'You two were...?'

'Shame you didn't share that teeny tiny nugget of information with me before you got me pregnant. Your daughters are fine, by the way. Good of you to ask.'

Finn's face falters and his eyes flick to the floor. 'I never wanted children. They're not part of my plan. I told you if you went ahead with the pregnancy, you were on your own.'

I raise my index finger and point it at his chest like a pistol. 'And on my own, I have been. Through the nappies, bottles, reflux, toilet training. Through the good days, the bad days, and every damn day— and I wouldn't change a single thing.'

Lucas has turned the same shade as the white fluffy clouds lining the sky. 'How could you?' His torso twists to Finn, accusation heavy in his tone.

Finn raises his hands in protest.

'You didn't think to mention any of this to me?' Lucas's mouth tightens in a grimace.

'He probably thought I'd keep my mouth shut and get on

with it like I have done for the last seven years.' I fold my arms across my chest. 'But it seems everyone else in this world is entitled to shoot their mouth off, so I figured it was my turn.'

Finn's eyes are so wide, they look like they might explode. 'Those girls probably aren't even mine,' he snorts.

'You're damn right they're not yours.' Ronan appears from nowhere, his palm splaying across the base of my spine. 'They're mine now. I'll be a better father to them than you could ever be, you spineless fuck. Just because your wife's okay with you being a cheating shithead, I'm not. This woman,' he motions to me, 'deserves so much better.'

The sight of Ronan, sweaty and apologetic, sends a shiver of relief through my ribcage. He's okay. We're okay. My disappointment he got delayed dissipates. He's here now. He'll always be here for me. I don't need him, but I want him more than ever.

I turn to Finn, who's eyeing Ronan with a wary trepidation, and rightly so. 'You didn't call once. You never sent a single cent. Not that I'd have taken it. I didn't need it and I certainly didn't want it, but you didn't know that. What kind of a man are you?'

'Not the kind we want representing Coral Chic.' Lucas steps forwards with a thunderous expression furrowing his features.

'You've got to be kidding?' Finn's face is furious. 'I flew in from London for this. I cancelled a one-to-one training session with one of the Spice Girls, and tonight's slot on The One Show, and now you're telling me because of some slu–'

Ronan's fist connects with Finn's face and a sickening but satisfying crunch cuts through the air as Finn's nose breaks. Blood gushes across the front of his chest, crimson liquid flowing like a waterfall.

'You broke my fucking nose,' he screeches, catching it in

his hands, gazing at it like he's never seen blood before. 'You'll pay for this. You and your who–.'

Ronan steps forwards with a murderous expression glinting in his ice-cold irises. I place a hand on his heaving chest to steady him. The last thing I want is a lawsuit. He'd lose his job teaching, all because of a pathetic little shit and his sharp tongue.

Ronan growls. 'Don't you ever talk about my woman that way again. Or it won't just be your nose. It'll be every bone in your gutless body.'

'You'll be hearing from my lawyer,' Finn shouts over his shoulder as he staggers across the beach and up to the main road.

'I didn't see anything, did you?' Lucas inhales heavily and blows out a breath. 'Savannah, I am so sorry. I had absolutely no idea you'd had a previous relationship with Finn.'

'You weren't to know. But I couldn't let you go into business with him not knowing.'

'And I'm sorry if I misjudged you, too.' Lucas extends a hand to Ronan. Ronan eyes it for a second, then shakes it resignedly. 'You clearly care about Savannah a lot.'

'I love her,' Ronan says simply.

'It's not hard to see why.' Lucas crooks his lips and plucks his phone out of his pocket. 'I just need to make a quick call.' He backs, leaving Ronan and me alone.

'Where have you been?' Though truthfully, wherever he was, he's here now. And breaking Finn's nose more than made up for it.

'It was Jake calling on repeat this morning. Jess got airlifted to Dublin Maternity Hospital. He was out of his mind because he couldn't go with her, so he asked me to get there as quickly as I could.' Ronan rakes his fingers through his hair, genuinely distraught.

'Is Jess okay? The baby?' He didn't abandon me. He's

nothing like Finn. He'd never hurt me. He's the best man I know.

'She is now. She's out of surgery. They had a baby boy.' Ronan's eyes well with emotion. 'Jake just sent me a picture. You should see him, Sav, he's the tiniest thing I ever saw, but my god he's so gorgeous.'

'You're gorgeous.' I take a step towards my man and his hands hook around my waist.

'I'm so sorry I let you down, baby.' The sincerity in his tone leaves no room for doubt or insecurity. Especially given he just punched my ex in the face. There was something so fucking hot about having Ronan stick up for me.

Lucas steps closer, having finished his phone call. 'So, it looks like I'll be needing a new male ambassador...' Lucas says to Ronan.

Ronan's eyes capture mine with an unspoken question, and I nod. This shoot was what brought us together. It's only fitting that we do it together.

'In that case, get over to hair and make-up.' Lucas points to the marquee. 'And separate changing rooms, you two. This is a family-friendly brand.'

'There's nothing family-friendly about what I'm going to do to you later,' Ronan murmurs, his hot breath tickling my earlobe.

'I heard that.' Lucas tuts. 'You are one lucky, lucky fucker.'

'Believe me, I know.' Ronan's lips land on mine and the rest of the world melts.

Chapter Forty-Four
RONAN

For a man who hates the camera, I'm doing a good job of hiding it. The crew instructs us to strike a million different stances.

'Now, Savannah,' the lead cameraman shouts, 'if you could lie on your back and float with your arms stretched wide and a grin up at the sky like you're living your best life.'

'I *am* living my best life.' She shoots me a grin.

After almost two hours in the water and seven different outfit changes, my skin is turning blue and my teeth are chattering despite the afternoon sun. Savannah's nipples are like bullets, and I am dying to do something about it.

'That's a wrap,' Susie shouts, beckoning us out of the sea.

'You did it, baby. You faced all your fears today.' My hand slides across Savannah's peachy ass as we wade out of the water.

'I know.' Her head angles up towards mine, the sunlight dancing over her cheekbones. 'Thank you for facing them with me.'

'You look like you need a hot bath.' I grab the thick fluffy Coral Chic towel Susie hands me and wrap it around Savannah's body, pulling her into me. Cameras click behind us, despite the formal shoot being over.

'I'd love one. But we have an interview to do first,' Savannah reminds me.

'I've spent the entire day counting the seconds until I can bend you over, devour you, and then fuck you until you scream,' I rasp in her ear.

She sucks in a short breath. 'There's that filthy mouth I love again.'

'You're going to love it even more when it's devouring your pussy.'

'Better not say that on camera. Coral Chic ambassadors are supposed to be "wholesome".' Savannah uses her fingers to make an air quote, then presses a kiss to the tip of my nose.

'Let's do this.' The quicker we get it done, the quicker I can do her.

Lucas steps in front of an iPad secured by a freestanding ring light and taps the screen. He counts down with his fingers to show we're going live. He lets it run for a few minutes, presumably to maximise the viewers. Eventually, he clears his throat and starts.

'Hi, I'm Lucas Beechwood coming to you from Coral Chic's swimwear shoot at Velvet Strand beach. I'm sure most of you are aware of the scandal surrounding our new brand ambassador, Savannah Kingsley, this week.' He pauses for dramatic effect, beckoning us over.

She had to take the lead on facing Finn. She's not going to have to take the lead on this, too. As we stride forwards, I keep my arms firmly wrapped around Savannah's shoulders.

'This is so weird,' I mutter in her ear as we stand in front of the iPad, and she giggles.

'Don't worry, I'll do all the talking. I know you hate it.'

She steps in front of me, her back flush to my front, both of us still wet from the water.

'Do I just talk into the camera like someone is actually listening?' I frown. The sun isn't helping with the visibility.

Lucas laughs. 'Someone *is* actually listening.' Lucas laughs and points to a number at the corner of the screen, which is increasing by the thousands with every passing second.

Savannah opens her mouth to speak, but I silence her with a quick, fleeting kiss.

Lucas clears his throat pointedly and nods towards the numbers again. 'Okay, well in that case, I'm here to tell you that I am in love with the woman many of you know as Single Sav. Coral Chic's brand ambassador. And Lucas, you couldn't have picked a better one to represent your business.

'I became obsessed with Savannah the day she totalled my Aston Martin two years ago, and I'm still obsessed with her.'

Her cheeks flush crimson as she grins. 'The feeling is mutual.'

'She came to me looking for swimming lessons to prepare for this very shoot, but we ended up falling in love. Savannah has experienced a huge backlash for coming out as my girlfriend. She's been called a hypocrite by people who are supposed to be her fans. She's not a hypocrite. The woman is a goddamn hero.'

'Language. Wholesome, remember,' Lucas murmurs.

'She was hurt so badly by the father of her children, she thought she'd never let anyone in again. The fact that she's brave enough to do so now shouldn't be condemned, it should be applauded.'

Savannah squirms next to me, and I tilt my head to face her instead of the stupid camera. 'It's true, baby. I love you so much. I'm so proud of you.'

I catch her lips with mine and Lucas hits a button to end the live broadcast.

'Well, that will give them something to think about,' Lucas chuckles. 'I fully expect the new range to sell out in seconds. We might be a wholesome business, but sex still sells, and you two are radiating it.'

He's not wrong. Which is why we need to go home and make the most of the girls being at their sleepover.

'There's a launch night in the Shelbourne in two weeks to celebrate the new range. As brand ambassadors, I do hope you'll both be there.' Lucas extends his hand again.

'Of course.'

'Thanks Lucas.' Savannah presses a kiss against his cheek. 'Everyone else had pretty much written me off but you.'

'The only thing I'm writing is your cheque. You did brilliantly, both of you. I hope we can work together for a long time.' His deep brown eyes crinkle at the corners as the angles of his mouth turn up. 'I still can't believe you're with him when you could have had this,' he jokes, pointing to himself.

'Careful, Lucas,' I warn playfully. 'I was just beginning to think you and I might become friends.'

'Funny you should mention it. I was thinking the same thing. I have a business proposition for you.' Lucas roams a thumb over his chin. 'I'll call you next week.'

'Do.' I'm not in the mood to hear anything other than the moan of Savannah as she writhes beneath me.

Forty minutes later, we're home, and the house is blissfully silent. As much as I love those girls, I love this time with Savannah even more.

'What are you waiting for?' She heads to the fridge, grabs a bottle of Bollinger and two champagne flutes, and motions to the stairs. 'Let's fill the jacuzzi.'

I like her thinking, but I'm going to have to get creative. I wasn't joking when I said I've been dreaming all damn day about kneeling between her parted legs and licking her until she comes undone. Watching her parading around in that sexy swimwear was almost as sexy as seeing her stand up to her prick of an ex.

When I reach the bathroom, she's leaning against the side of the tub, waiting for it to fill. Bringing the Bollinger bottle to her luscious lips, she tears the gold foil with her teeth, then pops the cork.

'I like your style.' I take the bottle, pour it into the glasses and hand her one. 'Have you got any panties on?' My fingertips skim the underside of her tiny skirt.

'Yes.' Her pupils dilate and her nipples visibly stiffen beneath her flimsy top.

'Be a good girl and take them off for me.' I step back to watch the show. The bath isn't even halfway full. I bet I can make her come before it's anywhere near overflowing.

She places her glass on the mosaic tiles at the edge of the bath. Her fingers disappear beneath her skirt and two seconds later, we both watch a scrap of white lace descend over her thighs and float to the floor.

'Such a good girl.' Her eyes rise to meet mine, loaded with lust. Her fingers go to her waistband, but I grab them and stop her. 'Leave it on.' I love the idea of my head under her skirt.

I nudge her backwards until the backs of her legs touch the ceramic of the bath. 'Sit down, open your legs and drink your champagne. We have a lot to celebrate.'

She perches on the edge of the tub, clutching her champagne like the queen that she is. My queen. The heart-shaped eyes she's throwing me only further fuels the caveman inside.

Mine.

She's all mine.

I drop to my knees on the hard-tiled floor, part her thighs wider with my hands, and then bury my face in her sex, and worship her with every flick of my tongue without taking my eyes from hers. I love watching her get off. I love being the one to get her off. But most of all, I just love her.

Her pink painted fingers rake through my hair, nails dig into my scalp. She squirms and writhes with every stroke. Her legs begin to tremble and tighten. The hand holding the champagne trembles as she brings it to her mouth and sips. We don't break our stare.

She watches me, on my knees for her. I'll get on my knees again for her very soon, for a very different purpose, but for now, I want her to feel adored. To know how special she is. To understand that I will do absolutely anything for her. Everything for her, if she'll let me.

I'm going to marry her.

I'm going to put my babies in her stomach.

And I'm going to give her everything she never had before.

Security, stability, but most of all, love.

'Ronan,' she moans. 'I'm going to...' And she shatters as I work my mouth over her, worshipping her until she protests and pushes my head away.

The bath isn't even three quarters full.

Satisfaction coils in my core.

'Your turn.' She smooths the denim back over the tops of her thighs and stands shakily.

I rise from my knees, kiss her mouth, then spin her around until she's facing the bath. 'Turn the water off. I'm nowhere near finished with you yet.'

She bends over and I get a flash of her glistening folds. She twists the taps off. The room goes oddly silent, bar our ragged breathing and the furious beating of my heart.

I place my palm on the small of her back, motioning for her to stay bent over the tub, in the exact angle I've been fantasising about all day. Her head cranes and her eyes meet mine with understanding. I tug my shorts down and immerse myself in Savannah's tight, hot walls, inch by life-affirming inch.

'I love your pussy.'

'It loves you too.' Savannah thrusts backwards, her ass striking my skin with a sexy slap.

'I've wanted you so badly, for so, so long.' My hands grip her hips, fingertips sinking into her skin as I drive into her.

'I'm yours, Ro.' White-tipped fingers grip the side of the bath as I give her everything I've got.

Fire builds in my groin, the temperature rising with every passing second. I can't hold on much longer. I reach around, my fingers skimming Savannah's soft satiny flesh, searching for her sweet spot to drag her into devastation with me. My thumb circles as my hips drive both of us over the edge.

Her walls tighten in a vice-like grip and my dick doesn't stand a chance. Static blurs my vision as her pussy pulses on my cock and a million stars shoot through me, catapulting me sky-high into my personal hedonistic heaven.

Afterwards, she sits between my legs, her glossy hair secured high on her head as it rests against my chest, and we sip our champagne. The jets spray against my shoulders, massaging every ounce of tension from my muscles.

If I died right now, I'd die a fucking happy man. But I'm not planning on checking out yet. Not when things are finally starting to go my way.

EPILOGUE
One year later

Savannah

My ivory silk dress cups my breasts and accentuates my narrow waist before extending all the way to the floor.

My hair is loose in bohemian-style waves, embellished with an orchid rather than jewels.

My veil is short and light, but it makes a satisfying swishing noise when I tilt my head, exactly the way I imagined it would when I was a child.

My feet are bare, the sand warm beneath my toes.

For a woman who never went to the beach, I've certainly made up for it since. The sun beats down on our shoulders as we stand under a floral archway mere metres away from the Atlantic. Not the Irish side. The Dominican Republic side. Punta Cana, to be precise. There was no way I was relying on the Irish sun for an event this important.

My gaze roams over the crowd, taking in each and every one of our guests.

Steve and Stuart sit in white wicker chairs in the front row, Stuart dabbing his eyes with a brilliant white handkerchief while Steve rubs soothing circles on his back.

Ronan's mother, sisters, brother-in-law and baby, Mark, sit beside them, Mark grabbing fistfuls of Rachel's hair and laughing.

So many of our friends made the trip to be with us, including Lucas Beechwood, who sits three rows back with his new girlfriend, Felicity, a former Miss Ireland.

After the Coral Chic shoot last year, Lucas offered Ronan a partnership in the business. As well as designing and manufacturing sophisticated sculpting swimwear, they're now producing a practical swimwear range for professional athletes world-wide.

Ronan still teaches swimming at St. Jude's but only during the week these days now he no longer has to make excuses to see me every Saturday morning!

And as for me... I finally opened my own store on Grafton Street stocking my designer infant clothing range. My latest book, *Sassy Sav's Guide to Dating After Kids,* was a bestseller and I'm currently outlining another one loosely called *Sassy Sav's Guide To Getting Married*.

I glance down to where Isla and Eden flank my side, each clutching a bouquet of colourful, tropical blooms. In matching pastel pink dresses, they're the cutest flower girls I've ever seen. If the way Ronan's pageboys, Joseph and John, are looking at them, they think so too.

Ashley and Holly, my bridesmaids, stand to my right, wearing the same shade of pink as the twins and holding a more elaborate version of the girls' bouquets. Ashley brushes back a single tear from her cheek, while Holly beams like a kid in a candy store.

My stare returns to my almost husband standing in front of me. In navy dress shorts and a white fitted shirt, he looks every bit the poised groom. Rolled-up sleeves reveal strong tanned forearms, and the open collar flashes a hint of the smooth muscular chest beneath. A smile the size of a stadium stretches his lips and silver specks glitter the edge of his irises.

Ronan catches my hands, and a surge of electricity slithers over my skin. Our pupils lock as he slides a glittering diamond wedding band onto my fourth finger.

'You may kiss the bride,' the registrar announces.

Ronan's face inches down as I stretch up on my tiptoes until our mouths collide. He parts my lips with my tongue as he tugs my body flush to his. He is mine and I am his. And I probably was since the day I totalled his Aston Martin.

Our guests erupt, yelling, cheering, and clapping, but none so more than our daughters.

'Dad, that's gross,' Isla shouts. 'Put Mam down.'

The girls never asked Ronan if they could call him Dad, but they started the second he moved in with us, and it felt like the most natural thing in the world.

Ronan's palms roam over my ass, which he squeezes promisingly before releasing me. The love and light shining in his navy eyes are the mirror image of mine.

'We'll continue this later, wife.' His rich, deep baritone sets goosebumps soaring over my spine.

Our friends and family shower us with love and confetti as servers pass around trays of champagne and canapes.

A DJ sets up on the beach, blending rhythmic beats and reggae. Large circular tables are set with sparkling crystal for dinner right here on the sand as the waves caress the shore.

It's everything I ever dreamt of and so much more.

When the sun sets and the stars twinkle in the deep purple sky, the DJ calls us up for the first dance. My eyes shift to Ronan, then to Eden and Isla.

'Are you ready?' Ronan drags me to my feet as Beyonce's *Rule The World* floods the speakers and the four of us break into the dance routine Ronan and the twins made up all those months ago. Our guests cheer and roar with laughter.

My heart is full.

And so is my tummy. At only eleven weeks pregnant, I'm not showing yet. But that doesn't stop Ronan from stroking his huge hands over my stomach every night.

I've been called Single Sav, and Sassy Sav, but my favourite name, apart from Mam, will always be Mrs Rivers.

AFTERWORD

Dear Reader,

Thank you so much for reading Savannah and Ronan's story. Hope you enjoyed their steamy romance. Poor Savannah had been through enough- there was no way I could write a third act break-up for her and Ronan!

Ashley's story is set to release spring 2025. There's a good chance it will be earlier, but I'm planning on spending the rest of this year writing my L A Gallagher books....

If you haven't already seen Wreck Me, you can check out the blurb here...

Wreck Me

In the meantime, if you're not already part of my Facebook Reader Group, Lyndsey's Book Lushes, come hang out with me here...

https://www.facebook.com/groups/530398645913222

Lots of love,
Lyndsey xxx

ALSO BY LYNDSEY GALLAGHER

DATING FOR DECEMBER

Ava:

My perpetually single status hardly serves as a shining advertisement for HeartSync, the dating agency I own. Nor is it likely to convince my incredibly successful movie star brother, Nate, to invest in my business. Which is precisely why I agree to fake-date Cillian "can't-crack-a-smile" Callaghan for the month of December.

Sure, his role as a stoically single father and a notoriously grumpy divorce lawyer is far from ideal, but his silver eyes, sculptured shoulders and sharp tongue tick all the right boxes.

Even boxes that are supposed to remain, ahem, unticked...

One mistletoe kiss sparks a lust that could melt Lapland, and frosty fake dates blaze into something feverishly real...

Cillian:

I'm the country's most successful divorce lawyer. It doesn't take a genius to figure out why I don't date. Add in the fact that I'm a full-time single dad, even if I had the inclination, I don't have the time. But when my cheating ex blows back into town, the only way I can convince her it's over for good is by fake-dating someone else...

Enter Ava Jackson, with her infectious laugh, long legs, and luscious lips.

Throughout December, her witty one-liners and effortless bond with my daughter thaw my every defence.

She's everything I never knew I needed.

I'm an expert at breakups... but maybe it's time to master a love that lasts.... Dating For December

Dating For December

A FAKE DATING CHRISTMAS ROMANCE

Lyndsey Gallagher

FALLING FOR THE ROCKSTAR AT CHRISTMAS
SASHA

Ten years ago, I inherited our family castle and sole care of my youngest sister. More Cinderella, than Sleeping Beauty, at the mere age of twenty-eight I have a teenager to raise and a hotel to run. If the hotel is to survive past Christmas, I need a lottery win, a miracle, or Prince Charming himself to sweep in with a humongous... wad of cash.

When my super successful middle sister announces she's coming home for the holiday season, I'm determined to put my problems aside and make this the most fabulous Christmas ever. Especially as it might just be the last one in our family home.

I didn't factor in the return of my first love, **Ryan Cooper**. Back then he was the boy next door. Now, he's a world famous singer/song writer. We were supposed to go the States together. He left without me. Now he's back. Rumour is he has writers block. Apparently this is a last-ditch attempt to find inspiration before his record label pulls the plug permanently.

And guess where he wants to stay? You have it in one- the most inspiring castle hotel in Dublin's fair city.

Every woman in the city wants to pull this Hollywood Christmas cracker. Except me. I'm going to avoid him at all costs.

Easier said than done when he's parading around under my roof, with enough heat exuding from his molten eyes to melt every square inch of snow from the peaks of the Dublin mountains...

FALLING FOR THE ROCKSTAR AT CHRISTMAS- click to learn more

Falling For The Rock Star At Christmas

THE COLDEST HOLIDAY OF THE YEAR JUST GOT HOT...

Lyndsey Gallagher

FALLING FOR MY FORBIDDEN FLING
CHLOE

Even the name **Jayden Cooper** sends a hot flush of irritation through my veins. His rockstar brother might be about to marry my darling sister, but that does ***NOT*** make us family.

Thankfully, there's a continent separating me from his ridiculously attractive but super-smug face. And his arrogant tongue.

I'm rapidly carving my name in the glittering world of celebrity event management... and what better event to manage than the final farewell tour of my sister's fiancé, Ryan Cooper.

It's the biggest gig of my career.

Eight cities.

Eight concerts.

Eight opportunities to propel my business to a global level.

I couldn't turn it down if I wanted to.

The catch?

It involves working with closely with Ryan's agent- his brother, Jayden-Super-Smug-Cooper.

Going on tour with Jayden is almost as inconvenient as the hate-fuelled lust that steals the air straight from my lungs every time he's near.

Someone somewhere is testing me, but I've survived worse. And I'll survive him.

As long as I don't melt under the intensity of his smug but admittedly smouldering stare ...or fall foul of the talents of the aforementioned arrogant tongue...

Especially when technically...like it or not, we're about to be related.

JAYDEN

I've been through hell to get to where I am today.

I'm *the* best agent in Hollywood's cut-throat industry because I clawed and dragged myself there inch by excruciating inch.

Which is why I refuse to be bossed around by a pushy, Prada-wearing princess when it comes to organising my Rockstar brother's farewell tour. I've got bigger fish to fry, starting with upholding a promise I made a lifetime ago...

But Chloe is about to find out the hard way, what goes on tour stays on tour.

FALLING FOR MY FORBIDDEN FLING- click to learn more

FALLING FOR MY BODYGUARD
VICTORIA

As a student doctor, I deal with bullet wounds on a regular basis, but one teeny nightclub shooting is all it takes for my sister and her rock star husband to send me a new bodyguard/ babysitter.

The last person I expect to turn up is Archie "can't-bear-to-look-you-in-the-eye" Mason.

Now we're roommates until graduation. I can't turn around without tripping over him. If only I could trip underneath him. Because he is every bit as alluring as he was five years ago. And equally as unavailable.

But when my night terrors result in us sharing the same bed, our situation sparks a brand new danger.

One that could hurt both of us irreparably...

ARCHIE

I've been *obsessed* with Victoria Sexton for years.

If my boss and friend, Ryan Cooper, had any idea how bad I have it for his wife's little sister, he'd sack me on the spot.

Living with her is testing every inch of willpower I possess.

How can I watch her back when I can't stop imagining her on it?

FALLING FOR MY BODYGUARD- click to learn more

Falling For My Bodyguard

Lyndsey Gallagher

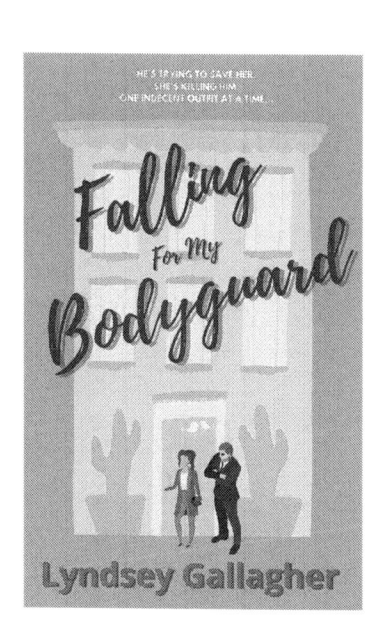

*HE'S TRYING TO SAVE HER.
SHE'S KILLING HIM.
ONE INDECENT OUTFIT AT A TIME...*

LOVE & OTHER MUSHY STUFF
ABBY

I need a man. Not in my bed, but for my radio show. I'm an eternally single agony aunt responsible for dishing out romantic advice to the nation. It would be funny if it weren't so tragic. I desperately need to up my ratings.

What better way than to employ one of the country's hottest rugby players to offer his take on love and other mushy stuff to the frenzied females of the nation?

Callum Connolly is the classic example of male perfection.

He's everything I need for my show and everything I don't need in my life…

CALLUM

I'm not looking for *the one*, merely for *the next one*. That is, until my teammates bet I can't keep the same woman long enough to bring to my best friend's wedding.

How hard can it be to date the same woman for three months?

When I bump into a beautiful DJ in a hotel spa, we strike an unlikely but alluring deal. I'll feature on her show and help up her ratings, if she fake dates me until after the wedding.

I don't bank on falling for her.

Especially when nailing her proves harder than nailing the most elusive touchdown ever…

https://mybook.to/Love_OtherMushyStuff

LOVE
& Other Manky Stuff

LYNDSEY GALLAGHER

LOVE & OTHER GAMES
<u>EMMA</u>

I spent one mind-blowing night with the country's hottest rugby hooker.

It was the best night of my life.

Transcendent, in fact.

And foolishly, I believed **Eddie Harrington** when he swore the feeling was mutual.

But it turns out, the man is a notorious player off the pitch, as well as on it.

They don't call him "Hooker Harrington" for nothing.

One year later, I board a flight to my best friends beach wedding, dreaming of sun, sea and sangria. The last person I expect to find in the seat next to mine is Eddie "love-them-and-leave-them" Harrington.

His best friend is about to marry mine.

I *hate* the ground he walks on, but to keep the peace, I'll play nicely.

Even when a mad twist of fate forces us to share a romantic, idyllic honeymoon suite, complete with only one ginormous, rose petal-covered bed.

Eddie is certain his practiced tactics will earn him a replay, but this time around, I'm sticking firmly to my game plan.

Even if the chemistry between us is hotter than the Croatian sun...

https://mybook.to/Love_

LOVE
& Other Games

LYNDSEY GALLAGHER

LOVE & OTHER LIES
<u>KERRY</u>

Who's unlucky enough to get sacked and evicted in the same week? Me. That's who. But a chance phone call with a witty, velvet-voiced stranger provides a stunning solution to both my problems.

Nathan's looking for a live-in nanny for his sunny five-year-old daughter and as fate has it, I have a degree in childcare, even though I swore I'd never use it.

Taking this job will force me to face demons I've been hiding from for a long time, but I have no choice but to accept.

It's only when I reach the magnificent Georgian house, my new home for the summer, I realise Nathan "the velvet-voiced stranger" is actually Nathan Kennedy, Ireland's most successful rugby player, and the only man I ever kissed when my boyfriend and I were on a break.

I can only pray one tiny (hot as hell) blip in my past doesn't ruin my future.

I need this job more than I've ever needed anything.

And worryingly, now I'm here, I want it more than I ever wanted anything too.

As the summer heats up, so does the escalating chemistry with my new boss.

Nathan's advances are becoming harder to resist.

And this time round, he swears he's playing for keeps...

https://mybook.to/love_and_other_lies

LOVE
& Other Lies

LYNDSEY GALLAGHER

LOVE & OTHER FORBIDDEN THINGS

AMY

I've always been a good girl, but for the first time in my life, I'm ready to do something bad...

Hot, half-naked men lurk everywhere I turn. But the one whose soul screams to mine wears the number six jersey, along with a look of sheer uninhibited desire.

Six has always been my lucky number, but it's hard to see how this will end auspiciously for either of us.

Ollie Quinn is my brother's teammate. And thanks to my recent appointment as the team's physiotherapist, he's now my patient too. He might be newly single and ready to mingle, but he is utterly off-limits.

Does that stop me?

Of course not.

Chemistry crackles like an invisible circuit between us but when sparks fly, one us will get burned...

OLLIE

Injuries sustained on the pitch seem minimal compared to what Eddie Harrington might do if he finds out I'm sleeping with his little sister. But Amy is everything I never knew I needed and I couldn't give her up if I tried.

Is it simply the temptation of tasting the forbidden fruit?

Or will forbidden turn into forever?

Love & Other Forbidden Things

LOVE
& Other Forbidden Things

LYNDSEY GALLAGHER

LOVE & OTHER VOWS

MARCUS

Once upon a time, I was the captain of the national rugby team, surrounded by the loyalty and laughter of my teammates, basking in the glory each winning match brought our country.

Now, I'm a stay-at-home-dad to my two beautiful, bubbly, busy girls while my stunning wife, Shelly, slides, shakes and shimmies her pert little ass all over national television as part of the newest, sexiest, celebrity dance show.

I don't resent her.

She's my world.

But if I tell you I'm struggling to adjust, it's an understatement.

SHELLY

After years of flying solo with the kids while my husband travelled the world with his teammates, the light has finally emerged at the end of a long and lonely tunnel.

Living in Marcus's shadow has been hard but now, I'm finally getting my chance to shine.

I never dreamed I'd be offered a place on the hottest new dance show around.

Nor did I dream I'd be paired up with Marcus's oldest rival either, though. And they weren't just rivals on the pitch.

We have a whole lot of history. And history has an awful habit of repeating itself.

Marcus and I vowed to stay together through sickness and health, but can we survive the pressure brought by fame and wealth?

https://mybook.to/love_and_other_vows

LOVE
& Other Vows

LYNDSEY GALLAGHER

THE SEVEN YEAR ITCH

Twenty-seven-year-old **Lucy O'Connor** has been asked to be her future sister-in-law's bridesmaid despite the fact they don't see eye to eye. The last thing she expected was to fall in love with a complete stranger at the hen weekend. Which wouldn't be a problem, apart from the teeny tiny fact that she's already married to somebody else...

Is it a case of the **Seven-Year-Itch**? Or could it be the real deal?

Lucy needs to decide if she's going to leave the security of her stale marriage in order to find out if the grass is indeed greener on the other side, or whether it's worth having one more go at watering her own garden.

Could this party-loving, city girl really leave the country she loves for a farmer from the west of Ireland?

Is there such a thing as fate?

What about karma?

Is John Kelly all that he seems?

★★★★★ ***Love can be insane, gut-wrenching, and dizzying***

https://mybook.to/The_Seven_Year_Itch

ABOUT THE AUTHOR

Lyndsey Gallagher lives in the west of Ireland with her endlessly patient husband, two crazy kids, and and an even crazier boxer puppy. When she's not dreaming up the next boyfriend, she's circuit training, sea swimming, or eating more chocolate than is healthy.

Hang out with her in her private reader group, Lyndsey's Book Lushes. https://www.facebook.com/groups/530398645913222

Or subscribe to her newsletter @ www.lyndseygallagherauthor.com

MEET MY ALTER EGO...

If you're still with me... well done! ;)

I've recently started writing under L A Gallagher in addition to publishing under Lyndsey Gallagher. Spice and sass levels are similar but a different branding attracts a different audience, some readers simply don't like the cute covers, while others won't buy the male model ones, so I decided to do both.

Introducing **The Beckett Brothers Series...** turn over for a sneak peak...

WRECK ME
SCARLETT:

Months away from graduating from Dublin's most prestigious college, I'm down to my last hundred euros, my landlord's just doubled my rent, and I have no way to pay the final semester's tuition fees.

That is until my best friend scores me a pole dancing job at the most exclusive 'Gentlemen's Club' in the country.

After years of hiding in plain sight, finally, I feel seen. Wanted. Desired. The heat of all those eyes on my body is intoxicating.

But none more than James Beckett's, a billionaire bachelor with a reputation as famous as his family's whiskey distillery.

Apparently, he's under pressure to settle down, until he conquers the next part of his empire, at least.

Which is precisely why he makes me a proposition.

One that could secure my future or shatter my world...

JAMES:

I'm a heartbeat away from being fired as CEO from my own family's whiskey distillery, unless I can prove to my father and The Board that I've shed my playboy reputation.

The last thing I want is a showpiece society wife.

Especially when I'm obsessed with The Luxor Lounge's newest pole dancer.

At only twenty-three, Scarlett radiates an innocence that drives me wild. Turns out, my little dancer is a virgin. Seems like every man in the club wants to proposition her.

But I've got the most enticing proposition of all.

Accept a lucrative job as my fake girlfriend until I complete my latest takeover, and prove my competence to my father and The Board.

I'll even tutor her through her final exams... and anything else she might require "tuition" in...

Fooling around with my fake girlfriend was *always* part of my plan.

Falling for her *wasn't*.

She's everything I crave, but everything my father forbids.

Even if I can convince him that Scarlett is the one for me, she's been keeping a secret.

One that could wreck me...

🖤Age Gap
   🖤Forbidden Romance
   🖤Billionaire Posessive hero
   🖤V FMC
   🖤Touch her and d*e vibes
   🖤Blush-inducing steam

https://mybook.to/Wreck_Me

Wreck Me is a tale of forbidden love, opposites attract, and the battles we face in the shadows, as worlds collide, and the lines between love and secrets blur.

⭐⭐⭐⭐⭐ **GOODREADS REVIEWER**
"Don't put this on your TBR. READ IT NOW!"

⭐⭐⭐⭐⭐ **GOODREADS REVIEWER**
"It's official, Lyndsey Gallagher is my favourite author!"

⭐⭐⭐⭐⭐ **GOODREADS REVIEWER**
"God, Lyndsey Gallagher just gets better and better."

ACKNOWLEDGMENTS

They say it takes a village to raise a child, well it takes one to publish a book too!

I need to say a massive thank you to my beta readers, Jennifer Brooks Brown, Kathy Mercure and Katy Pyle. I really appreciate your eagle eyes, screenshots and suggestions!

Huge thank you to my fabulous ARC team who read, review, and shout about my stories all over the bookish community! You're the best!

Thank you to my amazing Lushes who show up for me every day. Your friendship and support means the world to me.

Big thanks to my author friends, especially Margaret Amatt and Sara Madderson. The chats, support, video notes and FaceTime's are often the highlight of my week.

The biggest thanks goes to you, dear reader! Thank you for picking up my book, when there are so many amazing romance stories out there.

Printed in Great Britain
by Amazon